CHEF'S KISS

ANGI N. BLACK

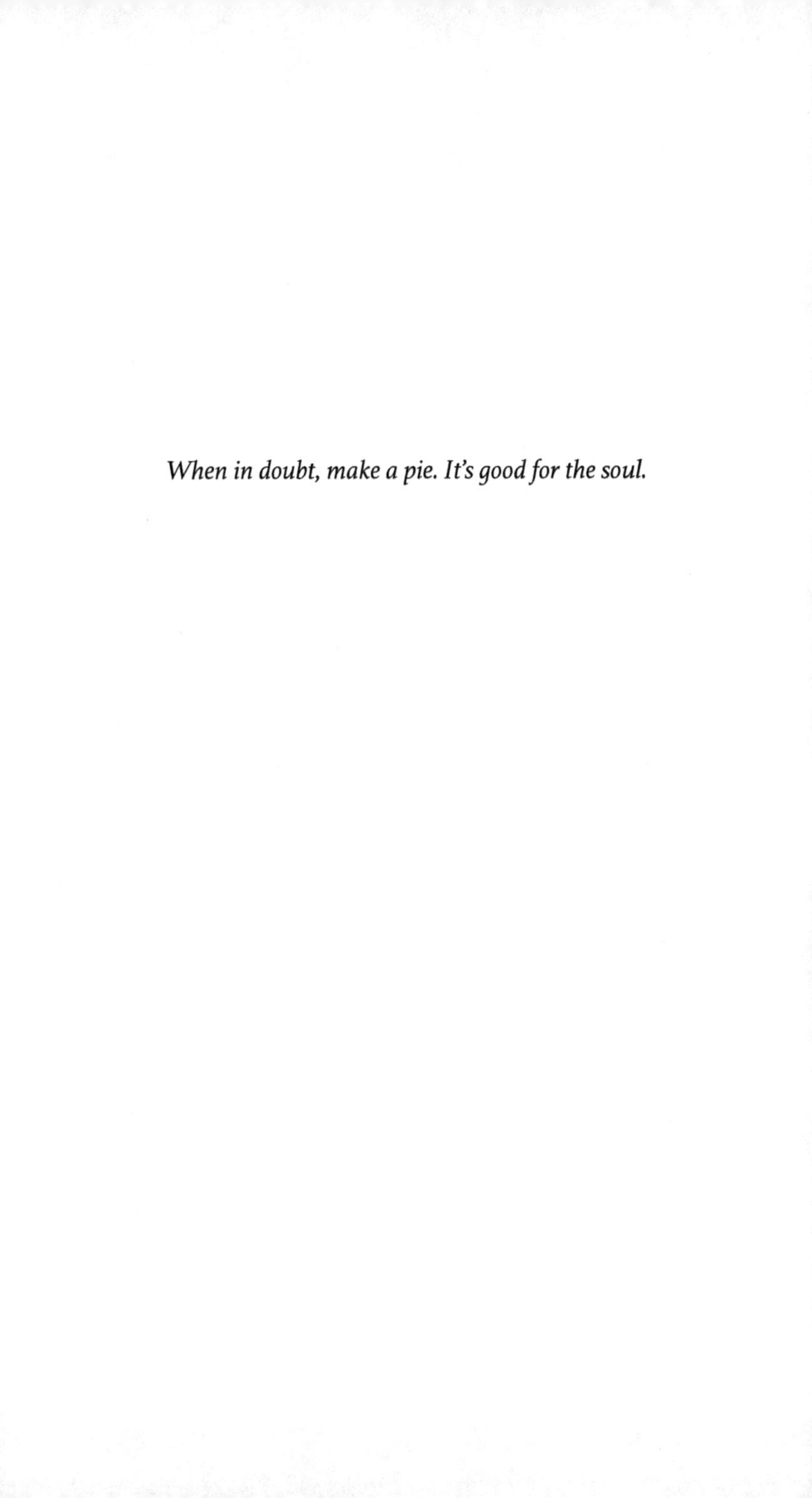

When in doubt, make a pie. It's good for the soul.

1

Helene

Kitty stood in front of me. "Don't worry. It's all going to be okay."

"What's going to be okay? Is something wrong?"

She smiled, half comfort, half bless your heart. "I promise. It'll be fine."

"Where am I?"

She didn't answer me, just kept that same smile on her face. It calmed my nerves as I yawned and rubbed my eyes. When I opened them, Kael was there. "What are you doing here?"

He shrugged, crossing his arms, a look of disdain on his face. "I think the bigger question is what are you doing here? Do you really think you belong here?"

Tears pricked at my eyes. "Why are you like this? I never did anything to you. And why is everyone speaking in questions?"

The room I stood in was unrecognizable. A neon signed flashed in the distance but I couldn't make out the name on it. I held a copy of *Food, Drink, Air.* I followed Kael's burning stare to the magazine in my hand.

I lifted it up. "What?"

"You know what."

I honestly didn't. What the hell was going on? I turned to see a small diner filled with people. This sign I could read, and it was flashing my name. I walked to the doors as my sister stepped in front of me.

"I need you."

"Okay. In a minute." I tried to sidestep around her, but she was right in front of me no matter where I moved. I could not get to the diner.

"Move. I have to go to work. My kitchen is over there." I pointed to the restaurant that was getting farther away. It blurred as it receded from my reach.

She scoffed. "You don't have a kitchen."

More tears fell down my cheeks. Kitty put her arm around me. "She's on your side, it will all be okay."

"What will be okay?" I practically begged to know the answer she was trying to give me, but her face faded away.

"Leen, Leen, Leen."

The bed bounced as my nephew jumped up by me, shocking me awake as he called my name over and over. Celia, my sister, poked her head in the door. "You okay? You look like you've seen a ghost."

I sat up to give my nephew, Jonny, a hug. "That was a wild dream."

Celia sat on the bed by me. "What was it?"

"I'm not even sure." I shook my head and tried to give her a rundown of the weirdness.

She was thoughtful, chewing on her lower lip as she processed the information. "What do you think it means?"

I stood up and stretched my arms over my head. "Not to eat Bolognese that close to bed."

She laughed and tossed a pillow at me. "Come on, Jonny. Time for school."

"Awwwww. Do I have to go?"

Celia lifted him off the bed and shooed him in front of her. "Yes. Auntie Leen has to go to work anyway."

I tried to shake off the cobwebs of sleep I'd been so abruptly ripped from. I hadn't spoken to Kitty in over a week. That was unusual and now she popped up in a dream. Couldn't be a coincidence. I did the math of time zones and decided it was too early to call her, so I put a note in my calendar to phone her at lunch.

Rushing through my morning routine since I'd overslept didn't leave me much time to contemplate the dream again, except for one part.

Why did Kael Ruggeman show up in there? We had a past, but that was just it – the past. A distance, ancient past that I didn't care to revisit. Good riddance. That man had been a thorn in my side and an ache in my head since day one.

He might have starred in a few lovely dreams, but he wasn't worth the heartache he'd caused me. Why did he pop up in that weirdness last night?

The subway bumped along the track as I tried not to think about him. If I was honest with myself, I used to think he was pretty great. Day one I thought he was cute. By day three, I was smitten. He was amazing in the kitchen. I'd never seen anyone do the things he did with food, creating perfect flavors and dishes out of the wildest ingredients. But that was all before he showed his true colors on the last day.

He doesn't get any more of your time.

I pounded the pavement of the last block before work, trying not to be late. As I reached the front door of the office building, my phone buzzed.

I stared at the screen. It was Kitty. What are the odds? As I answered the call, I grinned. I'd missed her. "Hello?"

"Is this Helene?" A voice I didn't recognize was on the other end.

"This is she."

"Hi. You were on the list to call. Kitty has passed."

Black spots clouded my vision as my world stopped. "What? When? What happened?"

"I'm sure you know, she's been sick for a while, but she took a turn a few days ago. We lost her last night. She wanted you to know she loved you and she said to tell you directly, follow your dreams because you can do it."

Leaning against the building, I clutched my chest. I couldn't breathe. I wasn't sure my legs were going to hold me much longer. "Thank you." I choked out the words, not convinced I was making sounds.

"Oh, she wanted me to let you know to expect a package in the next few days and to tell you it will all be okay."

With that, I lost it. That's what Dream Kitty had told me. Tears dripped down my face in rivers. She was gone. I thanked the caller, then dialed Celia to let her know. Kitty wasn't family by blood, but she'd been there for us when we needed her most. Celia did not take the news well, and in hindsight, I should have told her later tonight.

"Do you need me to come home?" I asked Celia.

"No. I'll be okay."

"Please remember to eat and pick up Jonny."

"I promise."

The call to duty of taking care of my sister snapped me back to reality. I'd have to save the tears for later. I pushed off the wall and took a steadying breath.

What would I do without Kitty?

I stopped in the restroom to clean myself up and made my way to my office. Jen, my assistant was waiting for me.

"I was about to call you. You're never late. Had me worried." Then she saw my face, red and blotched.

"Are you okay?"

I shook my head, sitting at my desk. "I lost a dear friend, she just passed."

She knelt by me, holding my hand. "What can I do for you? Need the rest of the day off?"

"I wish, but I can't. I'm reviewing two places today."

Jen stood and opened her computer. "Screw them. We can move it."

I shook my hands and then my head. "No. I need to work. I can't sit around and be sad. What will that do for me? Plus, Kitty would be pissed if I did that." I laughed. "She'd be so irritated if anyone made a big deal about it."

Jen smiled. "If you change your mind..."

"Thanks, Jen."

Not an hour later, a package showed up as promised. Inside was a book with Kitty's recipes and a note from her, all held together with a rubber band. They were her own things she loved to make, her favorites and a few more. It was old and beat up and the cover made a cracking noise when you opened it. Her perfume wafted up and out of the pages as I flipped through it. Tears threatened again, I pushed them down as best I could.

I set it aside and pulled the next thing out of the box.

Very official looking papers were in a manilla envelope. I

flipped through them quickly before I saw a letter with my name scribbled on it. My fingers closed around it, lifting it gently as if it might crumble at any minute. Opening the flap of the envelope, I pulled out a letter.

Lena,

I know I didn't let you know how sick I was, but you've had enough worry for five life-times and I didn't want to make you worry more. Just like I don't want you to worry now. Here's all my recipes. I hope you'll put them on the menu when you open your restaurant. Make sure to give them ridiculous names. (Everyone loves a ridiculous name!)

They are all for you to make your own. I wish I could see your place when you open it, but know I'll be watching from wherever and whatever is next.

I hope the music is loud and the food is good when I get where I'm going.

I've set up an account with some money in it for you. I hope you'll use it to start your own spot. Don't let anything stop you.

Love,

Kitty

P.S. If I'm gone by the time you get this, don't cry for me. It's all going to be okay. Just make a pie instead.

. . .

THE PAPERS in the manilla envelope had the account information and all I needed to access it. I sat in stunned silence. She'd given me her recipes and her blessing, plus start up cash. The best way to repay her would be to follow my heart. I intended to do just that but for now, I had this job to deal with starting by writing up my latest review.

But tonight, I'd talk to Celia and make a plan to turn my dreams into a reality.

Kael

MY MICHELIN STARS on the wall stared down at me, taunting me. *It's all downhill from here.* The glass of bourbon I held to my forehead did little to calm or cool me. Instead, beads of sweats dripped into my eye.

"Fuck. That burns."

I grabbed a towel, wiping away the sting. I downed the rest of the glass and poured another. What was my deal? It was just a review. I'd had a million. Okay, not a million, but enough. And they were all five stars plus three Michelins. I had more high-level accolades than any other chef except one and we were tied. But if this was a five star, I'd be best of the best.

And that's where I wanted to be, on top. The very top.

The kitchen of London House was clean and stream-lined with steel tables and appliances. The pots and pans hung neatly in rows, glistening in the bright light. I looked around my little kingdom and smiled.

This was peaceful. This was order. No chaos, just like I liked.

But the last week had been nothing but chaos, and I knew that's why I was on edge waiting for the review. The shitshow that had ensued when Helene Carnahan walked into my restaurant seven days ago should've been laughable, but I couldn't find the humor. The second I found out she was the one doing the review, I went to pieces. I wouldn't have been hired to work fries at a fast food place the way I behaved.

And that wasn't shade to fast food, it was completely directed at me.

Helene was there to decide if I deserved those last elusive five stars to solidify my status as the best.

And her stars meant more to me than the others. Her stars *counted*.

Not just because she was the most respected reviewer in the business, but because I'd kicked her out of my first kitchen. And we'd almost...I don't know what we almost did, but it was only an almost something and it stung my soul in a way I didn't like.

In culinary school, we'd been friends, or so I thought we were. And now I needed her to see I'd made something of myself and hopefully she'd let the past be the past. She was a professional after all, and no one knew our history.

If I was honest with myself, it wasn't my best plating or anything else that day. My stomach turned thinking about it, and it wasn't only the bourbon on an empty gullet.

Lou, my sous chef, hesitated as she entered the room, phone in her hand, the screen lit up. "It's here."

I braced in my chair, bourbon at the ready. I stared into the glass for strength. "Read it to me."

When she didn't say anything, I looked up. "Oh god. That bad?"

She shook her head. "No. Not bad at all."

"Not bad at all, or not all bad?"

She pursed her lips as she looked at me.

"Then what the fuck are you waiting on?"

"Nothing. It's just - Stef said to remind you this is about the restaurant, and we work as a team here."

I rolled my eyes. "Yes. Because London House is such a team affair. Just read the damn thing." I ran my finger around the top of the glass. It clearly wasn't the five stars I had been holding out for or Lou would've already been reading.

"Go on," I said again, waving my hand at her.

She cleared her throat and began.

London House – Everything you'd expect – and some I didn't.
Four Stars

"FOUR STARS. DAMN IT."

Lou stepped closer. "Hey. Four stars is great."

I shook my head. "It's not enough."

She waited until I lifted my glass for her to keep reading.

Eating at London House was...an experience. While each dish was better than the last, it was a meal I won't soon forget. Except it wasn't because of the food.

First, the good stuff. The atmosphere was lovely and very upscale. The color palette of the place was inviting and warm. The staff excelled at being on top of my needs before I knew them.
For dinner, I started with an appetizer of Foie Gras, expertly prepared by Chef Kael Ruggeman. Yes, that Kael Ruggeman. The one everyone wants their food prepared by. It did not disappoint. It was as moist and succulent as you'd expect from a chef with his reputation. Every accolade he has is well earned.

"See? That's good, right?"

I grimaced, knowing the blow was still to come. "She's simply saying I'm a good chef so it should taste like this. It's not...exceptional, it's routine. Keep going."

"She could say you're a bad chef."

"But she would never say that."

Lou raised a brow. "You know her?"

I took a heavy drink. "You've read her reviews. She's too eloquent for that." I waved my hand in little circles to get her to continue.

The salad, a play on a Waldorf, cleverly named the Astoria, had pear instead of apple, pecans instead of walnuts, and a little different take on the dressing. Very good with the right amount of acid to sweet.
Next, I moved on to two entrees — the roast chicken they are famous for and a braised short rib. Both rich and full, with the right amount of sauce for the chicken and the perfect consistency of potato and veggie with the rib.
I also appreciated each dish was more than a forkful.

. . .

"That's a great mention. She likes the portion. That'll tell people we're worth the money."

I rolled my eyes. Whatever was coming must be bad if Lou was buttering me up like this.

"We have a three month wait list. I don't think anyone cares about the portions."

"You know what..."

I raised an eyebrow. Lou took a breath after frowning at me and read more.

For dessert, I had little choice but to try a bite of all five offered that evening. A tiramisu, an upscale bread pudding with bourbon sidecar, an apple tart whose flake on the pastry I might never get over, their renowned chocolate cake, and lastly something between an ooey gooey cake and shortbread. All delicious, all worth getting.

Lou stared at me.

"What?" The impatience was getting the better of me. I was seconds from ripping the phone out of her hand and reading it myself.

"Remember, it's a team effort."

I finished the bourbon.

So why only four stars? While the food was everything promised, the meal felt rushed and hovered over. When I could have savored, I felt pressured to give an opinion and move on. And when I mean I had no choice but to try all the desserts offered on the menu, I mean Chef Ruggeman insisted on it and waited for me to do so.

He stood by my table, demanding answers instantly, barely giving me a chance to contemplate his often complex flavors.

Food is the language of love and that begins in the kitchen. Here, the customer might be enamored by the plates offered, but the chef seems to have lost his crush on the process, and it showed in each dish.

~Helene Carnahan~

Food Critic with Food, Drink, Air magazine

I STOPPED, empty glass in midair. "She gave me four stars."

"Well, not you per se. But the restaurant."

"No. She gave *me* four stars."

She said as much. I grabbed the phone from her hand and shooed her away. I scrolled the article and read through again. Yes, good food, loved the dishes. Even pointing out the proper acid ratio I worked so hard on. The chef was the problem. *Lost his crush on the process.* I pushed the poisonous words away and slammed down my glass.

A four-star review from Helene Carnahan. The shit of it was, I had only wanted to impress her. That five-star would've put me in a class by myself – the chef with the most five-stars and the most Michelin stars. No one could touch me with that.

At least she'd liked the food. It was me she couldn't stand. Great. I wouldn't even get a wave if she came in here now. And I didn't care because knowing her was a past life. That's how little she meant to me in the scheme of things. But four stars? That meant a lot. It hit the front and back of my brain over and over growing into a chorus of my first chef telling me as his sous, I'd never make it. I wasn't good enough. His voice asking, why was I even here?

I poured another drink and finished it.

"Screw her." I stood and made my way to my locker. I had three missed calls and a handful of texts.

I leaned my head back against the wall. Something must be wrong because my sister never called that many times. Actually, she never called.

"Cynth, what's wrong?" My sister was panicked, I could tell as soon as she answered me. Her voice was clipped, heavy breaths holding back tears. My stomach clenched.

"It happened. She's gone."

I sunk to the floor, back against the locker. "When?"

"Early this morning."

I sat in silence for a second.

"Hey, you there?"

I nodded. "Yeah, Yeah, I'm here."

The phone pressed to my ear with the line open, neither of us speaking. I didn't know what to say. Aunt Catherine was gone. She was the one who had believed in me, taught me the way around a kitchen to begin with. And now she was just gone.

"Was it...was it peaceful?"

"Very. But Kael, honey, you're gonna need to come home."

I bristled, standing back up. Every ounce of bourbon I'd sucked down threatened to make a reappearance on this floor. "Sure. I'll be there for the funeral, just send me details." I pulled my apron out of the locker, attempting to tie it on while holding the phone to my ear.

"No. There won't be a funeral. She didn't want one. But I mean, you'll need to come home."

I took a breath. "Cynth, you know I can't. I have a job here and a kitchen to run. Can't you guys take care of it?"

I heard her suck in tears. "No, honey. She left it to you. All of it, just to you."

I froze. "The diner?"

"Yeah." My sister's voice was so small when she answered.

"How do you know? You said she just passed. There can't have been time to see to anything formal yet." My mind whirled. She left me the diner. My aunt, the only person Cynthia and I had was gone and she left me the diner. Her diner. The institution that was her diner.

"She told me last week. She said when she was gone to make sure you knew right away. She didn't want to close. She wants you to keep it going."

"I...I don't. I can't. I..."

"Kael, you need to come home."

I paused. "She was this bad last week and no one called?"

"I did. You never called back."

I hung my head.

"You need to come home."

"Okay. I'll be there." The words sounded foreign, as if it wasn't my voice speaking them but someone holding strings to move me like a puppet. Cynthia said something else, but I didn't hear her. I had to go to the one place I'd tried so hard to get away from, and who knows when or if I'd be able to leave again.

I walked to the Stef's office, in a daze. I had no idea when I woke up this morning my world would be unrecognizable before noon. Could I do this? Just up and leave? I held a hand in the air, hovering for a second before knocking on the frame.

"Yes?"

"Hey. I just had a death in the family. I have to go."

He looked up at me. "Sorry for your loss. What can I do for you?"

I shook my head, unable to speak.

"When will you be back?"

I swallowed hard on the words I knew I needed to say but didn't know if I could get out. "I won't be back."

He stood. "That must've been a big loss." He raised a brow at me.

"So big I can't comprehend."

"Best of luck, Ruggeman. Stay in touch. Send in your Sous."

"Heard, Chef."

I told Lou she was needed in Stef's office. A laundry list of things I needed to do filled my brain, anything to push away the thought of Aunt Cat being gone.

Cancel my lease or find a sublet. Pack, arrange travel. *She was gone.* I'm sure there was paperwork to handle. Could I do this? *Gone, gone, gone.* I took my stars off the wall and held them. Lou was at my shoulder.

"I'm so sorry."

I handed her my apron. "Thanks. It's yours now."

And like that, my time in New York was over.

2

Helene

"Have you seen this?"

I twirled in my chair, head to the ceiling. "Probably, but you'll have to be more specific."

It was a slow day and I swear I didn't have any more restaurants in New York to eat at that I hadn't already. I was itching to get out of the city. I wanted a full plate of food, not three jelly things on a leaf.

I'd never been a super fan of the city anyway, but I was stuck here for the foreseeable future. Stuck, stuck, stuck. The money from Kitty was a lovely gift and a step in the right direction, but when I started doing numbers to open a place of my own, well. There would have to be a lot more saving done before I could get there. I stopped my chair before I got dizzy just as Jen hit my arm. "Another chef leaving London House."

"I mean, it's a dumb name. It's in New York and it doesn't serve any English dishes. I don't understand the popularity. I would leave too."

She scoffed. "You gave it four stars."

"The food was good." I shrugged and sat up to look at my assistant.

She pursed her lips. "Don't you think it's weird though? Another big-name chef leaving the city. What is going on?"

"Leaving the city or leaving London House? Those are different."

"It says leaving the city."

I grinned. "Maybe they can't handle my reviews."

She laughed as I spun my chair again. "You think Kael Ruggeman is leaving the city because he can't handle your review?"

I stopped my chair. "Ruggeman is leaving?" An unwelcome buzz went through me at the mention of his name.

She nodded. "Yeah. Wild, right? Besides you're not that scary." Jen turned back to her computer. "He's like 6'4" and those tats? Not scared of a few well-placed critiques."

I tapped the eraser end of my pencil against my chin. She didn't know the past, but he did have reason to be scared of me. I knew who he was. The man who pretended to be my friend and then when we were pitted against each other showed his true colors. "The food was great. Many other things that contributed."

I went back to trying to find a different way to describe salad in my review of Brown's, the new hot spot on 5th. "Besides, he's 5'9" at best," I added under my breath.

I felt Jen's stare as she turned in her chair, but I didn't

look up. "He's ridiculously hot. You have to admit that. Those curls, and those biceps."

"I thought you liked girls."

"I like both, thank you very much. I'm equal opportunity. Now, hot or not?"

I still didn't respond. She wasn't wrong. He was pretty to look at. *You should see him with his shirt off.* But no amount of good looks or tattoos, or that thing he could do with his tongue, could make up for his personality. I heard a creak and then more taps on the keyboard. I grinned again. I had a reputation as a hard ass and loved it. But still, each person wanted that five-star review from me. *Food, Drink, Air* was the biggest publication in the food world and I was the top critic. Restaurants and a chef's success could hinge on my thoughts. I tried to be fair and honest though, and never intentionally malicious, even with a jerk like Ruggeman. There was enough backstabbing and toxicity in the kitchens.

I wanted people to know where they could get good food. If I was honest about that, why did that make me the bad guy?

"Like what?"

"Like what, what?"

Jen came and sat across from me. "What else in your critique? The other factors."

I tapped the pencil on the desk. "I don't know. It just, was uncomfortable. He came out with the food."

"So? Don't all the chef's do that?"

"Yeah." Her red hair caught the light just right in the late afternoon and I lost my train of thought. She waved a hand at me and I shook my head to bring it back. "After the fact, but he stood there and waited for me to eat. He wanted a real time thought process and I don't work like that."

"He stood there?"

I nodded.

"At the table?"

"Yes!"

She clicked her tongue in agreement with my disdain.

"Exactly. And he wouldn't go back for the next course until I told him at least something about each dish. It was awful. And as it went along, he got more hostile and impatient, and I got more pissed he was being a jackass, so my answers got shorter, which seemed to make him madder. I could barely enjoy the food."

She went back to her desk. "Then the answer is hot to look at it, but not with the personality."

"Yeah, that covers it."

"But be honest, have you ever met a chef that wasn't an egotistical ass hat?"

I laughed. "Not yet. I don't think they make them with hearts, just an empty hole needing to be filled when you kiss their ass and tell them you've never had such excellent boiled potatoes."

Jen laughed and went back to her desk then whooped.

"It's here!"

"Whoa, slow down. What is?"

"Your interview with Food and Wine. Want to hear it?" She flashed me a smile.

I tried not to sigh out loud. It wasn't so much an interview as a profile and, honestly, I don't know why they wanted to talk to me anyway. I ate food. I talked about it. Other people then went and ate the food. This was not rocket science.

I wasn't sure it even mattered in the scheme of things. But it did pay the bills.

"Sure. Go for it."

I moved over to the couch and lay back on the uncomfortable leather cushions. Jen came and sat on the recliner next to me.

Today's look at People Who Love Food Like You Do is Helene Carnahan.

"I ALREADY HATE IT." I put the back of my hand over my eyes.

"Why?"

"I don't know. It feels weird. Who cares about what I do?"

Jen stared at me until the force of it caused me to look at her.

"You literally write about things other people do for a living."

I huffed. "Fine. Go on."

Helene completed culinary school at the young age of 19 and jumped right into the kitchen, landing a Sous position at a prestigious restaurant here in New York City. She soon learned a professional kitchen can be quite toxic. After a horrible kitchen experience, Helene left the industry but was still a food lover.

MY STOMACH TENSED. "Oh god. I cannot believe they put that in. They didn't mention the restaurant or chef, did they?"

She scanned ahead. "No, not that I see. I didn't know you went to culinary school."

I shrugged and crossed my arms.

Her new dream was to open a restaurant of her own, bringing her love of small-town diners and comfort home-cooking to one place with an upscale experience. Helene couldn't have foreseen the family tragedies that would make this an unrealized notion.

"You wanted to open your own place?"

I stood up and paced. "This is why I hate these things. It was a dumb thing I wanted when I was younger, but not everything works out. They make it sound bigger than it was."

Jen opened her mouth, but I held up a hand. "Truly. It was a long time ago."

She nodded, getting the hint and kept reading.

Fortunately for those of us who love food, she began writing a column about the smaller eating establishments here in the city, and soon worked her way up to the top. She's now THE première food critic and reviews the highest-profile places. Her reviews are legendary. Every chef strives for a five-star review from Helene Carnahan.

You can find her expert food opinions each month in Food, Drink, Air, a culinary magazine available in print and online by subscription.

"THAT WAS FUN. Your picture looks great too."

I took the laptop from her. It was an okay picture. I did have on my favorite green shirt in it. It was the one Kitty had given me a million years ago.

"How did you decide on that photo? That color looks great on you."

"I didn't. I sent five to them and they picked. And thanks. I love that shirt. A dear friend gave it to me a long time ago. It's my good luck shirt." I grinned, then quickly wiped it from my face.

"That's adorable." She went back to her desk. "Guess we should get to work."

I rolled my neck side to side. "I guess. That is what they are paying me for. Is there a better word for lettuce?"

"Better than what?"

"Um...lettuce?"

Jen laughed and I tried to pretend like I liked my job.

I STRETCHED AND BLINKED, adjusting to the bright overhead light. An hour had passed before I knew it. I poured another cup of coffee, even though no amount of caffeine would work today. I looked at the search engine I'd pulled up as I yawned, thinking back over the conversation Jen and I'd had about Kael. Over thirty high profile chefs or their seconds had left their posts in the last two years. Something was definitely happening in the industry. Her question had nagged at me all night. Why were so many kitchens losing their leaders? So here I sat at five am next to my coffee and my laptop trying to find the answer.

I counted on my fingers what time it would be on the other coast. I picked up my phone to text Deidre anyway.

Still eating at mom and pops on the road
while reviewing places to stay?

To my surprise, I almost immediately got a response.

You know this. It is my job. Why are you up
so early?

I smiled at the screen.

Why are you up so late?

Big after party for a première. Your turn.

My best friend's life was very exciting compared to mine. I mean my past was probably more interesting, but who gave a shit about that. I sighed.

Trying to figure out why so many chefs are
leaving the city.

They are working at the mom and pops. I've
seen at least three.

Where?

I wrote down the names and cities and sent a kissy face emoji.

I'll come see you soon.

Love you.

Mean it.

I looked up each one. She was right, they were all over. I put in the next chef's name on my list and sure enough, also at a small town diner. Not so much luck on the next couple but then two more showed up.

What were they doing there? What kind of food were they making? And most importantly, why?

I leaned back into the couch where I sat. I thought over the almost restaurant, the nearly real menu in my mind, the practically purchased décor. So much was a should've, could've, would've. Instead, it was *here we are now*. I was supposed to be one of those chefs, not in the city, but there, on a roadside. Travelers coming and going and once back in their car and on the road talking about the delicious food they'd recently enjoyed.

Instead, life happened. My dad happened. The funeral happened. And now I wrote about other people's food. Good god, my life was depressing.

I sat up and downed my coffee. I gasped as the too hot liquid hit my throat. I added the diners to my list of 'to visit' and tucked it away. It was hard to be away for too long these days. Celia and Jonny depended on me for a lot, and I had to be there for them. Plus, I couldn't do anything that would jeopardize my job now that I had a good one. The insurance alone was worth it. Well, it made it tolerable.

I thought about all the money I'd had saved up and the day I went to get it and the balance was zero. A wave of anger rolled over me, but I pushed it away. No sense dwelling on something I couldn't do a thing about.

"Auntie Leen?" A small head poked around the corner.

"JonJon, what are you doing up?"

"I had a bed dream."

"You mean a bad dream?" He came around the counter and hopped up in my arms.

"No, a bed dream. It was eating me."

"The bed?"

Tears rimmed his eyes.

I squeezed him. "Want me to check it out and tuck you back in?"

He nodded against me, but I could already hear his breathing leveling out. I carried him back into his room and tucked him in after a thorough bed inspection.

"No teeth detected," I said as I kissed his forehead.

I poured another cup of coffee. It was that kind of day.

Going through the calendar, I thought I could get away this weekend. It had been awhile since I'd devoted attention to my side project and I had the itch. The city was draining.

Plus, now I wanted to check out some of these diners with their transplant chefs. I started to text Didi again but glanced at the clock. *Oh shit.* It was almost seven. I filed away my thoughts and got ready for work.

Kael

THE SUN SHONE off the booths in the nearly empty diner. I leaned on the counter, trying to figure out how to keep this place afloat. I wasn't sure how Aunt Catherine had done it. I felt the resentment build that she'd left this responsibility on my shoulders. I was so mad at her. Mostly for leaving me here without guidance.

Guilt crushed in on me. Cat was the one person who had always believed in me and my dreams. I'd wanted to get out of this town for so long before I did and she'd pushed me out the door when it was time to follow my goals. I was a chef because of it, because of her.

And then I didn't even call the last week she was alive.

My mind put up a wall. I couldn't fall down this well again of torturing myself for something that I couldn't fix. The only thing I could do now was not let her down.

And if I failed now, I would be letting her down.

I mean I was a five star chef. Well, a four star chef according to Helene Carnahan, but that was irrelevant, right? I grit my teeth as my nemesis popped into my brain. My cell phone buzzed telling me it was desk time. My least favorite time of the day.

The office was cramped and dingy with an overflowing desk full of things I needed to handle. Small noted were pinned to a calendar that still had last month's dates on it. That's how far behind I was. I pushed the paper stacks to the back, somehow making the pile higher, to open my laptop and look at invoices.

How did she do this? I looked at Aunt Catherine's photo on the wall. "What was your secret?"

When I got no answer, I shook my head and opened my email. The first thing I saw was one from Danny. The subject line said: another Mystery review.

One day he'd learn how to use capital letters in the right place, right? But I was intrigued so I opened it.

Sure enough. Another review from the anonymous critic who had been doing mom-and-pops.

Nanny's Eatery
Papillion, Nebraska
Five Blue Plates
Great service, great food, great fun. Nanny's has been in business for fifty-five years and boy, does their food show it. The minestrone soup was possibly the best bowl of soup I've ever had.

I followed that by a French Dip with au jus that had been perfected by years of practice. The apple pie was the ultimate slice of Americana. Ruthy was a joy as she told me the history of the place, how Mr. Ben smokes too many cigarettes for her liking, and offered to give me the recipe for the soup. I would recommend this gem to anyone passing this way.
Anon H. Critic – Small Town Eats

I LOOKED around at my crumbling restaurant. "This is what I need," I muttered under my breath. "A good review to bring people in."

I leaned back in my chair and tried to think of how to get a review on this place. The mystery reviewer was anonymous and as far as I could tell, no one knew who it was. Not even Stef back in the city, and he knew everything.

"Happy anniversary," Danny said in a deadpan voice.

"Anniversary?" I asked as I closed my laptop.

"Yeah. It's been a year of it being Kael's not Cat and the Fiddle."

I huffed as I blew past him and began to chop carrots and onions. "It's still Cat's and it always will be."

Danny grunted. "I promise you, this isn't Cat's. She wasn't an asshole."

"True. But you still have a job, so shut up."

Danny and I were related somehow. I wasn't sure the actual path or name of the relation, but apparently, he came with this place. All I knew was he was a royal pain in my ass but all the same, I enjoyed having him around. Maybe it was because everyone else was easygoing and as it had been suggested in my life more than once, I only liked things if they were difficult.

I reread the review, not the Anon review, the other one. My London House review, the one I thought about every morning. Just like I did every day before I prepped for the shithole I called work. Okay, shithole was a bit much. I'd tried to fix it up a bit. New paint here and there, fixed the ripped leather on the booths. I was trying.

Cat's place, and Cat, were beloved in this little town. But then again, so was the abandoned Fina storefront that hadn't been lived in by anything except raccoons for ten years.

And for the record, Helene Carnahan wasn't the reason I left New York, but it didn't hurt. That review let me know it was time. *Lost his crush on the process.*

The thing was her words didn't matter to me. No. That was a bit off. They *shouldn't* have mattered to me, but they bounced around my brain constantly. I'd never gotten anything less than a five star anywhere. Ever.

And I only waited at the table because I wanted to impress her so badly. I needed *her* five stars. The shit of it was, I didn't know it was her until halfway through the meal. I just knew the critic worked for Food, Drink, Air and I sure as shit wanted a five from them. They were the only real rival for Michelin.

If she walked in here right now, I wouldn't know her, so why did she take up so much real estate in my brain?

That was another lie. I would know Helene anywhere. We'd started in the same culinary class. We were friends. Things...happened. And she was in my kitchen for a while. The first one I ran. I'd made her life a living hell. Not my finest moment, but she was so damn good. I had to push her. That's how it worked, right? Yes. I was right to, because she couldn't handle it and she wasn't at the stove anymore. She was a damn food critic now.

And she thought I was only worth four stars.

I stopped chopping during veggie prep so I wouldn't lose a finger to check the clock. "Two hours 'til open."

A chorus of *thank you chef,* and one *fuck you, chef* met my ears. I chuckled knowing I could always count on Danny to do his work but be bitter about it.

I had exactly three seconds of reprieve before Helene entered my brain again. Nice while it lasted.

The fact she couldn't cut it in my kitchen was the reason I needed to impress her so much. I had to let her know I knew why I did what I did, and I was right to treat her like that. I was right and she was wrong.

Even after we kissed. Even after that one night. Even after we had almost been...something. I shook my head. It was the right thing.

The little voice in my head that sounded suspiciously like Aunt Cat said, "If it was the right thing, why are you trying so hard to convince yourself it was?"

I put that wall back up and focused on today's recipe. Today's dish was potpie. One was in the oven about done but it was fall and I knew another would be needed. Between that and the blue plate, we probably wouldn't sell much of anything else.

I had no choice but to try all of them...

Ugh. Her voice, or what I vaguely remembered it sounded like, rattled in my mind. I could not get away from her. I wasn't even in that city anymore, but she was definitely here with me in this one. She meant nothing to me. The review meant nothing.

Except that it did. It was personal. The food was good, great even, but I was the reason we lost a star. I growled as I prepped, ending right back where I started in this circle of hellish thinking.

Danny bounded around the corner. "See the email I sent? Anon posted another review."

"I saw." But I grabbed the phone from his hand and scrolled the article again. Clearly someone in the business or formerly so. The language was too knowledgeable not to be someone who knew their way around a kitchen and a plate of food. Normal folk didn't say au jus, did they? Maybe they did. I had it on my menu, but I wasn't normal.

That didn't come out right.

"Nanny's gets five stars?" I slammed a pan down. I had so many five stars. A four shouldn't matter.

"I believe they're blue plates."

I shot him a look. Danny laughed. "C'mon. You know who it is, don't you?"

"No. How would I know?"

"Cause you know people."

"Not that person. And not anymore. Now get your prep done. It'll be a big day."

He grumbled as he went off to his station. Why would someone go around and review small town food anonymously? It made no sense. What were they getting out of that?

"One hour to open." I got the same response and chuckled again.

I would do fine here, eventually. Was this kitchen the line at London House? Or Frederique's. Or Belle Amour? No.

I didn't have the resources, or the food, or the produce, or the equipment. But here I didn't have to deal with any egos from other chefs.

Yeah, you're the only asshole here.

I rolled my eyes at the voice in my head.

I looked around the tiny speck of real estate I was essentially lord over now. Pans with the bottoms burned in desperate need of replacing or scouring hung haphazard on the rack. Everyone had on an apron, but they didn't match. The light held a yellow tint which took a minute to get used to and realize it wasn't the food that looked wrong.

I sighed, hands on my hips, head hung. How the mighty have fallen.

I went to the office, looking through the books. I needed to order matching aprons. That would help a little. I did some math and pulled up the supply place on the computer. I ordered aprons with Cat and the Fiddle stitched on the front, the same color blue as the neon on the sign.

It would be a nice gift for the staff, right?

Right. I hoped.

I went back to the kitchen, taking another look around.

This was an uphill battle I didn't know if I could win. But what else was I supposed to do? Let this place shutter like so many others in this town had? When Aunt Cat passed, I got the call to step up and I took it. No looking back. I looked at my crew. Small but mighty and I provided them with jobs, which everyone but Danny seemed to enjoy.

I turned back to the prep at hand and then glanced at the clock.

Nanny's got a five star and you didn't. I shook my head, getting rid of the thoughts like fog. Focus. "Fifteen minutes to open."

"Thank you, chef."

"Fuck you, chef."

Just as the clock ticked over, I heard the bell of the front door.

3

Helene

The small plane bumped along the runway sending a wave of relief over me. I needed to stretch my legs and get warm. It was still technically fall, but unusually cold and these little planes did not hold heat at all. A real advantage of taking these small planes was one, the cost was cheap or free. Especially since they were nine times of ten piloted by a retired vet who knew my dad at one point or another. They were generally bored and ready to fly, plus taking General Carnahan's daughter somewhere seemed to make them happy. They all loved my dad. It wasn't their fault they didn't know the asshole he'd been at home. The day the military called and said he'd passed I sat in the floor and cried. But it wasn't because I was sad. It was a release and freedom I'd been waiting for.

The news my mom was gone too hit harder. I didn't care what the report said, I knew she'd finally had enough of him. I pulled my arms around myself tighter.

Why was I thinking about this? Oh yeah. Because I had just landed in Nowheresville, Midwest, USA.

And that's the last place I remember being happy. Summers and falls in the Midwest had been my favorite. We've moved a lot as Dad had advanced his career, but the time we spent in this part of the world would always be my favorite. It was before I knew what happened at our house didn't happen at others, back when Celia was herself and I had my mom.

Then I'd only had Kitty. And Kitty's place was here and now that she was gone, I had to make sure it was in good hands.

I took my bundled self off the plane, thanked Jack, and went to the office to retrieve my car. These little airports had decommissioned cop cars and you could drive them around while you visited their towns just for using their hangers. It was the best. I could go and eat food, then head back to the tiny airports and there was virtually no paper trail. Plus, this was food I wanted to eat. Real portions. Not eighty dollar food on a toast point.

The kind of home cooking I craved and wanted to make myself. That's what my restaurant would've been. Blue plates and things that reminded you of Grandma's Sunday dinners.

I grinned to myself as I pulled out of the lot, the GPS chirping on in a British accent. Five minutes into a small town and the voice in my head sounded like a Norman Rockwell painting. I blasted the heat and drove straight to Kitty's diner. This place was legendary. I'd been informed their pot pie was the best by my intel – Deidre, of course. She would know. It was literally her job.

She reviewed small town hotels and when she did, she always made sure to eat at the local diners. That's how this whole thing started. I would go meet her and we'd eat. AS I was telling her all about the food, she encouraged me to review it.

"And what good would that do?"

She'd shrugged. "I don't know. So you could do something to make yourself happy. You could do it anonymously and would it would be just yours."

I nibbled a french fry. "I guess, except you just gave me the idea. And how would it go anywhere? I'm under contract at the magazine."

She smiled. "Just sent it to someone, like The Times or whatever. It'll probably just sit on a desk, but at least you'll know you did it."

And for some reason I still don't understand, I did. It was a hair brained idea, but to my shock, it picked up steam and grew a following. Now here I was, using my alter ego to check in on Kitty's place.

Deidre told me the cook was hot too.

"I'm telling you, Lena, he was smoking."

I'd grimaced. "Maybe something was burning in the kitchen."

She'd smacked my arm. "Can you just once go with it when I objectify a man?"

I rolled my eyes. "There are so few men worth objectifying and less of them are chefs."

She'd let it drop and instead went on about the potpie.

I pulled into the parking lot of Kitty's place, half frozen to death and ready for some good food. A blue neon cat moved the bow back and forth on their violin on the sign high above me.

The building looked like it might fall down at any minute. Honestly, I wasn't sure there was any mortar left in this brick-and-mortar establishment. Paint looked recently touched up though. Interesting. Someone was caring for it.

I walked inside, greeted by a charming ding above the door, and a waitress with salt-and-pepper hair piled on her head saying, "Hi Sweetie. Take a seat wherever."

I smiled and unwrapped my scarf from my face and neck to occupy the furthest booth from the door. The waitress, Sheila her name tag informed me, followed me and took my coat to hang on the wall hook beside my booth.

"Brrr." She said as she felt my chilly outerwear. "I guess that answers my next question, still cold out there?"

"Freezing."

She nodded and returned with coffee. "On the house. Warm up and I'll be back in a jiff to get your order."

I instantly loved Sheila. I held the small ceramic diner cup in my hands, letting the warmth soak into my frozen fingers. I held it close to my face to let the steam drift up and thaw out my nose. It smelled good and comforting in the way only roadside diner coffee can smell. I blew on it then took a small sip. Delicious. I sat it aside and typed a note into my phone. I couldn't use my regular note pad, because then people would know what I was doing out here.

Or maybe they wouldn't, but it wasn't a chance I could take.

I picked up the cup again. A diner mug fit in your hand so well. You could close your hands around it or hold it by the handle. And it held the perfect amount of coffee too. It didn't get cold because the mug was too big, and right as you were done, you could get a refill. As a bonus, a waitperson could fill several cups with one pot of coffee. Bougee coffee was for the birds.

After another satisfying gulp, I picked up the menu. It was blue and white with the logo and musical cat splashed across the top.

That design screamed Kitty. She'd been sentimental but always a little over the top. A neon cat musician seemed right.

Now, I had been to a million of these little mom-and-pop shops. Their menus read like books and each was about a hundred and fifty years old.

But this menu was different. First, it looked relatively new and was small. It had two sides only, no extra pages, and the lower front could be replaced with a slip-in menu making it easy to rotate each day. That was...odd. It was almost upscale. I looked around. The booths looked straight out of the fifties, except they didn't have much wear and tear on them, and the jukebox in the corner said out of order, though music filled the room. This place was not upscale.

I looked down the menu.

TODAY'S SPECIAL – Potpie. Served in a piping hot cast iron pan, have your own individual dish of flaky crust brimming with a stew of chicken and fresh veggies simmered for hours and baked to perfection. Served with mashed potatoes. No substitutions.

I READ IT AGAIN. Kitty was a poet about her food. That checked.

Under that an open face beef sandwich made on fresh bread covered with au jus.

I raised a brow. *Au jus.* I know several of these smaller

places served au jus, but only with French dip. Open face beef was covered with gravy. What the hell was going on here?

A permanent part of the menu below had a few things. I flipped to the back to find two more menu items, sides, and a massive pie selection that could also be changed day to day.

I sat the menu down. This wasn't a cook's kitchen. This was run by a chef.

A chef who was used to changing the menu daily. Another big city chef was here.

Commotion through the window peeking into the kitchen area caught my attention.

"Danny. C'mon man, I need you to keep up with the housekeeping of your station and do your damn job while you're at it."

Housekeeping? Yeah. That was chef talk.

"Whatever." The man on the receiving end of the conversation muttered.

"What was that?"

"Oh, by all means, yes chef."

The chef in question turned back to face the window and as he said, "Prick," we locked eyes.

The color drained from my face. Kael Ruggeman. He held up his hands. "Sorry. Didn't know we had a customer."

I looked back to the menu. My heartbeat fast and hard. This was it. I would be found out now for sure. It was all over New York how much he hated me for the four-star review.

But like, damn dude. Don't hover.

Especially over someone you have a past with.

Sheila came back to the table with an apologetic smile.

"Sorry about those knuckleheads. What can I grab ya, Sweetie?"

"I'll have the potpie and a piece of cherry pie."

"Anything to drink?"

"I'll stick with this delicious coffee, but I would like some cream and a glass of water."

"Sure, Sweetie. The lemonade is real good today too."

"Okay, I'll try some." I smiled at her.

I wanted to order the open face sandwich too, but that would be a dead giveaway to someone like Kael. Ordering more than one dish like that is something you're taught to look for as a chef. It's the best way to know if there's a reviewer in your midst.

What was he doing at Kitty's place? Surely, he didn't buy it. Anger built inside me.

This wasn't his. He shouldn't be here. Not in her place of all places. He wasn't good enough to stand where she stood.

More commotion from the kitchen as my order was put in the window. I rolled my eyes. Clearly he was the same jackass here he had been back in the city. He'd never had a reputation for being what one would call the nice guy. His food had more than made up for his attitude though. But did it? He'd blown through several restaurants back then. But geez, this was a tiny town. You couldn't act like that here.

You couldn't treat people like he'd treated me.

I saw him glance out the service window my direction. I busied myself with my phone.

Did he recognize me? That would be it. It would be over. I could make up a story about meeting my friend if it came to it, even though Deidre was four states over.

Why didn't she mention Kael was here?

Simple answer – she didn't know the hot chef was the hot chef who hated me most. This was a disaster.

And if he didn't recognize me, I'd be just as devastated. I thought we'd had something before I ended up in his kitchen and found out the asshole he really was. But in culinary school...it was different.

He'd been different. Or at least I'd thought so.

Before I thought it could be ready, plates were set on my table. I looked up to thank Sheila, but to my horror, Kael stood by the table.

"Just came out to apologize for the nonsense back there. Hope you like it."

"Thanks." I waited for him to say something else, but he stood there. Was he messing with me?

"Thanks a lot?"

"You're welcome. Sorry."

I nodded my head. "Again, thanks."

"Hmm. Okay. Just passing through?"

"Something like that. My best friend travels a lot and told me about this place." That was almost the story I concocted.

Then he sat down in the booth across from me.

He sat in my booth.

With me.

"She did? Well, that's cool. Where are you on your way to?"

I started to rethink my review of London House. Maybe he wasn't a jackass, maybe he an idiot who couldn't read a room. Who just sits at someone's table?

"Just around."

I didn't know how to answer without giving myself away. "Anyway, thanks again for the apology. I'm sure you need to get back to your kitchen."

He seemed to remember himself. "Yep. Wouldn't want to

hover." He frowned as he said it and now I knew he was messing with me.

I squared my jaw. "Yeah. People don't tend to like that."

He turned to look at me. "How's the food?" He just couldn't help himself.

"Haven't had any yet, but I'll let you know. Maybe you should give people a chance to eat before you demand answers."

He stared at me as I leaned across the table.

"What the hell are you doing here? Did you buy this place at auction or something? You know, the woman who used to own it, she was something special. This is her place. Why are you changing things?"

He sat back, his face agog. Then his jaw tightened, a glint in his eyes. "How do you know I did?"

It was my turn to look self-satisfied. "The menu."

His jaw fell open wider.

"Au jus on open face? C'mon. That's gravy and you know it. Plus what, you run four dishes each service so they can be the very best they can be and you hope every day someone comes in here to tell you your new little diner is five stars?"

My insides burned as I said the words, but he deserved them. He had and would always be an ass.

He stood, running his dish towel through his fingers, eventually clutching it between two fists.

My insides twisted with heat in a way I wished they wouldn't.

Sheila came over, stepping around him to refill my coffee. "Kael? Need something?"

He shook his head and grumbled as he stalked off. What the ever-loving hell was that? I blew out a breath.

"Sorry 'bout that. He hasn't realized he's in Kansas yet. Still thinks he's in the big apple."

"Oh?" Now this I could get behind. The tea about Kael.

"Yeah, the owner of this place died." Sheila looked at the ceiling as she counted on her fingers. "Died a little over a year ago, I guess. Can't believe it's been a year already." Sadness passed over her face for a minute. "Anyway, just awful and Kael came here to run her diner."

I softened a bit. That didn't line up with anything I knew about the ego-driven chef. Coming out here to run a small restaurant seemed somehow, honorable.

"He was in New York before?" I asked as if I didn't know.

She nodded as she stood there. "Sure was. Big time chef up there. You'll taste it in the food. He might be a pain in the ass, but damn, that kid can cook." She laughed a gruff smoker's laugh as she walked away.

So maybe his cooking was enough to make up for his attitude here too. I watched as she walked away. She reminded me of Kitty somehow and for a minute I swore I knew her.

My fork broke through the crust of my potpie. A delicious aroma rose up and I breathed it in. My mouth watered. Oh god. With a big forkful, I took a bite.

The crust practically melted on my tongue. The stew, the chicken, both rich and full. The veggies were cut and cooked to perfection. I devoured it and it was gone before I wanted it to be. The potatoes were next. Right amount of cream and consistency. The texture was textbook. I chugged the lemonade and as promised, it was so tasty.

I pulled the pie to me and right as I was about to take a bite, a low voice surprised me.

"How it is?" Kael yelled from the service window. People at the other tables looked at him and shook their head.

I looked at him and pointed to my chest. "Me?" I said around a mouthful of cherries and divine pastry crust.

"Yes. You. Do you like it?"

"It's very good."

He frowned and turned around and showed up by my table a minute later.

"Can I help you?" I said to him, irritated.

"It's our signature dish."

"The pie?"

He crossed his arms. "No, the potpie. Signature."

I blinked at him. "Signature dish? This is a diner in Kansas."

He pursed his lips. "So? I just wondered if you liked it."

"Why does it matter? I said it was good. Why are you bothering me? I'm not here working. I'm eating a meal."

He stepped back, clearly realizing what he was doing. "Sorry. I'm having...Sorry."

"Are you a dick to all women, or just me?"

His crossed arms flexed. I definitely did not notice how good his muscled and tattooed arms looked. Nor how broad his chest was when his t-shirt stretched across it. Nope. Did not notice. Didi's words came to mind again – hot chef. I tried to focus on my irritation, not his physique.

"I'm not. I wasn't. I...ugh. Food's on the house." He picked up my check and shredded it, letting the small pieces of paper fall to the table.

Well, one thing was certain. Getting out of the city sure as hell didn't help his attitude.

I got up and wrestled into my coat. I wound my scarf on, locking eyes with Kael as he held my gaze.

I shoved one last big bite of cherry pie into my mouth. I chewed it slowly as we stared at each other. Kael's eyes flicked down to my lips as I licked off the crumbs and an unwelcome spark jumped inside me. I straightened my shoulders and pushed that feeling far away.

Sheila tried to apologize. I shoved a twenty in her hand. "You were perfect. Believe me, it's not your fault."

I pushed past Kael, bumping his shoulder as I did. Heat bounced off him, me? I didn't know. I turned to look at him. His eyes raked over me as I stood there. I leaned in then righted.

Oh, get a hold of yourself.

The ding over the door wasn't near as charming this time. I plopped into the car and looked back to see Kael standing in the doorway, holding it open as he watched me go. I went back to the airport where Jack was waiting on me. I didn't think it was ego or oblivion, I was beginning to think my first opinion was correct and Kael Ruggeman was just an ass.

My phone dinged as I waited for flight check.

> How was it? So good right?

I grimaced at Didi's message.

> The food was great.

> And that chef? Hot.

> The chef was a jerk.

The phone rang and I rolled my eyes.

"A jerk? What happened?"

"It was Kael Ruggeman."

"Who?"

I huffed. "The one who hates me because I gave him a four-star? The chef that--"

"Ohh. Yeah. Fuck that guy."

I pushed out a short, hateful laugh.

"Did he recognize you?"

"Oh, for sure. He was an ass, then he was like, food's on the house when he...actually, I don't know why."

"Mm-hmm. I see."

"You see what?"

"You like him. You never get worked up like this."

"Ha! No one else is a jackhole like him." I half smiled at Jack and mouthed sorry. He just shook his head with a grin.

"Admit it though. Ridiculously hot."

I couldn't keep the smile from my face. "Maybe if he didn't speak. I guess."

"C'mon, you can't tell me you don't want to know what he really has cooking in that kitchen."

I knew already, but I wasn't going to tell her that. Rule number one is you don't sleep with the chef. Moreover, you don't sleep with the chefs you review. And you definitely don't tell anyone if you do.

Now I laughed fully. "Oh Didi, that doesn't sound as sexy as you think."

"It was meant to be dirty, so I think it landed fine."

"Okay, I'm taking off. Love you."

"Mean it."

I sat back and buckled in. Kael did have very pretty eyes. They were ice blue. Which thinking about it, was probably because his soul was a frozen wasteland. But he did leave his life to run a small diner. I couldn't reconcile those two people – the one who demanded respect and adoration for his food with a clearly humbling act of running a kitchen in Nowheresville.

Not only was he an ass, Kael Ruggeman was a mystery.

4

Kael

"**W**hat was that about?" Sheila met me at the door to the kitchen.

"Nothing. Just my nemesis dropping by."

Her scratchy laugh tickled my brain. "Nemesis?"

I slammed things around as I made the next ticket order. "Yes. It's someone from my past and I can't believe she just walked in here."

"Who was it?" She leaned against the wall, in no hurry to go back out to the customers.

I slowly turned to her. "Her name is Helene and it doesn't matter who she is."

She fought a smile, but her cheeks quirked up. "Okay,

Kael. Obviously a nobody." She chuckled as she went back to the dining room.

My insides burned as her new words compounded with her old ones. *And you hope every day someone comes in here to tell you your new little diner is five stars.* I squeezed my eyes close. *Lost his crush on the process.* I stalked out the back door, sucking in cool air to calm down.

Screw, Helene Carnahan.

IT HAD BEEN another week like any other. The only highlight, or maybe downfall, had been Helene, who ordered potpie, then left in a huff because I was a dumbass. I laid in bed and looked at the ceiling, dreading the reality of another day, like any other.

Shit. Even my mind was repeating itself.

Of all the diners in all the world. Ugh. Why had Helene been here? It was bugging me. This was far off her beaten path. I know she'd said a friend recommended, but all the way in Kansas? That made zero sense.

What friend was randomly in Kansas then said, hey. You should check this out. And she did all the way from New York? Zero sense.

But what made less sense was the way I had fallen apart around her. What the hell was I doing except the exact thing she had put in the review she'd given me?

In short – I'd acted like me.

What killed me the most about the whole thing? I wondered if she liked my pot pie. I was hopeless. But she was the best at what she did and I needed to know what she thought.

I rolled to the side, putting my feet on the floor and

looked at my phone. I was thirty minutes behind and had a text from Danny. Oh god. What could he want he couldn't just tell me at work?

Unless he wasn't coming in. That would suck. He might be a pain in the ass, but he was valuable in the kitchen.

I clicked on the message.

It's here. They finally got us.

A link was below it.

What the hell does that mean?

No answer.

Is this you, or have you been hacked?

Finally he responded.

It's me. Anon has struck again.

My heart beat hard in my chest and I opened the link.
It was from Food, Drink, And Air. That was…interesting.

Food, Drink, and Air *is happy to partner with Anon H. Critic to bring the best (and worst) of all walks of food. Our star reviewer Helene Carnahan will keep you informed of the must-eat places in greatest cities in the world. Anon will let you know where you should stop as you explore the best small towns of this great country, giving you the lowdown on can't-miss restaurants.*

Now, we proudly present our first collaboration with Anon H. Critic: Cat and the Fiddle.

.   .   .

Cat and the Fiddle
Four Blue Plates
Don't let the four plates fool you, Cat and the Fiddle is a must stop on your trek through Kansas. From the adorable neon cat on the sign out front to the love of the namesake and how long she'd run the place to the nostalgic music playing, it's a treasure. The décor and long soda counter gave me everything I was looking for in a roadside stop.
I had the pot pie they are famous for. I wasn't aware a blue plate diner could have a signature dish, but if this is it, it was a good choice. The crust was melt in your mouth perfect and the stew inside should have a shrine to its honor. The pie, the lemonade, the coffee, and my waitress Sheila were all just as wonderful. So why not a perfect rating? The head cook. He was unpleasant to his employees as well as the patrons. It's the only reason I can account for this place not being packed to the gills every day. With a little attitude adjustment now that the original owner isn't around, this place could easily be Five Blue Plates, but for now, I'll need to hold one back.
Anon H. Critic
Small Town Eats

I SLOWLY SAT down my phone as I seethed. Another review where I was the problem. I went back over every customer from the past two weeks since the last review Anon had posted. No one had come in and ordered multiple plates. No one had taken notes as they had eaten either. Who had gotten mad?

Helene. She did have potpie. But so did everyone else.

And I'd told no less than fifteen people it was the signature dish. Because it was. It was Cat's favorite and her recipe. So that was no help.

Three others had complained about yelling from the kitchen.

Damn. I did have a problem, didn't I?

Still, pointing that out in a review could hurt business. Damn whomever this person was!

And if they partnered with Food, Drink, Air then they had to be in the industry. I'd known it all along. And I bet Helene knew who it was since she worked there.

I angrily showered. My anger was measured by how many times I knocked over the shampoo – which was five today. I ran my fingers through my hair and gave it a good shake to get rid of extra water. A quick teeth brushing and I made my way to the diner.

Danny was already in the back when I got there.

"What's up, Four Star?" He snickered.

"Go to hell, Danny."

I took a breath. That wasn't going to fix anything. "Everyone – team meeting in thirty, in the dining room."

Three yes chefs, two groans, one fuck you chef. Perfect. Everyone heard me.

Head cook? Who the hell did they think they were? I was a chef, *the* chef, and this was my place and… I heard it as my mind rolled over it. I was a prick.

Hands on hips and head hung, I made my way to my employees waiting in a couple of booths. I sat on a barstool facing them.

"I want to address a couple things happening here. One – I know this isn't like it was when Cat was here. My aunt was great at this," I said as I gestured to the food, "but she didn't know how to run a restaurant, she knew how to cook and feed people. I know how to do both, so that's what I'm after. Preserving her legacy."

Danny opened his mouth but I held up a hand.

"Hear me out."

He nodded and I went on. "Two – I know kitchen morale hasn't been the best and one of the reasons I left the city was to get away from the dickhead chefs I had to work with there. And now I'm turning into one of them."

"Turning into?" Someone mumbled under their breath. Sheila tried to stifle a laugh.

"That's fair. I've been an ass."

"Does this have to do with the review?" Sheila asked.

I looked at the ceiling and blew out a breath through my teeth. "Partly. It was just the final straw. I want to not be that guy. So…I'd like a fresh start. Can we do that?"

A bunch of hesitant nods were my only answer.

"Great. I got you all new aprons." I passed them out. "Meeting over."

Danny stood up. "So, who was the reviewer?"

I shrugged. "How the hell should I know?"

He smiled and clapped me on the back. "You're nailing the not being a dick thing right now."

Sheila smiled at me, put on her apron, and wiped down the tables. I dragged myself back to the kitchen and glanced at the clock.

"Two hours until open."

Until then, I'll have to hold on to a plate.

"Danny? Can you cover my prep today?"

He looked at me, mouth open. "Um, yeah. Sure."

I grabbed my laptop and found a quiet corner in the diner. I didn't say anything to Carnahan after the review at London House, but this time…this time I could and would defend myself against my unknown assassin. Before there had been too much to lose, but now, I had something to gain. I could defend my little corner of nowhere and hopefully the review wouldn't hurt us. I'd explain things and then people would know that the reviewer, whomever it was, was the ass, not me. The readers didn't even know who I was. To them I was Joe Schmo. But I was Kael Ruggeman. I had Michelin stars, damn it. I put fingers to keyboard and typed out a response.

Dear Anon,

This is the "head cook" at Cat and the Fiddle. You recently reviewed my restaurant, that's right. It's mine. You gave us Four Blue Plates apparently because of me. Well, I'd like to defend myself and my staff as well as the institution that this place is. I have gone over every interaction over the last three months in my head. I can't think of one time the events you described happened. Only one customer comes to mind, but she had a bad attitude from the beginning and left in a huff. It was someone I've worked with before and they can be quite high strung. I think they brought some past experiences into the diner and that was the cause. Besides, that couldn't have been you, she only ordered one dish.

And our regulars seem to like it here just fine.

If you would come back and give us another chance for that fifth blue plate, I'll cook anything you want. You seemed to like the food well enough. So here is my open invitation to you, Anon H. Critic, come back and experience the Five Blue Plate meal you crave and I know we can provide.

K. R.

. . .

I looked over the response. I smiled with a satisfied grin. If this Anon was a professional, they would accept my invitation. If not, I'd shown most people liked eating here. I found the submission email for Food, Drink, Air – the last place to publish a review – and hit send. Making my way back to the kitchen, I felt better and better about it. There was no reason I shouldn't defend myself and honestly, I didn't care what they thought. I only wanted the restaurant to survive and thrive if possible. I didn't want to let my aunt down. The thought of this place closing squeezed my soul in a vice grip that kept me up at night.

I got back to my station to find Danny hadn't done any of my prep.

"Where the hell is Danny?"

"Out back having a smoke," Sheila called from where she wrapped silverware.

I stalked out to the stoop. "Damn it, Danny. I asked you to cover my station."

"I did. No one messed with it."

I hung my head, hands on hips. "I wanted you to do my prep. That's what watch my station means. Jesus Christ, Dan. Now, put out that cancer stick and let's fucking move. We're behind."

He crushed out his cigarette and muttered as he followed me in. "You're the one who had something to do right then."

I whirled on him, in no mood. "Yeah. I can go and do something if I need to. You should be able to chop a few god damn vegetables and check the stock in the pots. It's not anything hard. How long have you worked here, man? What did you do before?"

My chest heaved and I noticed Danny leaning back and away. I righted myself.

"Sorry, man. I just, I just need to know I can count on you."

He squared his shoulders. "It's okay. You can. Sorry. Cat didn't need me to do anything."

I turned back to my station. "I promise she did."

The rest of the day I tried to be on my best behavior and not cause anyone any problems. No one else would come in and say I was the problem.

Not even Helene Carnahan.

Helene

THE HEAT ROSE up my neck and across my face as I read the email. Rob leaned over my shoulder, reading from behind me.

"Print it."

"No!"

"Why not?" Rob asked. "It is the exact thing readers will eat up."

I shook my head. "Is that the kind of magazine we want to be? Don't we want to be a high class place where readers can find the best of dining, or have we devolved into some gossip rag perpetuating a feud?"

"Both." He had a smug look on his face.

"Both?"

"Oh hell yes. Do you know what this is going to do?"

"Make Anon look like an idiot for agreeing to do business with us?"

Rob spun my chair to face him. "No. It's going to make

people read not just your reviews, but also Anon's to see if they pissed off anyone else. Oh, this is too delicious. If Anon was here I would kiss their mouth. You can't buy this kind of drama. I can hear the clicks."

I turned back to my computer. "That's dollar bills you hear, Scrooge McDuck."

"Who is that?"

I rolled my eyes. "The duck that swims in money?"

"Don't know him, but he sounds great." He laughed as he strolled out of the office. I looked at Jen.

"How did we get here?"

"Do you want the cliff notes?"

I put my head in my hands. "No. I remember."

Last week was burned on my brain. Rob had smirked. "The Times sent us another one of those anonymous crits. Who the fuck is doing this?"

I'd been surprised it was so fast. That meant my secret reviews were gaining traction. But I didn't have time to be happy because my boss stared at me. I shrugged. "Why does it matter? They don't seem to be covering any of the places we do."

He'd looked at me like I'd grown a second nose. "Why does it matter? Because those are readers. Our readers. Or should be. Numbers are everything."

I sat down at my desk as he followed me into my office. "My numbers are fine."

Hands on his waist, he blew out a breath. "For now. Do something about this."

I'd looked at him as a sickness settled in my stomach. "What do you want me to do?"

He leered at me. "That's not my job, it's yours." He turned on his heel and left in a dramatic fashion. Sometimes I thought Rob had decided he was in an 80's movie, heading up a firm and way more important than he was.

Back in the moment, I thought about the response. "Shit."

Jen turned and gave me a sympathetic look. "Do you know who it is?

I raised an eyebrow to her. Did she know it was me? I shook my head, not able to form the words to lie to her. Especially since she was the one who gave me the idea that would save my ass.

"Maybe team up with them."

"How, Jen? It's anonymous." And how the hell was I supposed to team up with myself on this one?

"Place an ad asking them to send it to you and then we can print it and get the views Rob wants."

I smiled. "You're a genius. But I'm going to sleep for twenty minutes. Be on the lookout?"

She nodded, no questions asked.

I snuggled into the blanket I kept on the small couch in my office. Could I combine the two? I didn't know. And I wasn't sure I could keep this up much longer anyway. Did it really matter to these places? Some rando saying your food was good or bad and nothing to write home about. I sat up. That was a better name. Food to Write Home About.

"You okay?" Jen started as I bolted upright.

"Yeah. Um, yep. Sorry." I typed the name into my notes app and laid back down. This time I drifted off, seeing my two columns next to each other in my mind.

I was startled awake by Rob bumping my couch with his knee forcefully. "This is how you are on top of the rogue critic situation?" He folded his arms and stared down at me.

I sat up and stretched. "Sorry. Just a bit of a headache."

And I'm dead tired from traveling. "But I'm on it, Bossman. Jen gave me a great idea."

He looked over at my assistant dubiously, as if he didn't believe good ideas could come from her. She smiled at me though.

"And?" He tapped his toe with impatience.

"I'm going to place an ad asking them to contact me. Hopefully they'll send to us instead of the Times and then we can print them, get the views. We can run it with my column."

He nodded. "Could work. We can probably find a small bit in the budget to sweeten the pot. I'll have someone run you some numbers down today. Good work, Helene."

I crossed back to my desk, looking at the clock, seeing I'd been asleep for over an hour. "It was Jen."

He gruffed in her direction. "Good job." And with that he was gone.

"What an ass." I said as I clicked on my computer.

"I heard that," Rob said from just outside the door.

"Good," I answered back.

Jen just grinned. "Thank you for always having my back."

"Thanks for having mine and letting me sleep. Now, where am I eating this week?"

She handed me a menu for yet another fusion place. "And you have a plea to send to copy."

I nodded slowly. "I guess I do."

I made a mental note to set up a fake email for correspondence and I'd have to do something about pay if there was budget for it. This was getting out of control. I should just pull the plug before I got in over my head.

Kael's email stared me in the face from my computer screen, igniting my anger again.

"Shit." I said again. "I really don't want to print this."

She looked at me, pushing her hair over her shoulder. "You have to. Rob said so." She shrugged and half smiled.

I blew out a breath. It felt cheap and awful and how dare Kael Ruggeman write in. He was the worst. I mean, he must act on pure audacity. There's no other reason for this. And did he think this would make him look good? He totally shat on a customer, which happened to be me, but no one else knew that.

Who writes in to try and defend themselves, and in the process creates another problem? I couldn't understand how someone so brilliant in the kitchen was this much of a dumbass in life.

"Why does this bother you so badly? The chef is the one who looks like an ass. Anon can't hold you responsible. He wrote about a customer, like an idiot. I mean, I wouldn't go to his diner based on that alone," Jen said matter-of-factly.

I thought about that too. This could also hurt Kael and Kitty's diner. I didn't want that either.

"That's what I worry about. That diner sounds nice and I don't want it to hurt the other people who works there."

And Anon would hold me responsible because I was her and she was me and I was the bonehead who thought she could pull this off.

Jen nodded. "True. Hadn't thought of that."

But what could I do? I mean, bless him all over. His name was Kael after all. He didn't really have a fighting chance in this world, did he?

I swallowed my pride and prepared the email for publication.

But the more I thought about it, the madder I got. It was Chef 101 - you didn't respond to a food critic. There could be a million reasons they left the review they did and for that matter, I gave my reasons.

"Ugh."

Jen turned in shock. "What the hell?"

"Sorry. Just, that diner owner is an ass."

She leaned back and crossed her arms. "I already said that. So what are you not telling me?"

I shrugged. "I don't know what you mean." I typed and deleted as I tried to think of a way to introduce the response I was about to publish and start a firestorm.

"Yes, you do. You know who the diner owner is, don't you."

I looked at my assistant trying to keep my face as serene as a calm pond. "How would I know that? They only put initials."

"I don't think it would be too hard to look up who owns Cat and the Fiddle."

"It doesn't matter who he is, Jen. It matters what he wrote and the fact that he wrote something at all. You don't respond to critics. You just don't. It's about respect, which he clearly has none of."

She crossed her arms. "So what? It isn't like this is a professional reviewer or any—"

She stopped herself, causing me to look up.

"You know who Anon is."

I looked away, my coffee becoming very interesting. "How would I?"

"You can tell me. I will never betray you."

I nodded. "I know, Jen. And I'm sorry to disappoint, but I can't."

"Okay, have it your way. But you can tell me when you're ready." She went back to her desk.

Shit. That was close. But she hit it on the head. No one

knows who Anon is so no one can give them, well, me, the respect I deserve.

I chuckled to myself.

"What's funny?"

"Nothing. Just realizing I'm kind of a jerk, too."

She came over to me this time. "You're not. I promise."

"Thank you. I couldn't do this without you."

She shifted her weight foot to foot. "Well, I hope if you ever... leave this place, you'd take me with you. I hope you know I work for you, not the company."

I squeezed her hands. "It's a promise."

I heard a few clicks, then Jen screeched. "Kael Ruggeman."

My heart beat out of my chest.

"Where?"

"He owns the diner. That's why you're having this reaction. How did you know that?"

"Deidre told me." I didn't meet her eyes. And after a few minutes, I felt her stare melt away.

I tried to go about my day like normal, but I could not get that response out of my head. No matter what Jen said. I had to call Deidre.

I called as soon as I was far enough away from the office. "Didi, I have a problem."

"Your hot chef you keep giving not enough stars fired back?"

"I hate you sometimes."

"Only because you love me."

I huffed. "True. But yes. What am I going to do?"

"Hang on." I heard shuffling and heels clicking and I knew she was moving off somewhere private. "Okay, what do you want to do?"

"Go back there and tell him to his smug face how much of a problem he is."

"And?"

"And nothing."

"And screw his brains out. This is your problem. You've always had a thing for him."

I opened my mouth, but nothing came out.

"Before you disagree, which I know you were about to do, yes you have. You've had arrogant chefs before. You've had ones come out to your table—"

"They didn't hover."

"Yes they did. You just didn't notice."

I shook my head. "No, Didi. This was different. Plus I worked in his kitchen. He was so hard on me, in a way he wasn't to the other chefs. Why was I different?"

"You're not going to bring up culinary school?"

"Why would I? We were even then, on the same playing field. At least, I thought we were."

"You were better than him. I'll say it if you won't. Don't deny it, which I know you're about to. But you know I'm right. And he knew it too. That's his problem."

"What is?"

"That's why he was different to you. You're better than him and he didn't know what to do about it."

I sat back. "This response, this complete lack of respect? It's the internet equivalent of leering over the table."

"He doesn't know it's you. No one does. So tread lightly."

"It's still me, though. I know."

"Lena, listen to me. You have talked about Kael Ruggeman a lot. Before you went to his restaurant, after you left the restaurant, before he left the city, after he left the city. Then you show up at his diner—"

"Yeah. Who could've predicted that, best friend?" I

pushed through my building door and huffed my way up the stairs.

"I'm not sorry. I was hoping you'd go out there and get something out of your system. Instead, you poked the damn bear."

"Wait, isn't that what you wanted?"

"No! He was supposed to poke you!"

We both laughed and I did feel a little better.

"Seriously," she went on, "If he knew who you were, do you think he would give you the respect you deserve?"

I finally made it to my apartment and collapsed on the couch. "He only made one remark about our past. So doubtful." Was that what I was mad about?

"Write him back."

I sat up. "What?"

"Write him back."

"Absolutely not."

She guffawed. "Why not?"

"One, it's unprofessional. Two, there's no reason to shake this hornet's nest. What would it do?"

"It would let him know you're not to be messed with and also that Anon knows her stuff. And it is anonymous. So it definitely won't hurt anything."

I tossed the idea around in my mind.

"I do want to tell him to fuck off."

"Maybe don't say that."

I laughed. "Okay, Didi, but if this comes back on me, I'm blaming you."

"I assume responsibility. Maybe he'll come to New York to find you and then—"

"Don't say it, I know where your mind is. Plus, he doesn't know I'm in New York." I stuck my tongue out at the phone.

"Fine. Love you."

"Mean it."

I tossed the phone down next to me. Write him back. What would I even say? It did get a big response online today, as Rob predicted it would. And the comments confirmed what I thought, Kael was a jackass.

Now the real question I had to ask was – how did this help?

My phone buzzed.

> I know you're sitting there doing pros and
> cons. Just write the damn letter.

Deidre knew me too well. Normally I welcomed it, but right now I hated her all-knowing eye. Except she was wrong about one thing, I did not have a thing for Kael. I never had and I never would. He just got under my skin, and not in a good way. I couldn't believe she would think that.

Okay, maybe I had a thing once. But I was young and dumb and who wouldn't find someone who can cook like that, while looking like that, attractive?

I pulled out my laptop and opened up the email I'd set up to submit my Anon reviews. An email from Food, Drink, Air that I did not send sat in my inbox. It was a copy of Kael's response with one single line.

Care to respond?

I groaned. *Fucking Rob.*

I took a deep breath and set my phasers to destroy.

5

~

Helene

Dear Head Chef,
This is Anon H. Critic. I stand by my review of your diner and
my first, and only, visit will be sufficient. I understand you may
not be wise in the ways of the industry due to the size of your
establishment, but you do not respond to critics. It shows
disrespect and a lack of knowledge in their area of expertise.
While I appreciate your invite, I will be declining, if for no other
reason than how you spoke of your customer. She wasn't a part of
this and yet you felt the need to tear her down. If you will do that
to a stranger, I have no idea what you would do to your staff.
I still hold, your food is delicious, and I encourage people to stop
at the cuteness and deliciousness that is Cat and the Fiddle. But if
they want full enjoyment, I would advise they call ahead and see
if it's your day off.

Anon H. Critic

I hit send before I had a chance to rethink it. An angry knot formed in the bottom of my stomach. This was a mess I didn't plan on. I just wanted to tell people about good food. I poured a heavy glass of wine hoping it would put me to sleep so I could forget about what I had just done.

I woke up the next morning to my phone blowing up.

"What?"

"Get in here now, Carnahan."

"Rob? Why? Are we on fire?"

"Anon responded. I had Jen put it out and he has already sent a response!"

I sat bolt upright. "What?" My voice was hushed. No, no, no, no. This was a nightmare. I pinched myself to make sure I was awake, and to my disappointment, I was.

"Yeah, this is perfect. I'm giving you a bonus on your next check. This is such a coup."

"I'm on my way."

I hung up and called Jen. "Read it to me."

"It's not pretty. It mentions someone he knows."

"What? Why?"

"Because Anon mentioned the customer in the rebuttal. And he said they worked together."

My stomach dropped. "Read it, please."

"Are you sure?"

I held the phone between my shoulder and chin as I attempted to pull on my jeans. "Yes. I need to know what I'm walking in to."

She cleared her throat.

"Anon, I'm well-versed in the 'industry'. This isn't my first kitchen and this isn't my first rodeo. Respect is only given where it's deserved."

I clenched my jaw but let her continue.

"Such as the customer I referred to in my letter. As I said, we worked together in the past, and there's a reason she now reviews. You know, those who can't do teach? Well, those that can't cook, have to get out of the kitchen.

But I was still willing to let it go after I said my piece. Now I have a new mission – find out who you are and take you down. Yours sincerely, K. R."

I vibrated with anger. Who the fuck did he think he was?

"Helene? You there?"

"Yeah. Yep. I'm here. Hey Jen, can you cover for a few days? I have to...take care of something."

"You got it."

I hung up. No questions asked. She definitely knew. Next I called Jack to get the plane ready.

"You sure you wanna go now?"

"Why wouldn't I? I know it is weird I'm going somewhere I've already gone, but it's an exception."

"It's just this time of year..."

I rolled my eyes. "Can you take me or not?"

"Yeah. I can. See you at four."

I threw clothes in a bag. I would go to...wherever it was Kael Ruggeman was... and give him a piece of my mind to his face. He couldn't pursue my identity. I could not lose this job. Everything depended on it.

I picked up the phone again. "Celia, hey sis."

"Everything okay?"

"I have to go out of town for a few days."

"Now? Are you sure?"

What was with everyone today?

"Yes. Now. Will you be okay?"

She hesitated before answering.

"Celia?"

"I'll be fine. I'm just worried about you."

I rolled my eyes. Now wasn't the time for her to play big sister. "I'll have Jen come and check in and take you to the store."

"That'll be great." It could have been my imagination, but I swear I heard a smile in her voice.

"I'll be back in like, a day, two tops. Give Jonny big kisses from Aunt Leen."

"Okay, sis. And hey, be careful."

"Always will be."

Jen's eyes were round when I came in. "I thought you were going somewhere."

I sat down at my desk, diving into the things I had to wrap up before my impromptu trip. "I am. I'm not here. But I didn't want to drop everything in your lap."

She sat down across from my desk. "Hey. I know where you're going and why."

I looked at my friend. "To see Deidre. Because she..." I couldn't think up a good lie, and honestly, I didn't want to.

"Right. Deidre. Obviously. It must be important."

I nodded.

"Anything I can do to help?"

I smiled. "Hold off Rob."

Her answering grin made my smile wider. "With pleasure. Anything else?"

"Can you check in on Celia and Jonny? They need to go to the store tomorrow."

She stood and squeezed my hand. "Of course."

I'd just put in my last review when Rob came around the corner. He saw my travel bag next to my desk. "What's this?"

Doing my best to not be a deer in the headlights, I rifled through my rolodex of excuses as fast as I could. "Gotta head out of town for a couple days. No biggie. I've filed all reviews, correspondence done, and next two reviews set up."

"Where are you going?"

I stood and leaned on the desk. "Are you not approving my PTO?"

He frowned at me. "I already did, but I came down to see what the hell was going on."

"Then are you asking as my employer what I'm doing with my personal time? Or as a friend?"

His frown turned to a scowl. "A friend."

I grabbed my bag and checked the time. I took a step toward Rob. "We're not friends."

I waved at Jen as I practically ran to the elevator. Barely enough time to make the plane.

I'm heading back there to let him have it.

Deidre responded right away.

And you know what else to do.

I won't be doing that. Only putting him in his place.

The phone rang. "And what will this do? I just want to make sure you've really thought this through."

Exasperation filled me. "You're the one who told me to do this."

"No. I told you to answer his letter."

I tapped my toe as I waited for a brilliant response to come to me.

"Lena, I know you're mad. He gets to you. But you don't have to prove anything to him."

I choked on unexpected tears. "I know, Didi. I have to prove it to me."

"Then go get him, tiger. Love you."

"Mean it."

The plane left the ground as I braced. Did the man who had messed with my life for so long think his words didn't have consequences? Well, they did. And I would prove it to him. Kael wouldn't know what hit him.

Kael

IT HAD BEEN MOSTLY dead all day. We were down to only needing one flat top on and I'd sent everyone except myself and Sheila home. A big weather front was about to roll through which meant only locals today. A few people sat in the dining room, grabbing a bite before heading home and hunkering down. We'd had a ton of to-go orders but not much else.

I was contemplating giving everyone free pie with their meals so I wouldn't have to throw it out when I heard the bell ding. It was late for someone to just be coming in. I had wondered more than once why we did a late dinner service. But that's how Aunt Cat did it, so that's how I would do it.

I tried to do as much like her as I could and still make this business successful.

She had only cared about the customer, I had to think about the bottom line. She had a safety net of money I didn't have. So I'd have to be content to land somewhere in the middle. I remember her talking about making sure they were open for evening travelers. It was lonely out there, she'd say.

Yeah. No shit it was lonely.

Sheila poked her head back through the door. "Someone here for you."

"For me?'

She nodded.

"Can't you handle it?"

She smiled. "Not this one."

I wiped my hands and grumbled as I walked out to the dining room. My heart stutter-stepped as I froze in my tracks. Helene Carnahan stood with her arms crossed, toe tapping. From her knitted brow to her pursed lips, impatience was all over her face. Fire lit in her eyes when she saw me. But it wasn't a fire anyone would welcome. It wouldn't keep you warm. This one would burn down your house.

"Can I help you?"

"I don't know. Are you going to write about me in some little tiff online?"

My mouth fell open. "What?"

She pulled out her phone and read aloud. "*Only one customer comes to mind, but she had a bad attitude from the beginning and left in a huff. It was someone I've worked with before and they can be quite high strung.*" She looked at me and I half expected her to stomp her foot. I pushed my lips together, trying to keep the sound inside, but I couldn't help it. I burst out laughing.

"Is that what you came back here for? To accuse me of saying something about you? How do you know it was you if you weren't the one with the bad attitude?"

Her face turned red as I watched and I took a step back. A tremor hit my stomach.

"Are you saying you ran off more than one customer in the last few weeks? And it was someone else that you worked with?"

Damn. She had me there. "No. I mean. I'm just saying, I asked you about your food—"

"You sat down at my table. Do you sit at everyone's table, or can you just not respect my space? You kept asking me to tell you about it right then. I was eating. Nothing else. How dare you bring up our interaction like that."

I crossed my arms. Something in my brain tingled.

"And then to say the words, those who can't cook, should get out of the kitchen." She turned her head away and then zeroed back in on me. "It wasn't enough to run me out of yours? How dare you."

Her voice shook and eyes glistened. She looked like she was about to cry and as she said those words out loud, I actually heard them. It was too far. An apology was owed, but I went on the defensive.

"You know who Anonymous is, don't you? Is that why you're so worked up? And why do you care, anyway? There aren't many in the food circles of New York that know you were in my kitchen."

She took a step back this time. "Plenty know."

I tightened my jaw. "Because this online tiff, as you call it, is between me and..." Well, I didn't know who anonymous was actually.

"You and who?" Her features rose in fear. Is that what covered her face?

"This anonymous source. But it's published out of Food, Drink, Air in New York. You have to know."

"I don't. It's just an email account." Her shoulders

dropped about five inches and visible relief settled through her. "I can cook."

I leaned back against the counter. "Look, I am sorry I brought it up. I was defending myself. I didn't think about how that would hit you. How could you I know you'd read it?"

"Oh, I don't know, because you clearly responded to a review my magazine put out?"

Dumbfounded could never describe the look on my face. A family of little green aliens could have come into the diner at that moment and I would've had a better grasp on what to say next. I stammered. "This reviewer, critic, whoever it is. They gave me four blue plates and it—"

"Bruised your giant ego?" She crossed her arms and stared directly through my soul.

"No. A little, I guess."

"A little."

"You wouldn't get it. You don't..." My words dropped off when I saw her face.

She lowered her chin as she stared at me. "I don't what? Have my own kitchen? Make food for people? I wonder why that could be."

I was at a loss. She wasn't wrong, but she was in my restaurant calling me out like this for simply defending myself. But before I could say anything she went on.

"I mean, someone comes in, takes time to eat here and then write about your food, and you have the audacity to respond like that and bring another person into it? What the hell is wrong with you? Why did it bother you to begin with is the question?"

"Okay. Then why do you care if I responded? This business means a lot to me. And you don't even know me."

"You don't know me either!"

"I do know you, Helene."

Her lips parted and eyes softened. But she regained her form quickly and lowered her voice. "Not anymore."

She turned and paced a little, hands waving in the air. "It's the disrespect, that's all. Everyone knows you don't respond to critics."

I stepped closer. "No. Not everyone knows that. Only people in the business."

She looked at me, frozen in place as I spoke.

We stared at each other, as time stood still. The world could've passed by and I wouldn't have known. It was only me and her locked in this moment.

When she spoke, her words cut deep. "No matter what you might think about yourself, Kael Ruggeman, you aren't the end all be all in this world. And I know you've run many kitchens, but why aren't you still in any of them? Now you're here in the middle of nowhere, frankly bringing shame to this place. You're so convinced you have all the answers, you never stop to check if anyone asked a question. You're the reason I'm not in the kitchen, not because I couldn't do it."

That hurt. I pushed her because she was good. I snapped back in that response because I was trying to prove...what?

"You're the problem here." Her jaw set.

I whirled on my heel, heading behind the counter. She matched me step for step, only a length of steel and a Formica-topped counter between us.

"You're the reason I sent a response." I leveled her with my eyes, trying not to look at her mouth. Her pout was getting to me.

"Me? What? How?"

"You gave me four stars and then whoever this nobody is gave me four blue plates and it set me off."

She leaned forward over the counter. "You bad behavior

is not my responsibility nor the result of me doing my job." She began to gather her things. "Besides, you don't know this is a nobody. It could be anybody, someone important."

A lightbulb went off.

"Then why are you hiding behind Anonymous?"

A laugh erupted out of her. "Me? You think it's me?" Her voice raised an octave. Then she burst into full laughter. "Have you ever met my boss? Like I have time to get away."

"You're here twice." Heat rose in me as I watched her chest heave with anger.

"I was meeting a friend. I came back here to tell you to your face what an ass you are. I didn't think anything else would do it justice. And believe me, it was worth the trip."

I slowly rounded the end of the counter, coming close to her. I drew in a breath and caught the soft sent of maple and brown sugar coming from her hair. She squared her shoulders, not backing down. I didn't know if I wanted to yell at her or kiss her pretty face off. Maybe both.

"Oh, I know it's you. There's no reason you'd be here otherwise." My voice was low, but she didn't so much as lean away.

Definitely kiss her. My breath rose and fell like hers as we stood toe to toe.

She shook her head. "You're crazy. You want so badly to be mad at someone, you will accuse the first person to step in front of you and call you on your bullshit. Kael Ruggeman, the great chef. Fleeing from New York because no one there wanted to deal with your ego and your impossible kitchen behavior. You never think of anyone but yourself and you thought you could come here, wrapped in the memory of what this place was and reclaim something that was never yours to begin with. But you can't. That isn't who you are."

We'd drawn a crowd. Every employee stood and watched. A customer sipped their coffee and Sheila absent-mindedly refilled the cup as they were engrossed in the scene, too. I knew they weren't on my side. Helene took a step forward, pointing a finger in my chest.

"Then you fire off a response to someone you don't even know and bring up a customer, me, in your fight? You brought my integrity into question for no other reason than to spare you from your inadequacy. I came here to let you know your actions have consequences. I thought when I gave you four stars for hovering over my table, it might get through that thick head of yours. But no. You had to see your shortcomings as a character flaw of mine."

I swear she didn't even take a breath before she continued.

"Yes, I do know the food world and I thought you did too. But I never thought you were so arrogant to fall to this. You might make some of the best food I've ever eaten, but it's barely tolerable because I know the man behind the stove."

Her chest rose and fell harder as she called out each of my insecurities one by one.

"And you do it all here in the kitchen of a great woman. How fucking dare you."

My shoulders rounded, defeated. She was right. I had no right to assume she was anonymous. Of course she would be defensive of another person in her field. I would defend another chef, even if they were a rival. No one got how hard it was to do what we do.

Or what she did. And I got it. She'd taken personal offense.

"I'm sorry. You're right. I shouldn't have included you in my response."

She stood her ground. "You shouldn't have responded at all."

I nodded, penitent.

She looked around to everyone in the diner, as if she remembered where she was, or more accurately, *who* she was. "Sorry, this is incredibly unprofessional behavior. I apologize." She made her way to the door.

I should keep my mouth shut, but having the right to remain silent and the ability were not both traits I possessed. "I still believe what I said was right."

She looked back, door open, the cold air whipping around her. "Of course you do. When have you ever thought you were wrong?"

The wind left my sails with her as she exited the diner. I looked around, wringing the towel I held through my hands. Expectant eyes, curious for my reaction, stared at me. Danny grinned from the kitchen window like he'd seen his favorite team win the World Series.

"Get back to work. Everyone else, eat up before this weather comes in. And take a piece of pie with you on the house. Want you all to be safe."

Sheila leaned into me as I tried to get in the kitchen. "If you keep giving away food every time she comes in, it won't matter what any review says."

I rolled my eyes as I made my way to the freezer and shut myself in. Damn her! Why would she come all the way back here? And what was she really doing here the first time?

6

Helene

I pulled my coat closer around myself. The wind whipped through me, chilling me more than Kael's demeanor. Who did he think he was? I shivered, not sure it was from the cold or from how close he'd gotten to discovering I was Anon.

Or maybe it was just being that close to Kael.

I hated how he could still get to me. It shouldn't be like that after all this time. I tried to push Deidre's words from my mind. I did not have a thing for that arrogant, cocky, always-has-to-be-right jackass.

I crossed the street to the car. Fingers numbed, I fumbled the keys in the freezing wind. Shit! It was so cold all the sudden. The door closed behind me, shutting out the gusts, but I could hear it howl as it curled around the car. I peered at the sky through the windshield. It was an eerie blue-gray, a winter sky ready to burst open.

I cranked the engine, willing the heater to work quickly. I called Jack to tell him I was heading to the hanger.

"Sorry, darling. There's no way we can take off and get out of here fast enough."

"Fast enough? What does that mean?" I asked as the first snowflakes hit the windshield.

"The storm. It's gonna be a doozy. That's why I asked if you wanted to make the trip. We can't get out of here anytime soon."

I sunk back against the seat. "The storm? There's a storm?"

I heard him chuckle. "You're the general's daughter, all right. Just head off to your objective without a thought to what happens next."

My back stiffened. "I guess." I bristled. I wasn't like my dad. I couldn't be. That man was a monster.

"Better get a room. Don't worry. I have a place to stay."

"Okay. Thanks. Sorry for the trouble."

"No trouble at all, darling."

I turned off the engine and grabbed my small travel bag I carry just in case. Already parked at the hotel, I opened the door to snow hitting me in the face. It was coming down hard. I pushed through to the sidewalk. The small lobby was as charming as the diner, except better because Kael Ruggeman wasn't there. I shook off the snow and cold as I stepped in.

"Can I help you?" The woman behind the desk asked me.

I nodded. "A room, please."

"Just for a night?"

I looked out the window. I could barely see across the street now. "Better make it two."

She typed into the computer while I waited.

"Luggage? I'll get it for you."

I held up my small bag. "This is it. Wasn't planning on the weather."

She handed me the keys, actual real keys. Complete with quintessential keychain you'd expect at any roadside hotel. "Here you go. Room 5."

I smiled. "Thanks."

I walked back outside, the snow swirling around me. My hair blew in my face. I fought to hold it back and keep my footing. This storm came out of nowhere.

I thought back to Jack knowing about the weather and my sister's questions and worry about me taking a trip and maybe it didn't. I was too riled up by Kael's response to notice anything else.

Who was the self-absorbed one now?

I made it to my room, which was thankfully close to the office. I pushed open the door, then leaned back against it to close it as quick as I could.

I tossed my bag on the bed then tossed myself down next to it. I shouldn't have acted the way I did in there. It was unprofessional and even if the things I said were true, I still didn't have a right to say them. The quiet of the room was peaceful and a welcome warm filled my body. It gave me a chance to regain my anger. I sat up.

How could he think he was right? You don't respond to critics. You don't double down. And you definitely don't bring up customers in your communications.

Especially ones you have a history with.

I can cook, damn him. I know I can.

"Grrrrr." I stood up and paced. What the hell was I going

to do stuck in this town? I had my laptop, except I left it in the car. I called Jen.

"Hey."

"How are you? Having a good trip?"

I grimaced. "Not really. I'm snowed in. I'm not sure when I'll be back. Can you do the biggest favor and cover for me?"

"Of course. Where are you?"

I took a deep breath. I really hated not telling her everything. But I had to keep it in. Too much was riding on it. "Middle of nowhere and like a dope didn't check the weather."

It was mostly true.

"Okay. Stay safe and I'll see you when you get back. I'll let Celia know."

"Thanks. I owe you."

I paced, not knowing what to do next. Antsy didn't cover what I felt. I called Deidre.

"I'm here and I'm snowed in."

Her laughter pierced the quiet of my room. "I know how you can pass the time."

I rolled my eyes, putting her on speaker and flopping back on the bed. "You have to let that go."

She chuckled. "Seriously, how'd it go?"

I cringed thinking about my performance in the diner. "Oh, Didi. It was awful." I told her all that went down and waited.

"That sounds awesome. I wish I could've been there."

I huffed. "It was hella unprofessional. I kept telling myself to shut up but the words just kept coming."

After a beat of silence, Deidre said, "I'm not going to make the joke you left dangling in front of me, but I'm proud of you."

I sat up. "You are? What for?"

"You always make a choice for everyone else. What is best for them, or your job, or whatever. You never do something for you. And you did."

"Great. When I finally do something for me, it's to make an ass out of myself in front of strangers, saying things that I would never usually say. Perfect."

She laughed again. "No, it's good. How bad is the weather?"

Checking the window, the snow was already piling up.

"Bad. I need to go find food before I can't get out."

"Okay. Love you."

"Mean it."

It just hit me I hadn't eaten all day. I started this morning in New York. How was this the same day? Plus, I needed my laptop if I was going to be stuck in here all night. Pulling my coat on as tight as it would go, I shoved the keys in my pocket and stepped out in the storm. The sidewalk was completely covered. Snow crunched under my feet, soaking through my shoes, chilling my feet.

I got my computer from the car and put it in my room quickly then walked down the sidewalk. A small ding met me when I pushed through the door to the office. "Hi. Do you have anything to eat?"

The lady behind the counter shook her head. "No. Not a thing. There's a diner across the street if you want to brave the snow."

I turned to look out the window. The light from the neon at Kitty's place burned through the weather, placing a pit firmly in my stomach. "Thanks." I didn't look back before I stepped out the door.

I went back to my room. I could make until tomorrow without food, right? I checked my bag to see if I had any snacks but no luck there.

I did not want to go back out in this. But the longer I sat there, the more my stomach rumbled.

This was silly. It was just across the street. I could make it. But it felt a little like tucking my tail in defeat going over there to get a meal.

For the first time in my life, I'd gotten the last word in and it'd been good too. I'd waited years to tell Kael what I thought of him and his attitude. Now I had, but to go back and be like, oh yeah, by the way, I'd like to buy a sandwich, that took the sting out of my bravado.

I lowered my head and trudged on through the snow.

Kael

I PACED THE KITCHEN, the storm beating against the front of the store. The diners had cleared out. I should go up and lock the door, but who was going to come in in this weather? There was only one person I wanted to come back through that door, but I knew she'd never grace my doorstep again.

Cleaning the kitchen did not occupy my mind like I wished it would and it wandered straight back to Helene and her fucking review.

If I thought the first visit was awkward, it was nothing compared to this one. I shouldn't have brought her up in the response, she was right about that. I would be pissed too. But she didn't have to come in here and tell me off like that in front of the whole diner.

Even if she had been right about what she said.

I blew out a big breath that sounded like a growl. Obviously she wasn't Anon. She would never come back here if she was.

I paused. Or maybe she would. Maybe that's exactly what she would do.

I stopped and looked at the dates of the review. Did that match her visit here? I didn't know. And I didn't know how to figure it out.

But it was another four blue plates. So if it was her, I would like her to tell me exactly why. Then I could tell her what she could do with that fifth plate. I should've confronted her about that before she left. Couldn't really do more damage at this point. Now I probably wouldn't get a chance. I was chained to this place and there was no way I could get away long enough to take this woman to task. But she was long gone and that was that.

I went back to wiping down the grills, making them cleaner than they had ever been. Good thing about being pissed as hell – my kitchen would shine. I thought I heard the bell. I froze, listening. I didn't hear anything else so I went back to cleaning.

A couple minutes later, a familiar voice met my ears. "Hello? Are you open?"

My blood boiled and I knew I turned red all the way up to my ears. I could feel it. I rounded the corner into the dining room.

"What the hell—" I stopped. Helene stood there with a too thin jacket, snowflakes still glistening in her hair. Cheeks were pink with cold. She crossed her arms around herself. She wasn't angry this time, she was cold.

She was so pretty, I melted a bit.

No. You're mad. She's your nemesis. I squared my shoulders.

"Hey. Sorry to bother you. But it appears I'm stuck here. And I need dinner. Are you still open?"

My first instinct was to ask her what I could make for her. I was angry at this woman, I reminded myself. I ran my towel through my hands, convincing myself not to pull her up into a kiss.

"I just cleaned the grill."

She shifted from foot to foot. "Okay, is there anything in the case or cooler? I'll take some pie, even."

I stared at her, not budging, trying to muster a frown. *You're mad.* But she looked so much like the person I used to know, not the one who had told me off an hour ago.

"Um, I'm happy to cook it myself. I know my way around a kitchen. And I'll clean up after."

That shook me.

"You're going to cook it?"

She nodded, snow falling from her hair as it melted. I wanted to tousle her hair, giving her a chance to get warm. "Sure. I mean, it's your kitchen. So your call. If you think I can cook and all."

That again took me aback. She'd worked in a high level kitchen. My kitchen even and I'd insulted her for no good reason.

"I'll go with you. Don't want you breaking anything, Miss Four Stars."

"I give what's earned."

That one got me and my jaw went slack. She rolled her eyes as she passed me, not waiting for anymore permission. I wanted to go outside and bury my head in the snow. Why did I need to be an asshole to this woman? Oh yeah. She gave me four stars.

And told me all the things I feared about myself were true.

And said them in front of other people.

I followed her as she put her coat to the side and pulled her hair up in a messy bun. I tried not to notice every curve and how she moved as her arms reached up to her head. The way her neck tilted as she stretched. She turned to me and I snapped my eyes up to hers.

"Sink?"

I tossed my head toward the far wall.

She looked over to find it hidden in the corner.

"Not really in the pattern, is it?" She furrowed her brow and pursed her lips.

"In the pattern? Haven't been out of that kitchen that long, huh?"

"Everyone has a kitchen." She pushed past me, the smell of brown sugar rising up. I was drawn in and followed her. She looked back over her shoulder.

"Do you not need personal space? Or do you just enjoy mine?" Her cheeks went pink. I did not understand this woman.

"What?"

"You hover at tables. You came out there to ask about my food before I could even process it. Now you're right behind me."

I took a step back. "Sorry."

She raised an eyebrow.

"Sorry? That's it?" She pulled pans and a pot from the wall and checked the bottoms of them.

"They are the best we can do right now."

"I wasn't judging." She placed them on the stovetop, then looked around to assess the kitchen. Nerves needled my stomach. I needed her to approve for some reason. It really mattered. She put an arm out to move me as she went to the produce bin and then to the fridge.

"I don't think I hover any more than any other chef."

"Yes, you do."

"I don't though. I mean, maybe you're just more aware of me." I wanted to shove those words back in my head but they were already out there.

She glared at me as she gathered ingredients. "I can read and also do simple math like two plus two. Other reviews said you were over-bearing, not just mine, and when I came here you said people don't like it when you hover." She cracked an egg in a bowl. "Including me, which I know was a jab at the review but it's clearly something you're aware of." She held up jazz hands. "Look at me, a genius!"

I scowled but it was hard staying mad as she made her way around the kitchen, cracking another egg and beating it soundly. She was gorgeous and she spoke her mind. Plus, watching her work in the kitchen had always been something to behold. I leaned back and took her in until she looked over.

"What?"

I shook my head, very aware I was staring. "What are you making?"

She looked back to her bowl. "An omelet, maybe a hash. Want some?"

I nodded. "Sure, what do you need me to do?"

"If we're doing a hash, potatoes?"

"You got it, Chef."

She smiled, before she remembered who she was with and pulled it from her face. My insides lit up like the neon cat outside, sending me soaring. Helene chopped the onion, peppers, and mushrooms with ease. I diced potatoes and heated my pan. She put the pot back. "I guess we don't need this after all."

"What were you going make with that?"

She shrugged. "I don't know. Sometimes you just have to put out the tools and let them tell you what to do."

I stopped to stare at her.

She looked back. "What?"

I shook my head. "Nothing. I've never thought about it that way."

She focused as she put eggs in a pan, swirling them to make a perfect circle. After waiting the appropriate amount of time, she added her veggies. "Shoot. I should've made sausage."

I went to the cooler. "Actually, I made too much this morning. We were slow because of the storm." I handed her a small container of cooked, crumbled meat.

"Thank you." She took the container and our fingers brushed. Our eyes met and lingered there. Brief, but there. She gave a tiny shake of her head. "Thanks."

Dumping in the sausage, she stirred the food until it was perfect.

"I thought you were making an omelet." I raised an eyebrow.

"Changed my mind. It's been known to happen."

I grinned, I couldn't help it. There was something else, though. The scent of the food rising and filling the kitchen plus Helene beside me felt like home. It was the only way to describe it.

Helene was...familiar. And cooking next to her was exhilarating in a way it hadn't been in a long time.

"So, where did you work most recently, because this isn't home kitchen cooking you're doing."

She side-eyed me. "It is. But nowhere since..."

I held out a plate and waited for her to finish.

"Yours was the last kitchen I worked in."

I plated the potatoes and she piled them with the scramble.

"I'm really sorry."

She waved her hand, brushing my words away. "Have any hot sauce?"

I grinned which she surprisingly returned. I grabbed a bottle of Cholula, and we made our way to the dining room.

She doused her food with the sauce and dove in. She closed her eyes as she held the first bite in her mouth. She reached for the salt, made the adjustments, took another bite and smiled.

I watched her as if I'd never seen a human eat. And honestly, maybe I hadn't. Watching her make the food and enjoy it, this is why I was a chef, but I hadn't experienced this before. Not like she did.

I leaned in, drawn to her, forgetting to eat off the plate in front of me.

I sat up tall and righted myself. No. She was the bane of my existence. *I was mad at her. So mad at her.* I sunk slightly in my seat as her tongue darted out to catch a bit of food from her lip. She closed her eyes again, savoring the bite.

Angry, remember?

I shoved a forkful of eggs and potatoes in my mouth. "Fuck me, that's good."

She ducked her chin. "Thanks. It's a recipe I used to make with my grandma."

"This is yours?" I immediately regretted the surprise in my voice.

She bristled and pulled away. "Yeah. Well, me and grandma. Why is that surprising?"

I chuckled. "I don't know."

She set down her fork. "I should expect it. I think you

made it quite clear what you think of me and my abilities. For everyone to read, too."

"I said I was sorry."

She nodded as I took the last bite of food.

"Sure. Those who can, do. Those who can't, critique. Everyone heard that, but only I heard I'm sorry."

The anger returned. "Why do you need everyone to hear me say I'm sorry? That sounds like ego, Helene."

I've never seen someone's face turn so red so fast. "Oh really?"

I picked up my plate, the knot in my stomach growing. "That's what they say."

"Do you think so?" She stood, almost vibrating with anger.

"Um, yeah. No. I don't know. Maybe. But probably not I guess." I made my way to the kitchen and she was hot on my heels.

"You know, Kael." There was distaste as she said my name, like she'd had a bad bite of food. "Maybe you should say everything in your head once before you say it out loud. And then you should decide not to say it."

"What the hell does that mean?"

"Because every time I think, maybe you're just awkward and have no idea how to talk to a human person, you prove me wrong and I see again you're just an asshole." Her chest heaved. I had really insulted her. The thing was, she was right. I was awkward, but I was kind of an asshole, too.

But I was trying not to be.

I turned to her, took her plate and dropped them in the sink. "Helene." I emphasized her name, the ridiculous of the second syllable. "Be honest, is it really Helen and you just want to be fancy?"

Her hands balled into fists. "It's a family name. You are

named after the least appealing leafy green. What the hell is wrong with you?"

"Like I haven't heard that one before. Sorry, sticks and stones, love."

"I'd like to have a stick and a stone right now. You, me, and love don't ever need to be in the same sentence." She leaned into me and I found I was leaning into her. She ran her tongue absentmindedly along her bottom lip. "Move. I'll clean up and get the hell out of here."

I didn't move.

She looked up at me. "Do I need to say the magic word?"

"I'll clean it."

Her jaw locked and she spoke through her teeth. "Fine by me."

As she turned to go, a loud boom rang out and then we were in darkness.

7

~

Helene

In the pitch black, I was hyper aware of Kael standing right behind me. My body responded in a way I didn't want to welcome but could barely help. I froze in my tracks. "Oh shit."

"That didn't sound good."

We walked in silence to the front of the diner, looking out to see the snow still coming down, not a light in the distance, and much to my dismay, a bank of snow piled against the front door.

I pushed against it but it didn't budge an inch.

"How can we get out of here?" I turned to Kael, my eyes adjusting to the darkness, the small amount of light from the moon helping.

"We can't."

"What?" My voice was low.

He turned and put his hands on the counter, head hung, defeated in his stance. "The back door has a time release lock that needs power to work. I've been meaning to replace it but haven't had the funds."

"So we're stuck." I plopped down in a booth.

He nodded as he faced me. "Basically."

"This is not how I thought today would go."

He sat across from me. "What was your plan then?"

I laughed, small and bitter. "I'm not sure I had one. I came here to tell you how awful it was you mentioned me in your response and that you even responded to a food critic. It's so disrespectful, but I get all crazy when I'm around you."

"Crazy?" Even in the dark, I could see the glint in his eyes.

I opened my mouth, but Kael's phone buzzed. I watched him as he put the phone to ear, his eyes never leaving me.

"Hey Sis."

I could hear her over the line checking on him.

"I'm fine."

"Yes, it's storming, we just lost power." He rolled his eyes. And I grinned.

"Okay. Okay, Sis. Love you, too. Bye."

He hung up the phone.

"Allie?"

He flushed. "You heard that?"

I nodded. "Come on, spill."

He blew out a breath, clearly annoyed. "It's my first name, well, Allan."

I made a face. "So you actually choose to go by Kael?"

"Hey," he protested.

"Sorry." I tried not to grin.

"Allan Kael Ruggeman. Also a family name."

"I see." I crossed my arms, fighting off a chill.

"But I didn't think people would take me seriously if…"

"No one would respect the Dread Pirate Allan?"

He laughed. "Something like that. Cold?"

"It's cooling off fast."

He stood and offered his hand. As soon as I took it, I felt warm all over. My eyes crept up over his tattooed-covered arm to his handsome face. Were his eyes always this blue? I looked away. "Thanks."

We stood there, me holding his offered hand, him staring at them together. I tried to clear my mind of the almosts and the never-weres from culinary school, of how it felt to kiss him. I did not want to think about how his arms looked now versus then. He had more tattoos and his hair was longer.

How would those arms feel wrapped around me and would those tattoos be scattered other places if his shirt was off?

He ran his thumb over the back of my hand, bringing me back to the now. I cleared my throat and pulled my hand away.

He snapped back to the moment, leaving me to guess where his mind was. "We better figure something out because it could be a long night."

I shadowed him to the kitchen, following the light of the flashlight on his phone, and looked around. "Why do you have a gumbo pot?" I asked as I lifted up a big metal multi-quart pot.

"It's a stock pot."

My cheeks colored. "Oh yeah. Sorry."

"You're from the south?"

I shrugged as I put three kitchen bricks in the bottom of

the pot. "My grandma was. I'm not from anywhere. Military brat."

"That explains a lot."

I shot him a look. "The brat part?"

He had a shit-eating grin on his face that was so damn adorable. "No. You don't seem like you're from New York City. And I mean that as a compliment."

"I'll take it as one, I guess."

I poured enough oil in to soak the bricks. "Have a small bag of chips around?"

He went to the front and came back with a mini bag of nacho cheese chips. I pulled a lighter from my pocket and lit the bag. Dropping it in the pot, a whoosh then a small fire burned in the bottom of the pot. "That will help."

He looked at me, awe covering his face. "Anything you can't do?"

I smiled. "Just lived through a hurricane or two. This will burn for a while."

Kael went to the back and returned with some fire blankets. "This is all I have for us. Not fancy, but it'll be warm at least."

We settled down into the pile of blankets and Kael pulled his around him then I did the same.

We faced each other in weird little blanket volcanos. Which felt right, because being around Kael made me want to erupt. The heat from the pot filled the space.

He pulled out his phone.

"Danny?"

"Yeah, yeah, no. But I'm stuck in the diner. When it lets up can you let someone know?"

I watched Kael roll his eyes then grunt a thanks then hang up.

"Hard to find good staff?" I asked, looking for sound to fill the space.

"Heh. This staff came with the diner."

I frowned at him. This was Kitty's diner. Why would he retain all the staff? But I let it alone.

It was quiet a couple minutes. "Your plan was to come to Kansas and tell me off and then what, just go back to the city?"

I shrugged. "I mean, I was hoping I'd get to make a blanket fort before I left, but otherwise yes."

His mouth twitched, fighting a smile. "Mission accomplished then, I guess."

We sat in the silence, a kind of silence that only a snowstorm can provide. The rare noise was a breaking branch here and there, or snow falling off a roof. Otherwise, it was that quiet you only hear in winter. It reminded me of Christmas mornings you see in movies.

"Of all the diners in all the world." Kael sounded almost whimsical.

"Well, you shouldn't have brought me up in the response that shouldn't have happened and I wouldn't be here."

He looked at me. "Why do you care so much?"

I looked ahead, trying not to meet his eyes. I couldn't tell him how personal it actually was. "It's just a respect thing. Why did you leave New York?"

He smirked. "Nice deflection."

I waited for his answer, not giving in. "Come on. It's going to be a long night. We might as well swap stories."

"I'm not really a swapping stories kinda guy."

"That checks." I frowned and huddled into my blanket further.

The silence stretched and I jumped when he spoke again.

"Tell me a secret shame."

I raised an eyebrow. "A secret shame? What does that mean?"

"You know, an indulgence of some kind, something you do behind closed doors you'd never do in front of others."

I grinned at Kael. "But you won't swap stories? What if you write about this too?"

"You're the writer."

I grimaced. "Not really."

He started to furrow his brow but when he saw my grin he smirked. "We might be snowed in forever. C'mon. We're stuck in here. Why not share some embarrassing things?"

"Fair enough."

I thought, what was something I did alone? I sent a side-eye to Kael. Except for what I would be doing back in my hotel room, thinking about the man beside me, what did I do alone?

"Hmmm. I like to get tanked and watch the Twilight Zone. I pause it after five minutes to guess if it's a lesson about racism, misogyny, or aliens. Then watch the rest to see if I'm right."

Kael busted out laughing. "That's amazing."

"What about you?"

He didn't hesitate. "I buy frozen dinners, one from each brand, make them, then narrate my own 'cooking' show, describing them as I eat as if they are food made by the contestants."

I stared at Kael. "That is hilarious. Do you rip them apart?"

"One hundred percent."

I shivered.

"Still cold?"

Very. But I wasn't going to tell him that. "I'm fine."

"Have it your way."

We sat in silence as the time dragged on. Five minutes or five hours, I'm not sure, but as we sat there, my head grew heavy. Only my shivering from the cold brought me back.

Kael was up, adding more fuel to our makeshift heater and he turned to see I was awake. "Helene."

"Lena."

"Lena?"

"That's what my...my friends call me."

"Are we friends?" He half-smiled as he joined me back on the floor in our pile of blankets.

"Not really, just trauma bonded."

He chuckled. "Fair enough. Come over here. I'm not trying to pull anything, but it will be warmer if we sit together and put both blankets around us."

My body responded quickly to the thought of being bundled up against Kael.

"Next you'll tell me we should take off our clothes too." I meant it as a joke, but I flushed and looked away.

"That is what they say."

I scooted over and he opened the blanket to let me in. He was warm and I molded myself into his side, but that felt very much how you'd sit with someone you were dating. I shifted around, trying to get comfortable and eventually my back was against his chest, his legs outside of mine, his arms holding me close.

"Is this good?" I asked meekly.

I felt him nod. He shifted and settled in, pulling the blankets around us adding mine to our little fort of sorts. His back was against a second oven across from the small fire we'd made. The orange glow filled the room just enough.

"It was really nice of you to install a fireplace for us." I giggled as I said it. I was loopy from tired and coldness.

His body moved gently as he laughed. "Anything for an esteemed guest."

"Now what?"

I felt him shrug. "Association game?"

"Like what?" I half turned my head, my cheek leaning into him. He leaned down against me. It was too easy, I could just reach up...I looked back to the front.

"How about what groups of things are called?"

I raised an eyebrow. "What do you mean?"

He pulled the blankets tighter around us. "Like a murder of crows. Get it?"

"Ooh. I have one!"

"Can't wait."

"A parliament of owls," I said proudly.

"Is that what they are called?"

I shook my head and felt him smile on my cheek he'd leaned down against.

"A bunch of wombats are called a wisdom."

"Really? Are wombats smart?"

He shrugged. "Apparently in a group."

Our bodies shook with gentle laughter.

"The obvious – a tuxedo of penguins."

"Perfect. Oh, I got one. A destruction of cats."

I looked back at him. "That cannot be right."

"It is. I promise." He held up a hand under the blanket.

I shook my head. "That sounds like you hate cats."

"What?" He leaned away a bit, letting in some cold. "I didn't make it up."

I tugged the blanket, pulling him close again. "Got it. Kael hates cats."

He guffawed. "I do not! I love cats."

I grinned. "Oooh. You're a cat guy? Roger that."

He slumped against me. "You don't play fair."

"I'm sorry, were we supposed to? Is that in the rules?"

It was quiet for a minute, then Kael's voice rumbled in his chest as he spoke. "I left New York for many reasons. But I'd be lying if I said your four-star wasn't a factor."

I stiffened. "I'm sorry. Your food was amazing."

"I know, it's just me. It always has been. You were right about the other reviews."

I shook my head. "I doubt that. You worked steady and you seem to have left on your terms."

I felt him shrug. "To a point, but also, that life—"

"It's a grind. That's why I got out."

"What do you mean?"

"I was in your kitchen until I wasn't, but it was toxic all over. That's why I didn't go back to it." His arms tightened around me, pulling me closer, and I tried to ignore how good it felt. "I love food, the making, the eating, the giving it to others to see their enjoyment, and I felt that dying."

He lowered his face closer to mine, our cheeks almost touching. "Yeah. I couldn't put it into words like you, but that's exactly it. I felt the anger taking over my love of all of it."

"How'd you end up here?"

He shook his head. "I think it's your turn to share."

I pushed back against him so he couldn't see my face. "I'll say it fast, and then let's not talk about it ever again."

"Deal." His arms somehow grew tighter, his hands sliding closer to mine. "My parents died."

"I'm so sorry. Both of them?"

I nodded. "Yep. It was awful. My dad I was glad to be rid of, but my mom. I miss her." I took a breath. I hadn't said this stuff to anyone out loud in such a long time. "But my dream was to open my own restaurant. Carry on the traditions of certain dishes so they don't get forgotten. A place people could go and feel the warmth you crave from food, or at least what I crave. I felt happy back then, eating comforting food"

"But how did you get from losing your family to cooking and baking?"

I grinned. "Breakfast casserole and blueberry lemon cake."

His voice was low. "What?"

"My favorite foods and I learned it from someone very dear."

"Go on."

I grinned. "You start with tater tots. Eggs, sausage, cheese. It's so delicious. A place like this would do well with it."

He stiffened. I felt it, but I wasn't sure why.

"And the cake?"

"It's another breakfast dish. I think I just really love that meal the best." No response from Kael, so I went on. "The key is the buttermilk. But you—"

"Have to make your own."

I turned to him as best I could. "That's right, how did you know that?"

"How did you?" He looked at me with suspicion.

It might have been cold, but it was suddenly stifling in here. "Before my parents' died, I'd removed myself and my sister from them. It was a bad situation."

Kael held me closer.

"I met this woman who was so kind and she took me and Celia, that's my sister, in. She taught me how to cook and such. I was about to open my own restaurant when my parents died."

"Can I asked what happened?"

I blew out a breath. "Official report says it was an accident. But I think my mom just got tired of things..."

"Oh my god. I'm so sorry. I..."

"It's okay if you don't know what to say. No one does."

We sat in silence for a few minutes until Kael broke it once more. "What was your restaurant going to be like?"

I shivered. This wasn't the Kael I had come to know. This was the person I thought he was to begin with, a long time ago.

"A little diner like this. I wanted to open a place filled with music everyone knows and food that comforted people. I started making cakes with my grandma on Saturday mornings. I had a countertop I sat on. In her little red and white kitchen. It's so clear in my mind, and might not be what it was at all, but it's what I remember. I want to give that to other people, you know? That's what food should do. Comfort and fill them up."

I felt him nod against me.

"Why didn't you open your restaurant?"

"When I went to get my money I'd saved, it was gone. My dad had spent it all. Then my nephew was diagnosed – you know what? Let's just say he has medical challenges, and my sister isn't up for dealing with anything on her own. So I put that aside, worked my way up at Food, Drink, Air after..."

He waited.

"After I left your kitchen and now I take care of them."

"You're amazing, Lena. That's selfless."

I pursed my lips together. Kael calling me Lena did something to my insides. Selfless wasn't how I saw it at all. It felt cowardly. Like I took the path of least resistance. "That's one way to look at it?"

"There's another?"

"Maybe I'm just a scared little girl who knew she wouldn't succeed at the other."

Kael's fingers wound down around mine, squeezing my hands. "Or maybe you're a woman who sacrificed what she wanted to do for what had to be done."

I caught my breath. "Kael…"

"Call me Allie."

"Allie. I…" I wanted to tell him everything suddenly. He would understand. He would get it. And I'd probably never see him again when I left here. But I couldn't bring myself to say more. I just leaned back into him, letting him hold me, pretending this night would never end.

Kael

I HELD Lena close as she relaxed against me. "That's how I ended up here. I came to pay my respects, and then I ran into you." Her voice was heavy with sleep but I was wide awake.

"What do you mean pay your respects?"

"The lady that used to own this. Kitty. She was the woman who took me in."

"That's how you know my aunt's favorite recipe."

She shifted around to face me on her knees in front of me. "Your aunt?"

I nodded again. "Yes. My aunt Cat. You know Cat and the Fiddle?"

She smiled and the warmth it radiated could have

melted all the snow on earth. "I knew her as Kitty. I never knew that was her favorite, I only knew it was mine."

I loved the look on her face and how we had this thing in common. "It was. She died and left this place to me. The only thing she left anyone actually and I couldn't let it close. She left everything else to the animal shelter."

Helene frowned but then she smiled. "Tell me about her," she said in a voice rich and full of excitement. I wanted to be more than I was, better than I was. I wanted to be a person who could deserve the woman in front of me. But I wasn't, so I talked about the greatest person I knew instead.

"Cat...Kitty was a wild woman. She used to tell me stories of nights with the Rat pack and crazier. She's been everywhere."

"Yeah. Her Mardi Gras stories where insane."

"The one where they made the giant King Cake?"

"Yes!" Helene leaned forward as she laughed.

I tightened the blanket around us as best I could.

"She always believed in me though. I never doubted I could do this because of her. Sheila, our waitress, was her best friend. They've had every adventure together." I fished a hand out of the blanket and pointed to a stainless counter-top. "I used to sit over there while she made pies and cobblers. My own counter to sit on. She'd talk me through the steps and then eventually, she'd say, "Allie Bear, can you tell me how to make a pie? I just can't remember.""

I wrapped my arms around Lena's waist, holding her close, pulling her up into my lap. As if we'd always been here.

"Allie Bear," she repeated softly as she reached up and stroked my cheek.

I closed my eyes, but she pulled her hand away quickly.

"Of course she could remember, but I learned how to

make things that way, what to watch for, and then she'd do that with all the dishes she made. I couldn't bear the thought of the only thing left of her not being in this world. It's an institution plus—"

"Places like this need to exist. They are our food history, our collective comfort, our—" she stopped herself.

"Why you'd stop?"

"Some people think I'm a lot."

I put my forehead against hers. "Some people are wrong."

I kicked myself for ever being like I was to her. We could've had these conversations from the beginning, I would've been there for her. We could have baked together with my aunt. "I'm sorry."

She pulled back. "For what?"

"For me."

She put her head back against mine. "I'm glad you kept this going. Places like this are important."

"Yeah. You get it. But I got here and the staff and the kitchen were such a shitshow. I've barely been treading water."

She looked at me with a tilted gaze. "You seem to be doing pretty well. Your aunt would be proud."

I felt my eyes glass over before I looked away. I felt her eyes on me before I looked back and saw a night long ago, two kids in culinary school, hands cramping from hours of chopping and prep work. She'd stretched her fingers or tried to.

"Here." I took her hand and massaged her fingers open, working the knotted muscles free. She'd locked her fingers in mine and I pulled her close.

The yearning of that night overwhelmed me.

Now, in this moment, I held her. I cupped her cheek in

my hand as she leaned into me. Heat filled me and the want I'd been fighting since the first moment I saw her bubbled over. She laced her fingers in my hair, pulling me close. I held her impossibly near as I laid her down gently. She looked in my eyes, stroking my cheek with the backs of her fingers.

"Allie." My name felt gentle on her lips. Falling over me like the soft snow.

She closed her eyes. "I need to tell you something."

I put a finger on her lips. "Not tonight. Let's just let tonight be."

She stiffened. "What the hell am I doing?" She started to get up, but I held her firm.

"It's cold out there."

"It is."

"Can I warm you up?"

8

~

Helene

I wound my arms up and around him, pulling him on top of me, feeling the crush of his full weight. The only answer I could muster was a slow and lengthy kiss, one that heated my body head to toe. I closed my arms on his bicep and felt it flex under my grip. His lips moved to the side of my mouth, planting soft kisses over my jawline, and down my neck. Cold air snuck into our cocoon of heat as I arched my head back, letting Kael have his way. I played with his curls and something was so familiar to me. He felt like h...

No. I would not say that even in my mind. I pulled at him to help his mouth find mine. Kael was the one person I'd thought of over and over through the years, the lone regret. He was my what if. What if we could've talked through our feelings. What if we hadn't landed in the same kitchen. What if he hadn't been like he was. None of those things mattered now though. He was here in my arms, kissing me and holding me close to ride out the storm together.

His kisses worked their way back down my throat, his lips soft but firm against my skin. I'd dreamt of this. His hair tickled me as he explored. The chill in the air where the blanket fell lax was a welcome contrast to the heat I felt where he touched me. I closed my arms tighter around him, playing with his hair. We weren't in a rush tonight. It felt as if we had all the time in the world.

And maybe we did. Perhaps we were the only two left in this world and Kael was my reward for all the heartache I'd been through.

It was as if not a moment had passed and we hadn't lost all the time.

But remembering all that had happened in those years, all that heartache, pulled me back to the moment. How I'd cried when I left his kitchen the last time, broken and defeated.

I pushed away.

"We shouldn't do this."

"Why?"

Was I serious right now? "You don't sleep with the chef."

"I think that ship has sailed."

I looked away then back to the man in my arms, hovering above me. "We're different people now. It's all different now. Our lives could be affected or ruined by this."

He kissed my forehead then rested his against mine. "Or maybe this is a second chance. No one has to know. What are the odds we were here together when the world stopped?"

"Allie…"

He rose up as I said his name.

"It's a snow storm, not the apocalypse. We can't do this." My eyelids were heavy as I fought the urge to give into him.

He looked into my eyes, a little defeated, propped up on an elbow beside me, my body missing the weight of him immediately. "You need to sleep. I mean actual sleep."

"I do. I'm exhausted."

We rolled until my back was to him and his arms were tight around me.

"Good night, Lena."

"Good night, Allie."

In the dark, only the crackle of the fire bricks, the blanket of snow outside and Kael's soft breathing filled the space. His chest rumbled against me when he did speak.

"I was only hard on you because you were so damn good. I didn't know what else to do. You intimidated me. It was my first kitchen and I didn't know."

I didn't respond.

"I'm sorry, Helene. Truly."

He waited then he sighed.

He kissed my temple and then I was out.

Kael

HOLDING HELENE – Lena – even on this hard floor in a cold room we might never get out of was the best thing I'd ever felt. Wrong, kissing her was. Her soft breathing leveled out as she lay in my arms. I tried to fight the urge to wake her up and kiss her again.

She was Miss Four Stars. She'd called me out in front of my entire staff and some patrons. I should be furious, but I couldn't be. She was so passionate when she cooked, talked, reviewed. How could I fault her, because if I was honest, nothing she'd said was wrong. I'd had my ego hurt was all.

And she'd always been the one that got away.

Now I was holding the woman I'd been in love with since she walked into culinary school all those years ago.

I wondered if she knew how many nights, and honestly mornings and days, I'd thought of her like this, wrapped up in my arms, sleeping against me.

She sighed, rolled over, and burrowed deeper into my arms. I held her close and kissed her forehead. I didn't want her to leave and go back to the city. What would I do when she left? There would be a hole that had always been there, but it would be deeper and darker and never be filled.

Maybe I could go with her. Could this place run without me? Doubtful. But if I did go back to the city, I'd find a kitchen no problem. That wasn't the issue. The issue was would she want me around. Could we have a relationship there due to her job? I knew me and I would never be able to keep my feelings for Helene to myself. Everyone in the world would know how lucky I was to stand beside this woman.

I pulled her closer, willing time to stop and keep this moment forever. All that was ridiculous anyway. She was hurling insults at me less than twelve hours ago and this was just a matter of convenience.

I was a matter of convenience.

You don't sleep with the chef.

My jaw tensed. But back then I wasn't a chef, not really

at least, when we had our one night together. She'd never pursued anything since either. Ever the professional.

So why would this be different? I crushed her to me, smiling when she burrowed closer.

Her job was there. And it would compromise her integrity if we were to see each other probably. She'd never agree to that.

Plus she had her family and that seemed to be a big responsibility. This really couldn't be anything. These were boyhood daydreams I needed to give up. I had to face that fact. But she was here and she'd come back. To give me, or the diner, a piece of her mind. Maybe she wanted to give it another chance. So maybe there was a chance for me too.

The next minute, Helene was shifting and sitting up. Even with her pulling away from me, it was warm. I blinked against the bright lights. It was morning and the power was on.

Lena scooted away a bit and folded her legs crisscross style, running her fingers through her hair.

"Morning." I said as I stretched and stood.

"Good morning." Her voice was small and meek as she spoke. I held out a hand for her and she took it to stand.

She took a step back, crossing her arms. "Power's back on it looks like."

"Yep." I gathered the fire blankets and shoved them into the basket with the napkins and towels that were waiting on their trip to the cleaners. They'd have to be washed before they could go back in the cabinet.

I watched her as she went out to the dining room. She came back with a frustrated look on her face. "Door is still blocked though."

I scratched the back of my neck, other hand on my hip. "Want some breakfast?"

She smiled. "Sure. I need to rinse my mouth out to be honest."

"Glasses are up front. Bathroom around the corner."

I couldn't help but watch those gorgeous hips swish as she moved to her destination. In ten seconds I was ready to go again and pick back up where we left off last night.

"Get it together, man," I muttered under my breath as I cleaned up the dishes we'd left in the sink.

Helene was by my side faster than I anticipated.

"I told you I would do this." She bumped me with her hip. "Go make coffee."

I nodded. It was so natural with her. Like we'd always been together.

But we hadn't been together yet. Not really. I closed my eyes, trying to remain a gentleman and not think about all the things I wanted to do together with Helene. I made coffee on autopilot then went and rinsed my mouth as well.

The strange thing was, it wasn't just getting her into bed that I wanted. Obviously, I wanted her. She was everything I could dream up if I got to dream up a perfect person. She loved food and to make food. She was smart and witty and could snap back and keep me in my place. Plus she was gorgeous. Which led me to the bedroom.

But what turned me on the most was doing the mundane with her. Last night, making food. Sitting and talking and playing those stupid games after the power went out. I craved more of that. The other stuff would just be icing on the cake.

When I came back with two steaming cups of coffee, Helene had the whole kitchen clean. She was sitting up on the counter I used to sit on.

"So what are we making? We had breakfast for dinner last night," I said as I handed her a cup.

"Should we make something sweet?" Her eyes sparkled.

"Whatever you want, chef."

She grinned and pushed herself off the counter, vaulting down to the ground. "Let's make French toast."

"Bacon?"

"Oh yeah. I'll never say no to that."

I turned on the oven and pulled out a sheet pan. Helene moved around the kitchen as if she'd been there since the beginning of time.

"It's organized well in here, Allie."

"Thanks." Her approval gave me a shot of adrenaline I didn't know I needed.

She placed two bowls on the counter and starting mixing things. I sat back and watched her work. It was just French toast for crying out loud. But it didn't matter. She was mesmerizing. I came up behind and put my arms around her, my cheek by hers. "Need help?"

"Allie – we shouldn't play with fire like this."

I leaned closer. "Last night was when we made the fire."

She giggled. "You're a dork. You know what I mean."

I nodded. I put my hands over hers as she stirred. "I'm just helping."

She leaned back into me. "This isn't helping."

I kissed her neck and lifted my hands away. "No?"

She bumped back with her hips. "Not so much."

"How is that encouraging me to stop?" I growled into her ear.

"Allie, you're going to make me burn the toast."

"Then let me help. Jeez, woman."

She smiled back at me as I reached my hands back down her arms, covering her hands with mine. She held a fork, turned the bread in the egg wash, dredging it then lifting it to the pan, sizzling as it hit.

"That toast feels how I feel."

I felt her cheek rise against mine while our hands moved together as she did the next one.

"You're a dope. I didn't know you were co cheesy."

"Please don't tell. I have a reputation to keep."

She giggled again and it was so damn cute. "You'd prefer to be known as an asshole?"

I shrugged but kept holding her. "Hey, they say when you're good at something…"

She kissed my cheek, catching me off guard. "Don't you have bacon to tend to?"

"Nope. In the oven."

"That's the difference between buying me a stuffed animal and winning it in a show of strength at a county fair."

I scoffed. "Trust me. It'll be worth it."

With the French toast done, I pulled the bacon from the oven and we ate right there in the kitchen, at that same counter. Helene was quiet while we did, and I could tell her mind was turning things over and again and I wish I knew what they were.

"How long do you think we'll be stuck in here? Wait. You said the back door would work now, right?"

I tried not to frown. I wanted to be stuck in here with her for infinity but there was probably a fine line between that and kidnapping. "I'll try it."

I punched in the code to unlock the door and gave it a push. It didn't budge. I tried to hide a smile. She joined me at the door.

"Let's try it together."

"Wow. Is my company that bad?"

Her cheeks flushed. "Not at all." She placed a hand gently on my arm. "I just have to get back to New York. I have a job, you know? I have...obligations. I've already been gone too long. I shouldn't have come in the first place." A frown twisted her pretty features for a second before she recovered.

"Fair enough. Push on three. One...two...three!"

It didn't budge at all, even with both of us leaning all our body weight against it.

"My guess is there's a drift against this door too."

"Well, we tried." She turned and went over to pick up our breakfast dishes.

"You don't have to do that. I'll clean it up."

She smiled back over shoulder as the water heated and poured into the sink. "You never leave a messy kitchen."

I joined her, and just like before, it was natural, wonderful, and I was getting used to this far too quickly. Our arms and hands brushed as we did the dishes. Just doing the dishes. The most normal thing. And I couldn't get enough. Helene kept glancing up at me then looking away just as fast.

She dried her hands on a towel then went to wipe down the counter and I did the grill.

"Welp, now what?" She turned to look at me, hands on the counter at her sides as she leaned back.

"I have some ideas."

Even though we'd just eaten, her eyes were hungry as I watched her take in my arms then back up to my face. "None of them good. I can't get involved like this, Kael. You know I can't."

I took a step in her direction, but kept my arms crossed, forcing myself to not reach out and hold her. "Why?"

She held up her hands. "My reputation. If it got out I'd sl...been involved with a chef I'd reviewed, it would ruin with me."

"Been involved? That's not what you were going to say." I drew my thumb over my bottom lip. "What's on *your* mind I think is the better question."

I stepped close, my hands on either side of her against the counter. She put her hands on my chest. "It's a bad idea."

"Bad ideas make the best stories."

She closed her eyes. "Only if you can tell the story. A secret can be torture."

I whispered in her ear. "This is a road we traveled already, no one has to know we circled back."

She looked at me, her gaze flicking down to my lips.

"We're in the middle of nowhere, snowed in. Who's going to know?"

She gripped my shirt in her hands. "What did you have in mind?"

I could think of so many things. I watched as she licked her bottom lip again. It drew my eyes down to her mouth. Her head tilted up to me as I took her in my arms. Our lips crushed together, her hands in my hair. She held on to me as I kissed her, our tongues pressing into each other. She tasted sweet, like syrup and brown sugar, which matched the enticing way she always smelled. The bitterness of the coffee finished it off, like the perfect bite. Her head tilted back, my hand at the base of her neck as I kissed down her throat.

"Allie." She moaned my name. A name I'd always hated, but when Lena said it, something shifted in me. I belonged to her. It was only her voice saying my name I wanted to hear forever. I pulled the shoulder of her shirt to the side and kissed across her collarbone. Her fingers tightened in my hair forcing me to look up.

"Kiss me." Her voice was liquid. And that liquid was gasoline poured over a fire. "Kiss me like you mean it."

"Oh, I mean it."

My mouth covered hers, but she devoured me, body and soul. She pushed against my chest until she had me back to the wall. I lifted her slightly, closing my arms around her. Her body slid down mine as I lowered her, the kiss never ebbing.

I held her tighter, feet off the floor, and spun her slowly until she was pressed against the wall. My fingers found the edge of her shirt and I closed my hand across her waist, her skin hot to the touch. I paused, waiting for her to let me know this okay.

"Tell me if you want me to stop, and I will. If it's too much."

She closed her hand on mine and pushed it higher.

"I want your hands on me, your mouth, your everything, Allie."

That was all I needed to hear. I pulled her shirt over her head as she gasped with pleasure. The smile on her face only fueled my need for her. I looked at this gorgeous woman in front of me.

"My god, you are beautiful."

The look of desire on her face almost did me in. She was self-assured and it was incredibly hot. This woman knew what she wanted, and I was happy to report, that was me.

I kissed her again, our bodies pushed together. She pulled at my t-shirt, lifting it up and off, tossing it to the side. Our skin pressed flush, singeing me with heat. One hand found her waist, the other behind her head to cushion it from the wall. I slid my fingers gently up her side, loving the little shiver it sent through her. I closed my hand on her breast, warm and full in my grasp. I kissed along the lace of her bra, followed by my tongue in the same place.

I pushed the fabric aside, my fingers finding her nipple,

giving a tweak. Helene drew a breath through her teeth. I took her in my mouth, suckling soft at first then adding more pressure. Gentle sighs came from the object of my desire.

She pulled my face up to hers, looking in my eyes.

"Lena, I…"

She cut me off with a kiss. Pushing me back, she twisted until I was the one against the wall again. She reached down, easily unbuttoning my jeans and making fast work of the zipper.

"Is this okay?"

I nodded. A woman had never asked me for consent before. It was so hot. Everything she did was only one more thing that made me want her. It wasn't just want, I needed her.

She worked my pants down just enough and freed me from my underwear. She smiled down at me and then looked back up. The look in her eyes was pure desire and I don't think I'd ever felt as wanted as I did in that moment.

She kissed down my chest and the center of my stomach. Her tongue drew a hot trail down lower. I moved my hands to my side, her head, my head, trying to find somewhere to be.

She took me between her lips, and I almost dropped. Her mouth was hot as she moved up and down on my shaft. Then pulling back and kissing the tip, before pressing back down in it, licking back up the length.

"Good god."

My knees were weak and yet, Helene kept on. I didn't know how much longer I could hold out. It had been a long time since…well, anything. Her hand reached up, splayed across my abs. I grabbed her hand and pulled her up.

She wiped her mouth. She opened it to speak, but I

kissed her, with force, spinning her until her back was against the wall once more, a breath huffed out of her.

I moved my hand down, finding the waist band of her jeans. I popped the button and slid down the zipper. Our eyes locked on each other, looking deep into one another's soul as I worked my hand down slowly. She never looked away. I loved her boldness. She was in every minute of this with me and it was fantastic. I felt the edge of her panties. I pushed past that, feeling her skin warm as I got closer to where we both wanted me to be.

"Yes," she moaned her desire.

My fingers were almost—

"Hello? Anyone in here?" Danny's voice boomed through the diner.

Helene and I shot apart looking for our respective shirts. She fought to get her jeans fastened as I tried to adjust everything as best I could and we had just finished straightening ourselves when he rounded the corner, eyes zeroing in on Helene.

"Oh. Hi," Danny said with a shit-eating grin.

Helene waved. "Hi."

He smiled at me, taking in our disheveled clothes and hair. I'm sure we were a sight.

"Oh. Oooh. Sorry."

I shot him a scowl and he wiped the knowing look off his face.

"Thanks for the rescue." My voice was gruff. I tried to slow my breathing and cool the desire brewing within. It was useless, but at least I tried.

Helene was pulling on her coat. "Thanks for not letting me starve or freeze."

"Yeah. Yeah, sure. You're leaving?"

She nodded. "Gotta figure out when I can get back to the city."

She turned to Danny. "Thanks for getting the door open." She stopped at the edge of the kitchen. "Goodbye, Kael."

I could only watch her go.

9

≈

Helene

The cold air washed over me as I took big, deep breaths, desperately trying to cool my insides. Kael was the hottest thing I'd ever seen. Being in the kitchen with him, the way he kissed me and touched me. He looked at me with passion and want, like I was all that existed.

He was something I think had always been at the edge of my brain, but I'd blocked him from my heart, and last night he came way too close to busting through those defenses.

I could still taste him and it made me hungry for more. I touched my lips wanting to feel him there again.

Maybe if I doused my head in the snow, it would get rid of this crazy notion that Kael and I could be a thing. But his lips on mine popped back in my thoughts and heat rolled off my body as I made my way across the street to the motel.

Over and over in my mind his hands were on me. And they were so close to what I wanted from him. That wasn't the only thing I wanted, but in that moment it was. What a terrible time for a rescue. I blew out a breath, following the cloud made by my heated breath until it dissipated.

I went into my room, shutting the door behind me. I collapsed on the bed. What the hell was I doing? You didn't get involved with chefs. Definitely not ones you reviewed.

Especially not ones you had a fling with a million years ago.

This was a disaster.

I stood up and paced, trying to burn off the sexual tension I felt. I picked up my phone to find I had many missed calls and texts. First, I texted Jen to let her know I was still here.

Second, I texted my sister and let her know what was happening. Then I called Deidre.

"Hey Doll face."

"Didi, I screwed up."

"Tell me everything."

I gave her the details of last night.

"Oh, he should fire the guy who walked in on you."

I chuckled. "That is what you got out of that?"

"That and you should go back over there and bang Kael Ruggeman."

"No, Didi. I have to get out of here. I almost told him I was Anon."

There was a pause.

"Didi?"

"You did what? Helene, why would you want to do that?"

I sat on the edge of the bed, head in my hand, phone to

my ear. "I don't know. I wanted to tell him everything. I told him about the restaurant dream, my dad, the money. All of it. He was just so…"

"So what?"

I blew out a breath. "So comfortable. But exciting. I don't know. I've never felt that way before."

"Tell me again why you won't go back over there?"

I stood up, pacing again, sure I would walk a hole in the carpet. "Because it doesn't matter if I like him. I live in New York, he lives here. I have obligations and a job I need to keep. He has a diner that can't run without him. It means too much to him. I can't ask him to go and I won't stay. Plus, you don't sleep with the chef. The end. And all of that is insane because it was literally one night in a diner. And nothing really happened. Oh god. What am I talking about?"

"It's more than one night."

"Not much more."

"You're talking like you're in love with him." She laughed then stopped suddenly. "Oh my god, you're in love with him!"

My stomach tensed, because that was the word my mind had been rejecting when it came to Kael for years.

"No, I'm not. I just actually met him for real yesterday. I don't think I ever really knew him before then. Love doesn't work like that."

"It absolutely does. Or can, I think. I mean I'm no expert but, you're in love."

"Why did I call you again? This isn't helping."

"I knew you'd fall in love with a tall, tattooed, chef that you couldn't stand to begin with."

I frowned. "He's not that tall."

She laughed now for real. "Taller than you."

"Like that's hard. And what do you mean you knew I'd fall in love with a chef?"

This time her laugh was filled with glee. "It's too perfect. The food critic and the chef. Oh, I wish I could be there right now."

I rolled my eyes. "Didi, focus, what am I going to do?"

"You know my advice."

I huffed. "Besides that."

"Honestly, Lena, you should tell him how you feel. Then he can decide for himself."

I thought about that and how batshit crazy that seemed. "Let's say I did that. What do I do? How does that look? Walk over there, through the snow by the way, and say oh hey. You know how we just met for real then shared our souls, well, I like you now. You kiss good. Wanna do something about that? Also, I'm the anonymous person you hate. I'd sound like a maniac."

"I think it's charming."

I smiled. "That's because you love me."

"What's not to love?"

"Okay. I have to run and figure out how I can get out of here before I make more terrible decisions. Love you."

"Mean it."

Deidre's words stomped around my brain. Should I tell him I feel something? Bigger question. Did I actually feel something or was I just trapped in a diner with a hot chef overnight and now my brain was sex-laden and clouded?

Probably the latter. Who just falls in love like that? No one in real life.

"Solves that."

I called Jack.

"It's still gonna be another day, at least, darling. No way of flying today. We'd catch the storm. Can't risk it."

"I understand. Thanks, Jack."

Now what?

You should go back over there and bang Kael Ruggeman.

I clenched my eyes shut. "Damn you, Didi."

Instead of focusing on that nonsense, I showered. I brushed my teeth and dried my hair then paced about the room. Kael's kiss, his hands, the way he held me was all my mind filled with. Those blue eyes, watching me, waiting for me to give the go ahead, his mind thinking only of me. A shiver ran through my body.

I looked at my phone for the time. It was almost lunch. I guess I could go to the diner and see what the special is today. No harm there. They served food and I needed to eat. I did come here to give it a second chance originally anyway.

No, you didn't. You came here to let Kael know he was out of line and you did.

But I was hungry. Lunch wouldn't hurt.

I pulled on my coat and stepped back out into the snow. It was piled in weird shapes courtesy of the wind last night. The sun was out, but there wasn't any warmth. I trudged across the street, my feet freezing cold by the time I got to the diner.

I pushed through the door. The ding over my head set off alarm bells in my body. Kael was near and every inch of me knew it.

"Hello?"

Sheila poked her head around the corner. "Hey there, sweetie."

I cleaned my shoes off on the mat by the door as best I could. "Are you open?"

She leaned back toward the kitchen. "Are we open?"

"Limited menu. Just open face sandwich and mash." My

body responded to Kael's voice in a way that wasn't unwelcome.

She turned back to me. "Does that work?"

"Sure does. And a coke?"

She nodded with a smile. I found a booth and slid off my coat. I didn't want to be out here. I should be back there with him. Right by him, next to him, under him. My body would not be still. I was close to Kael but so far away. Too far away. I wanted him out here with me.

Oh, the irony.

"Order."

He put the plate up in the window and froze when he saw me. His entire demeanor changed. It wasn't Kael, gruff chef. It was Allie, the one who held me through the storm. To my surprise, he pointed out to the booth to ask if he could join. I smiled and nodded.

"Taking five."

I thought someone said thank you, chef but it almost sounded like fuck you, chef. I pushed my lips together to not laugh. Kael brought the plate out himself and Sheila brought my drink.

I looked up at her. "Thanks."

She raised an eyebrow at Kael and I gave a tiny nod to let her know it was fine.

He slid in the booth across from me. I tried not to look disappointed. Oh no. I'd gone from *no chef ever* to *wish he'd sit by me* in a few hours. I pursed my lips together. I was hopeless.

He held up his hands. "Hey. I can go. I asked to come out."

"No, it's not that." I lowered my voice. "You're so far away."

Fire lit in his eyes promptly setting me alight in turn. "How long are you staying?"

I took a bite. The meat practically melted in my mouth. "Kael, how did you make this so good so fast?"

"I started it yesterday. That was the plan for the special today."

"Mmmm." I closed my eyes as I chewed my food, letting the tastes and textures mingle in my mouth. I took another bite. He started to speak, but I held up a finger and took another bite. "God, this is so good. Delicious."

"Five blue plates?"

I popped my eyes open. "Why would you say that?"

He sank in his seat. "Because that anonymous review only gave me four. Same as the amount of stars you gave me. It haunts me."

I put my hand on the table, stretching across until he looked up. I didn't want to lie, but I found I really meant what I said. "If I could give it that, I would. But I'm not impartial."

To my shock, he smiled. "As long as I know what you think."

I leaned toward him. "Allie, I don't have enough Blue Plates for you."

The look on his face took my breath away. It was elated and charged and somehow, I could tell it meant everything to him.

"Thank you."

I'm not sure my words or opinions had ever meant so much to someone. More perplexing was why that mattered to me. I wasn't a person who really cared what other people thought. I wasn't cold hearted, it was just my job. It wasn't personal. But it mattered very much to me what Kael thought and that he was happy.

"You should open your restaurant."

I was taken aback. "What? Where did that come from?"

"You should open your restaurant. The world should have your food and love of food. It would mean something to people."

I wiped at my eyes, pricking with tears. "Thank you. You don't know what it does to me to hear that."

He leaned in. "I'm sorry I ever made you doubt yourself. I'm not being arrogant, like it was all me." He paused. "But if I played a part in your decisions, I'm so sorry."

I pushed my lips tight as I got myself together and nodded my head in acceptance.

"So, how long are you staying then?" He asked again.

"Oh, at least until tomorrow. No flying apparently and driving would take me just as long as waiting for the plane."

Kael leaned back in the booth, picking at the stitches in between the colors in the leather of the seat. "What are you going to do with your time?"

He looked at me, those blue eyes burning straight through.

"Didn't have any plans. I only know one person here."

"You should do that then." His cheeks colored. "I mean, spend time with them, not do...unless you wanted. I, uh, gotta get back to the kitchen."

He was so adorable. I can't believe I ever thought he was a jerk. He stood to go and I found an ache in my body for him that surprised me.

"Allie?"

He turned.

"Thanks again for last night." I held out my hand and he took it. It looked like a handshake to everyone else, but his thumb smoothing over the back of my hand was anything but. I lowered my voice again. "Room five."

He nodded once and went back to the kitchen. I finished, paid and walked back slowly through the snow, letting the cold wash over me, hoping there would be a knock on my door before the plane was ready.

Kael

MY HEAD SPUN. Helene just invited me to her room. I had never had less interest in making food or running a kitchen than at this moment. The only thing I'd ever wanted to do was the only thing I didn't want to be doing currently. I glanced at the clock.

"Think we'll be busy today?"

Danny harrumphed. "I don't even know what we're doing here now."

I put my hands on my hips. "Go if you want."

He shook his head and wiped down his station. "No. I'm already here."

I smirked. He just liked to bitch. Sheila scared me by speaking up behind me. "You know, you could go. The food is made and when we're out, we're out. Danny and I can hold down the fort."

Shelia reminded me of my aunt so much. They had been close and she was the nearest thing I had to her. The look in her eyes right now told me she knew where I wanted to be. It's the same look Cat would've given me. I took off my apron and hung it without even double checking. I kissed her cheek.

"Thank you."

"Go get her."

I felt my cheeks turn red as I left.

I walked to my truck, but what was the point of trying to get home and back. What if I got stuck and couldn't get to her? Sheila and Danny lived way closer than I did, but I might have trouble as far out as I was. I turned and headed to the motel instead.

The snow was cold and I'd forgotten my coat in my haste to get to Helene. I tightened my arms, shoving my hands in my pockets as I walked over. The snow was very deep in some areas and didn't look like it was going anywhere soon. I wondered how long that meant she'd be here. She could come home with me instead of being stuck at the motel, maybe.

I stopped, standing in a small pile of snow.

What was wrong with me? That would be creepy, right?

Hi. We just really met. Come home with me. I think you're the one.

Yeah, no. Won't be saying that. And yeah, no? I officially sounded like I was from the Midwest. I shook my head and looked up to find myself in front of room number five without consciously going there.

I raised my hand to knock but hesitated. Was I ready to do this? Or even expect anything.

Could I let her go after?

I wasn't sure. Maybe it was better to hold on to last night and just leave it at that.

But this might be my only chance, and the one thing I knew for sure was if I let her go now without telling her how I felt, I'd regret it forever.

I put knuckle to wood and knocked on the door.

Helene's voice answered from the other side. "Who is it?"

Who else could she be expecting?

"It's, uh, Kael?" Why did I say it like that? I was, in fact, Kael.

The door flung open. "Hi."

"Who did you think it was?"

"I'm a woman, alone, in a strange town. Did you want me to just open the door?"

I hadn't thought about that. "Good point. Can I come in?"

"Sure, sure."

We sat a small table by the window. "I don't have anything to offer you except half a Coke from two days ago."

I smiled at her. "That's it. Then I'm leaving." I winked.

She smiled the most beautiful, playful smile. "Anything I could do to convince you to stay?"

I stood up, nervous, and decided to let the words fall out like pasta from a pot. "Hey, um. I know this is a little nuts. But you don't have to stay here and spend money. You could come to my place. If you like."

When she didn't answer, I looked back to her and found her staring at me. Maybe she was trying to decide who I was, or if she could truly trust me, but whatever it was bore through my soul.

Those eyes cut through me, directly to my heart. As if she knew every little thing I was thinking in this minute and all the ones to come. But she still wanted to know more. Most people looked at me and saw me for who they thought I was – an arrogant chef, angry at the world, a little full of himself – but she looked at me like she wanted to see the real me. And I knew her somehow, too. I knew that's what she was thinking.

The fact I wanted to show her the real me was the shocking part.

What an odd sensation. To know a total, well, almost total, stranger. No words. Just a look between us. Same as when you visit a new place and it feels like home. That was Helene. She was home to me.

"Yeah, I think I'd like that."

A huge smile spread across my face. "Let's get your stuff and get you checked out then."

She grabbed a small bag. "Ready."

"That's it?"

She shifted weight, foot to foot. "I wasn't planning on staying, remember?"

I nodded. "Okay, let's go."

We walked down to the lobby, the cold beating against our skin.

"Where's your coat?" She looked up, appalled by my lack of outer wear.

"I left it at the diner. I came here...in a hurry."

Her cheeks flushed and she pushed through the door.

"Hey Betty."

"Kael."

"Need a room?" Betty eyed me, then saw Helene and her demeanor changed. What if I did need a room? My diner was across the street. Maybe I couldn't get home. I frowned at her. "Not today."

No one here thought I would come back and keep Cat's place alive, and once I did, I clearly hadn't done a good enough job in their eyes.

Betty turned her attention to Helene. "Checking out?"

"I think so. Thanks so much for the hospitality."

"Anytime, honey. Come back and see us."

She eyed me again. And something sparked.

"Betty, come on in for the special next week. My aunt

always said you loved the French dip and that's what we're having. It'll be on the house."

The surprise on her face was refreshing. "Thanks, Kael. I will."

Helene smiled at me and took my hand. Warmth flooded me. Again, her approval meant more than it should. We walked across the street to my truck.

"Go get your coat. What if we have car trouble, or something."

"Whatever you say, Chef."

I ran in and right back out to find her already in the cab, looking like she belonged there.

I got in and cranked the engine. It fired right up and soon we were out on the snowy road, navigating our way to my place.

We didn't talk in the car and it didn't matter. I'd never been with someone like this. Comfortable in the silence.

We pulled into my driveway with no trouble at all.

"That was uneventful, just like I like it," she said and hopped down out of the truck. Then she disappeared with a small yelp.

I moved around the truck as quick as I could to find her on her backside in the snow. A goofy smile covered her face. "Shit."

I reached out to help her out. She grabbed my hands and just as she was about to get up, she gave me a tug and I was on the ground with her.

"Oh, you're going to pay for that." We rolled in the snow, her high pitched laughter ringing out in the quiet world. Snowflakes littered her hair. I brushed it out of her face as we came to a stop, her body underneath mine.

I lowered my lips to hers. Her eyelids shuttered as we

kissed, her arms closing around me. Her fingers tangled in my hair as the kiss went on.

"Allie?"

"Yeah?" I asked in between kisses.

"I'm freezing."

We laughed as I stood and helped her up. I kissed her nose. "That was your doing."

She shrugged, smacking the snow off my ass. "It was worth it." She brushed herself off. "Ugh. Now my clothes are all wet though."

"I've got stuff you can put on."

"Thanks." Her voice was small, shy.

We made our way into the house, the warm air surrounding us. I turned my face up to soak in the warmth, letting it seep in and fight off the chill. "Feels good in here. Come on. Let's get you out of those clothes."

As soon as it left my mouth, I wish I could've put it back in. I turned to look at Helene when she didn't answer right away.

She leaned against a door frame, hair falling over one shoulder. Spots where the snow had soaked through showed on her jeans. But still, she stood there, looking at me as she pulled on the bottom of her shirt, lifting it up and over her head. "Okay."

She was the most gorgeous creature I'd ever seen. I was to her in a second, my arms around her, holding her close as I carried her to the bedroom.

"You lift me like I'm nothing." She kissed my neck as we made our way down the short hallway.

But she was the opposite of nothing, she was everything.

"How am I supposed to lift you?"

She paused and tilted her head. "I'm not sure, but it's been an issue."

I turned her in a circle as she smiled and held on tighter.

I gently laid her back on the bed, undoing the button and zipper of her jeans. I took off her shoes and socks and sat them on the heater vent to dry before returning to her.

"You're very thoughtful."

She leaned back on her elbows, lying there waiting for me.

"I try to be. I'm not always successful."

I grabbed at the waistband of her jeans and peeled them off her legs. There she was, Helene, in my bed, in just her bra and panties.

"What are you thinking right now?"

The question caught me off guard. "What am I thinking? You're there, like that, and you want me to think?"

She chuckled, her breasts bouncing softly when she did. "Sure."

I moved toward the bed as I answered. "I'm thinking you're stunning, absolutely gorgeous. I'm thinking how glad I am you came back to my restaurant, even if it was to tell me off, and how lucky I am you're here." I put a knee on the bed, leaning over her. "I'm hoping you don't mind this kind of hovering."

"I do actually." I started to stand, but she put her hands on my shoulders and pulled me to her. "You're too far away."

I smiled. "What are you thinking?"

"That you have the prettiest eyes. And you're not at all who I thought you were. You surprised me, which doesn't happen very often."

We laid there in the silence, close to one another. I tried to process what she said, deciding whether to be offended or not.

"Truthfully, that's not it." Her voice startled me.

"What do you mean?" I could lay here with her forever.

"This is who I thought you were when we first met, then you...weren't."

"I'm sorry you had to put up with the other guy."

She placed a hand under the edge of my sleeve, squeezing my arm, then running her fingers down its length. Those same nimble fingers inched under the bottom of my t-shirt. I shivered as she found my torso and explored.

Helene pushed me to my back, straddling me. She lifted my shirt up and off over my head.

"Allie, you're so god-damned beautiful. I want to know what each one of these tattoos mean. I want to find every muscle, every curve, every piece of you." She leaned over me, holding her hair back with one hand, the other on my chest. "I want you." She leaned on her hand beside me, her hair falling around us as she did. "All of you. Both halves. I don't want you to feel like you can't be yourself."

I took her head in my hands, kissing her hard, our mouths a crush of passion and need. We rolled to her back, skin to skin. I kissed down her jawline, over the smooth skin of her neck. I moved the strap of her bra and kissed her shoulder. I ran a finger over the same spot then kissed it again.

"Has anyone ever loved you like you're meant to be loved?" I leaned up on an elbow. Our faces close.

Her eyes widened and her mouth opened and closed, as she was at a loss for words. "I...I don't know."

"I want to. Show you how you should be loved."

"I'm all yours."

"Tell me If that changes."

Those words were all I needed. Mine. At her consent. Because the honest truth was, I'd been hers since the first moment she walked into the culinary classroom so long ago.

It was confirmed the second she came into London House. And my fate was sealed the day she sat down in my diner.

I moved down her body, just above her, taking in a big breath. Smoky sweetness filled my brain and nose. She smelled like rich pastry and something sweet I couldn't place. The combination was intoxicating.

I ran my tongue along the lace edge of her bra. I was here yesterday, but this time no one would barge in at the wrong moment. Pulling the fabric back, I took her nipple in my mouth, my hand massaged her breast as I suckled her. Her back arched slightly, a small moan coming from her lips as her fingers tightened in my hair. I moved to the other side.

"Don't stop." She tightened her grip.

"I'm not," I smiled against her, "but I don't want to play favorites."

She reached under herself and with a flick, I felt the fabric loosen around her. I pulled the bra down her arms and tossed it aside.

Helene was a site to behold. Gorgeous curves. Strength and softness all in one. And she was there, waiting for me. I laid my head on her chest, holding her. She played with my hair, not saying a word.

I marveled that this would be enough. Just lying here with her would be all I ever needed.

But I could have more of her, she'd told me so and it renewed the need I felt. I kissed into the well between her breasts. I moved my way further down, kissing a straight line down her stomach, just like she had done to me.

I looked up to see her looking down at me. "Allie..."

10

Helene

Kael looked up, his blue eyes penetrating through me. Those eyes could set the sea on fire. And humans are mostly water, so I boiled. My head lolled back as he continued his descent. His mouth was gentle and soft against my skin, but hot, searing me with each kiss. His curls tickled my thighs as he moved lower. He leaned his head on my left leg as his fingers trailed up the inside of the other. He drew circles by the side of my knee, taking his time. His breath warmed my skin, driving me mad. As his fingers rose higher, just to the crease of my inner thigh, he stopped. I raised my head up to find him grinning like a devil at me.

I pleaded with my eyes, words failing me. He pushed aside the thin fabric, pushing in two fingers. I sighed and leaned back again. He worked slow and methodical, as if he had studied. The build would climb, then he'd shift, working from a different angle, until once again, my body heated. Suddenly his hand was gone and I whimpered. In one quick move my panties were off and he was right back to work. He positioned himself between my legs, one leg over his shoulder. His mouth was so close, but not on me, his breath heating me further. But his hand was unrelenting. I was close, arching my back, muttering his name incoherently, his hand closed on my hip and his mouth around my center.

His tongue delved deep inside and the wave of pleasure crashed over me. It rocked through my body, but Kael never let up with his mouth or hand until every drop was wrung from me.

He slowly worked his way back up my body, just as he had made his way down. As soon as I could reach, I grabbed him by those brown curls and lifted his face to mine.

His breath was soft and warm against my cheek, though he held back slightly. He caressed my cheek, taking all of me in.

"Lena."

I pulled him to me, closing the distance between us. My hands ran over his back, feeling the muscles flex under my touch. I pushed my fingers slightly into his waistband. "Take these off."

He stood. "Yes, chef."

I grinned. "God, you're hot."

His cheeks flushed. He took off the rest of his clothes, and holy shit.

Kael delivered on every level. We were brand new adults last time we were here and the years had been very kind. I knew it was good size from last night in the diner, but here, just him in all his glory, it was a sight to behold. I raised an eyebrow.

"Disappointed?"

"Not even a little. My memory did not do it justice."

He placed a knee on the bed and made his way to me, his body over mine.

He grinned his devilish smile. "So you've thought about me?"

I smirked. "Once or twice. What about me?"

"I can't count that high."

I gasped as he closed the distance between us, his hands pulled against my hip, then arms wrapping around me, pushing my body against the length of his. This kiss was bruising, like we couldn't get enough of each other.

His tongue pushed into my mouth, surprising me with its welcome force. It was warm. A sweetness but with depth. I pushed at his tongue with my own, a sensuous dance of passion. His kisses became short and soft, nipping at the corner of my mouth, right at the edge of my smile.

His body pushed against me as I spread my legs to show him what I wanted. He kissed across my cheek, catching the spot just below my earlobe. "Not yet. I want to enjoy you."

I growled. "I want to enjoy fucking you."

I felt his cheek curl up next to mine. "Oh, we'll get there."

"Allie, please."

He looked up at me, my eyes begging and my body hanging on his every whim.

"I guess we don't know how much time we have." He kissed the hollow of my throat.

"Don't tease me."

His eyes met mine. "I would never. Tell me what you want."

"Fuck me. You don't have to be polite."

He moved so quickly as he closed his mouth on my breast, drawing on it so hard I cried out. He relented only to push his body against mine, pinning me to the mattress.

"Is this what you want? Me to show you how much I want you?" His voice was commanding and raw and everything I wanted. I heard the rip of the foil packet and my heart raced.

"Yes. Allie, I want you. Now." I looked into those blue eyes.

He grinned that smile again, grabbed my thigh and slammed into me.

"Oh my god." My back arched to accommodate his size. But it felt so good. What in the hell had I been missing? His rhythm was punishing and relentless. The sweetness of a few minutes ago was gone. I scratched at his strong back, trying to find traction. I was floating, not bound to this earth, except through Kael. That's what I was attached to. He was my tether. The man with me, inside of me. I drew my teeth across his shoulder and heard him suck in a breath.

"Helene, you feel so fucking good."

With an arm around my waist, he rolled us in one fluid move, until I was straddling him on top. He took a breast in each hand, squeezing then releasing, over and over. His hands made their way to my hips as I made my own frenetic rhythm. His grip leveled me out, rocking back and forth, until we moved together, I leaned forward for a slightly different angle.

"Allie. God damn."

He smiled, eyes never leaving me. His fingers wound in my hair, holding my head at the base of my neck. We rocked together, harder and harder, my breath getting choppy. I couldn't get enough.

And I could already feel the build. It was too soon. I didn't want it to end. But the depth, the intensity. I was coming apart.

"Oh god. I'm—"

"Not yet." Just as I was almost there, Kael lifted me off him. He flipped me like I actually did weigh nothing and put me on my knees. He entered from behind. I reached back to hold on to his head, his arm around my middle.

I collapsed forward as he pounded into me, catching myself on my hands with his hand on my shoulder, his hips slamming against mine. He never lost steam and I was right back to the edge.

"Allie, Allie please." I begged for release or to make it go on forever. I didn't know. My thoughts were a jumble of nothing but all of him and how good he felt with his body next to mine. With him inside me.

Finally, I heard his labored breathing, the tell-tale moaning. His arm circled my middle and he kissed the spot below my ear.

He pumped against me two more times and my body exploded from the inside out as we came together, his arms the only thing holding me in one piece. He rested his forehead in between my shoulder blades, his breath hot on my skin. We melted down together on the mattress and he moved to the side.

He turned me to face him and kissed me softly, sweetly, brushing the hair from my face.

We were side-by-side, my leg draped over him and his hand rested on my thigh. I traced his cheekbone and jaw with my finger, kissing his eyelids and tasting his lower lip, slowly, in no rush. He smiled, completely content.

"I'm falling for you, Kael Ruggeman."

He closed his eyes. "That's so good to hear."

"It's really a problem."

He kissed me. "Why is that?"

"Generally, falling for someone you can't have is problematic."

"You can have me, Lena."

He laid his head on my chest as I held him in my arms. I was falling for him, but he was wrong. I couldn't have him. Kael would be a luxury, an indulgence. And I couldn't afford either of those things. My situation didn't allow for it.

My life was what it was and it wouldn't change anytime soon. That meant this is all Kael and I would ever have.

I played with his hair as he laid there, his breathing smoothing out. After he fell asleep, I snaked out of his arms and found my way to his closet. I pulled on one of his t-shirts, taking a big breath of Kael's scent that clung to it. I found my panties and once I was as close to dressed as I needed to be, I walked down the hall.

Kael's house was neat and put together. One wall had a bookcase of cookbooks and in front of it, a large stack of more of them sat in a haphazard way. An old chef cover was on the back of a chair. I ran my hand over his initials on the sleeve.

The kitchen was smaller than I'd imagined it would be, but it was fully stocked with all you'd need. I looked in the fridge. It was full too so I pulled out what I wanted to make chicken and cornbread and foraged the rest from the cabinets. Turning on some music quietly, soon I was lost in the ritual of cooking, loving every minute of it.

I opened the cabinets, innately knowing where he would keep things. I smiled every time something was in the same place I'd put it.

See how easy it would be?

I shoved those thoughts away and tried to hum along to the music as I prepared the food. But again, the feeling of familiarity and comfort took me over. I wasn't kidding when I told Kael I was falling for him, but it was more than that.

Deidre was in my brain. *You're in love with him.*

But what was I going to do about it? Simple answer? Nothing. I couldn't. He lived here and I lived there and neither one of us could really pick up our lives. Plus no one could know this ever happened. This was a completely different universe from reality and I'd never be able to visit this place of bliss again.

This was my one moment of normalcy and that would have to be enough. I put the cornbread in the oven and turned the chicken in the pan, wondering how on earth I got myself into this mess.

I jumped a mile when I heard Kael's voice.

"Hello Beautiful."

Kael

I LEANED AGAINST THE WALL, watching Helene work her magic, softly singing along to the songs coming from her phone. She was wearing my t-shirt and it was one of the sexiest things I'd ever seen. "Hello Beautiful."

She jumped. "Shit."

I grinned. "Sorry." I strode across the room and put my arms around her, pulling her close. Her kiss was welcoming and warm. It didn't feel like the first day, it felt like the hundredth day, the fifth year, the end of time and it had always been us.

"Hi."

I kissed her forehead. "Hi."

She kept her arms around my neck. "Rest well?"

I nodded, my hands on her waist. "I was sad when I woke up and you weren't there."

She pulled away to check on the food. "I'm making us some sustenance. Hope you don't mind."

"Not at all." I took a seat on one of the chairs by the island. "Make yourself at home."

"I did. Your kitchen is properly organized."

I gave her a playful smile. "Glad to have your approval." She couldn't know how true that was. Truer than it probably should be.

She smiled and checked the food. "Almost there." She leaned her elbows on the counter toward me. "So, come here often?"

"First time. But I suspect I'll be back." I took her in, trying to keep my composure. My t-shirt left little to the imagination.

Her answering grin brought up my own. "Repeat customers are the backbone of an establishment." She pulled something out of the oven. She put the chicken and cornbread on plates for us and came to sit by me.

The scent of the food met my nose and immediately made my mouth water. "That smells so good."

She smiled, ducking her chin at the compliment.

"Want some wine?" I asked her.

"That'd be great."

After pouring two glasses, I handed her one.

"Thanks for the hospitality." She took a sip.

"Anytime." I looked at her. "I mean it. Anytime."

She nodded and ate some food. It was of course delicious. "Damn, Lena. You can cook. You should open your restaurant if that's what you want to do. I know I already said it, but I mean it. I have no doubt you'd succeed."

She shrugged and pushed food around her plate, not meeting my eyes.

"I don't have the means. Or the place. Or the time. I have to keep my job because of family obligations."

I looked at her, trying to puzzle out what she meant.

"Insurance, you know?"

I nodded. "That's why you stay there? But you love it, too. Right?"

She looked at her plate. "Writing about other people's food. Sure. What's not to love."

I squeezed her hand. "You're incredible at it."

Her hand pulled away from me as she grabbed her glass and took a drink of wine. "I have no start up cash anyway. Or not enough. And who in New York wants a menu of roadside diner comfort foods?" She shook her head. "No. It's not a winning plan."

"Are there other family obligations?"

She waved a hand in the air. "Doesn't matter. I just need my job, that's all."

Her face clouded for a minute, the darkest I'd seen her.

I took a bite of chicken. "And I think there would be plenty of market for that. Like you said, people get tired of small bites."

"I guess." She got up, taking her plate to the sink. I followed with mine. "I just don't know where or how it would fit, but like I said, no money so irrelevant."

"Do you have to stay in New York?"

She didn't answer but instead took my plate and rinsed. I loaded them into the dishwasher after. Like we had done it a hundred times. Like this was always how it should be. I tried to shake off the feeling of home. Because that's what it was. Helene felt like home.

"Surely there's a way."

She turned to me, drying her hands on a towel. "Can we talk about something else?"

"What do you want to talk about?"

She pushed the sleeve of my t-shirt up. She touched the tattoo on my shoulder. "Tell me about this one."

I looked down at the ink lines I'd had on my arm for as long as I could remember.

"That is a cat and a fiddle dancing together."

She gave me a deadpan look. "Thanks. I see that. What does it mean?"

I took a breath. No one ever wanted to know this stuff about me. I was just the tattooed chef and that's that. "The cat is Aunt Kitty as you know her– real name, Catherine – and the fiddle is my mom, her sister. My mom was a musician and that was what they called themselves when they were young. Like the nursery rhyme?"

She nodded, hanging on my every word.

"My mom passed when I was very little and my aunt basically raised me and my sister. So when Cat got sick, I had this designed."

"That's lovely, Allie. And I'm sorry you lost them both."

I shrugged. "It happens. Okay, my turn to ask about something."

She put her hands on my waist, pulling me close. "We don't have to talk at all."

"Are you just avoiding telling me anything else?"

Lena leaned into me, her face softening as she grew closer. I crooked a finger under her chin, then cupped her cheek.

"Maybe. But time is finite. This can't last forever."

She nuzzled into my hand, her eye lids lowering. I brought my lips to hers, gently, trying to show her how precious she was to me. *This can't last forever.* Her words haunted me but I focused on the moment. She wasn't wrong. Any minute, the real world might call and say her plane was ready.

Her mouth moved against mine, slowly, languidly. Like we had all the time in the world, not just until the snow melted.

"You might have a point." My arms snaked around her, our bodies flush.

I held her there, holding her in my arms, kisses going on and on. Again, the notion that this could be enough hit me in the chest. Just holding her and kissing her. Doing the dishes, talking in the kitchen.

I wanted to watch dumb TV shows together. Take a walk as the sun set. Fall asleep on the couch together on a lazy Sunday afternoon.

I never knew this is what love could be. Or even that this is what love was. A series of small moments that meant everything even though most people thought they were nothing.

"You could stay a little longer. Just to make sure its totally safe."

"Allie, I'm here now. Can't that be enough?"

I lowered my hand, slipping it under the t-shirt she wore, splaying it open across her back as I nodded.

She slowly pulled away from me, her hand trailing down my arm until our fingers laced together. She looked back over her shoulder as she gave a gentle tug. I followed her as we moved down the hallway once more.

11

Helene

As I led Kael down the hall to his room, my heart pounded and my insides burned. I wanted him and I knew time was limited. But I also understood I was playing with fire. It was going to be hard to leave when Jack called and said the plane was ready. But I couldn't make myself stay away. My need for Kael was something bigger than just falling into bed, it was something I'd been searching for all my life.

But this felt like playing house.

More like, a home. And home was the one thing I'd never had and didn't even know I wanted until I showed up in this little town. I wasn't even sure I believed in the idea of home before now.

But I could see it, right in front of me. And Kael was the reason.

I turned to face him as we stepped into his room. A lamp on the bedside table illuminated the space in a candlelight-like glow. His face was beautiful in the shadows cast from the light. His eyes shone in the dusky twilight.

He stepped closer and turned me slowly. A mirror was in front of us, hung on one of the closet doors. From behind me, his head rested by mine, our cheeks together. His hands started at my shoulders and smoothed down my arms. He laced our fingers again and then wrapped our arms around me, so he hugged my middle still holding my hands. He lowered his head, kissing where my neck and shoulder met at the edge of my shirt.

"Look how gorgeous you are."

I shivered as his lips trailed up my neck and he released my hand and reached down, fingers trailing up the outside of my thigh, lifting my shirt just a little.

His finger traced the bend at my hip and around the outside. "This curve right here. Mm."

My breathing was shallow as his fingers traced my skin, his mouth only leaving me long enough to speak. His hand opened, squeezing my hip and pulling me against him. "Feeling you against me. It's enough to drive any one mad with desire." I moaned as he pushed against me from behind, holding me close with his other arm. "When do you have to leave?"

I reached back to run my fingers through his hair. "As soon as the weather lets me. I have to get back to work."

He sighed. "That's too soon." He looked at our reflection in the mirror. "Look how perfect we fit."

I leaned my head against his. "You have me now."

He drew his fingertips down my uplifted arm, turning

me to face him in the process. I kissed him, the fire burning in me. Each kiss could be the last and I hoped he could feel how much he meant to me.

Grabbing on to those curls, I pulled him closer as my tongue explored his mouth. His strong hands closed on my waist, locking our bodies together. I dropped my hands to his chest, pushing softly against him. He let go of me and took a step back to sit down on the bed. I reached down to take off his shirt.

Those tattoos over defined muscles made my mouth water. I still wanted to ask about each one, and I almost did, but now wasn't the time. I leaned over him as he rested his head against me. I kissed the crown of his head then he looked up, his hand on my cheek.

"What's wrong?"

I shook my head, not wanting to ruin the moment. "I'm worried I won't have time to ask you about your other tattoos. When did you get them and why? Do you want more?"

He smiled at me. "Why wouldn't you have time?"

I stood and looked away, crossing my arms. "Time is running out and when I leave here…"

He grabbed my hands and pulled me to him to kiss again. My lips tingled and ached in a delicious way, I knelt on the bed, straddling him as I sat in his lap. He supported my back and with his mouth worked his way down my neck. I leaned back over his arms. I felt his hands under the edge of his shirt I wore. And I helped him take it off me.

He found my mouth once more, closing those strong arms around me. It felt like the millionth kiss and the first kiss and somehow the last kiss each time our lips met. My head spun.

He stood, lifting me easily then laying us back gently on

the bed. He handled me as if I was fine China and he didn't want to break me. But it wasn't soft. I couldn't explain it. I felt cherished and adored yet I knew I was about to be ravished. I loved it.

Lying beside me, he traced the curve of my face. I kissed his fingertips as he got to my lips, holding his hand. Staring in his eyes, I placed his hand on my thigh and lifted it higher. He pushed the fabric of my panties to the side and slipped in his fingers. Slowly, gently, then finally working a little faster. Then deeper. I held on to the lover in my arms, tangling my fingers in his hair, drawing on his mouth as he worked my body to a height of pleasure.

I arched under his perfect machinations. He pulled away to watch my face as I broke apart at his touch. I whimpered as the waves of ecstasy rolled over me and I saw the excitement in his eyes. Heat poured from me as he slowed his movement once more.

"Lena, you're so god damn sexy." He kissed my neck.

"It's you. It's the way you touch me and look at me."

He slowly pulled the rest of my clothes away, never letting his eyes leave me.

He took my breast in his mouth, the wet heat sending me right back into a spiral of lust. The pressure was perfect, his hand squeezing as his mouth kept on. I pulled at his back, digging my fingers in as I tried to put him where I wanted, which was back on top of me. In me. With me. He rose up, eyes meeting mine.

I heard the rip of foil and he raised up just enough to roll on protection, then never letting his eyes leave mine, he slid inside me.

Again, my breath was taken away by his size. He brushed the hair from my face, our bodies moving together. And we were there, locked together, focused only on each other. I held on to his head, gently holding him to me.

But he moved stronger, deeper, faster. I closed my arms around him as he locked an arm under my leg, changing the angle just enough to feel even better, his lips locking to mine.

He rolled us until he sat up, me in his lap, legs around each other. Our hips rocked in unison as he kissed my chest and both my breasts. I leaned back as he took his time getting us there. He wasn't in a rush, and neither was I. I never wanted to be anywhere but here with Kael. My Allie.

I played with his hair, enjoying the feel of him. All of him. He locked eyes with me, pulling me into a deep kiss, our bodies never stopping.

"Lena, I just..." His face was flustered, eyes glassy.

"Shhh. I'm all yours." I smoothed his hair and kissed him again.

We rolled in one smooth movement. His chest flushed and he pumped his hips harder, faster, and I burned for him. My arms wrapped under his, holding on to his shoulders.

He moaned and slammed his hips into me. I bounced under him, loving the way he felt on me and in me. Everything was perfect- the build, the burn, the wave about to crash. I let my head fall back, riding this for all the pleasure I could get. It went on and just as I felt it beginning to break over me, Kael said my name and got there himself. He moved against me as the ripples of pleasure moved out through my limbs and back again. He collapsed on me, curling into my arms as we rolled on our sides. He pulled off the condom, reaching back to throw it away. I pulled him back to me, needing his warmth. It was cold when he wasn't there.

"We're pretty great together." I ran my fingers through his hair, finding a curl to twirl around my fingers.

He nodded and put his head on my shoulder as I held him. "I could get used to this."

"Mmmm," was all I could get out.

Because me too. That was the problem. I was used to it already and I had to acknowledge it for what it was – a moment in time. It wasn't real. It couldn't be. There was no way to make this something that could exist.

Who we were, where we lived, it wouldn't work. I would lose everything and he couldn't give up anything. Not to mention I was Anonymous and I wasn't sure Kael would forgive me for lying to him and creating this whole problem to begin with. There was no way to make this forever.

I shivered at the word. I'd have to settle for the very mediocre substitute of for now.

Kael

A SHIVER WOKE me up as I shook under the thin sheet that covered me. In the not quite dawn light, I fished around for my heavy comforter to no avail. I cracked open an eye against the purple light of early morning. I was alone.

I woke up every day alone, why was it strange now?

Last night came flooding back in a rush. Helene. I sat up and looked around. Her shoes were still in the floor, so she was here.

Of course she was here. What did I think? She ventured out in the snow back to the motel?

I got up and pulled on some jeans and a flannel.

Running a hand back through my hair, I made my way down the hall.

Helene was curled up, with my comforter, on the couch. She was beautiful. Her cheeks were a soft pink as she slept. Her hair spilled down over the edges of the blanket. Another chill went through me as I remembered the tickle on my skin from those same tendrils touching me last night as I looked at her.

I wanted this every morning. It was the first day we would have woken up together and it was something I already missed. How could someone walk into your life and fit so well so quickly that you knew you'd never be okay without them there.

I knelt beside her and pushed back a lock of hair from her forehead. She stirred under my touch, eyes fluttering open. A soft smile filled her face when she saw me.

"Hi."

"You stole my blanket." I grinned at her.

Her cheeks turned crimson. "Sorry. I couldn't sleep and I didn't want to wake you so I came out here, but it was cold." She opened the blanket to invite me in with her.

"You can always wake me up."

I slid into the warm cocoon next to her on the couch, my arms around her as she curled up against my chest. She pulled the blanket back around us.

"Here we are, in another blanket fort." She giggled and it soothed me as I held her.

"You're forgiven, but you could've woken me up."

She shrugged. "Some people are particular about their sleep."

As we lay there in silence, arms locked around one another, I didn't want to look outside to see if the roads had cleared. I didn't want to move to get food or coffee. I couldn't do anything to break this moment. If we got up for food or coffee, we could see out the window. And once we looked out the window and saw the road cleared, she was gone. Once we broke this moment, she might remember what an arrogant bastard I am. She'd remind us both how you don't sleep with the chef, then she'd be gone anyway.

"What are you thinking about?" I asked her, hoping she'd...honestly, I didn't know what I was hoping for. But anything besides 'I have to go'.

She sighed. "That I hope the road is clear today. I have to get back home."

I tried not to stiffen under her. That was the one answer I didn't want to hear.

"I get that."

"It has been nice to get away though."

"Yeah? You're welcome to stay."

She snuggled tighter to me. "I'd like that, but Allie, it's not possible. I have to go."

She sat up. The distant between us was too much even though we were still under the blanket.

I nodded. "But right now?"

"As soon as possible. I have...responsibilities that I have to get back to."

I clicked my tongue. "Responsibilities."

She looked over at me, then stood up. I was thrown off by her wearing my t-shirt again. I tried to focus, not get wrapped up in the curve of her thigh or how she bit her lip.

"Yes. I have a job and people who depend on me."

"People?"

She crossed her arms, her eyes glassy. "Yes. People. Why are you being like this?"

I shook my head and threw off the blanket. "I'm not being like anything. I just thought...you know what, it doesn't matter what I thought." I rolled out from underneath of her as she pulled the blanket up closer. I tried not to see the look of hurt on her face as I went to the kitchen to make coffee. I didn't really expect her to stay, obviously. And I was probably ruining the remaining time I had with her, but for some reason, I was angry.

Her voice was quiet as she spoke. "What did you think? I would come here to this small town and stay forever? That I didn't have a life? I didn't come here to stay for this long even. I came to say my piece and leave. I mean, there was a snowstorm. Things happened. We're adults. Did you think this was forever?"

Her words stung. No, of course I didn't think that, but it was what I wanted. I forced out one bitter Ha! "No. Why would I think that? I mean, it was just convenient, right?" I turned to see the hurt land on her face in real time and immediate regret filled me. I put my hands on the counter. "I'm sorry. I didn't mean you were convenient, I meant I was. I..."

"It's fine. I thought..." She pulled in her bottom lip and I knew she was about to cry. She turned to head back to the bedroom, but I met her and turned her to me by her shoulders.

"I'm sorry. I'm being a jerk because I don't want you to go."

She turned to me, her voice rising. "Then why don't you just say that? Why do you throw daggers before anything else?"

"I don't know. It feels safer. Then I can't be hurt."

She looked into my face. "Does that work, hurting others to protect yourself?"

"Not at all." I kissed her forehead and pulled her into a hug. "I don't want you to go. And I am sorry."

"I know. I'd like to stay, but I have to leave. There are so many reasons this wouldn't work. You don't want to be with me, and I can't be with you."

"What do you mean?"

She snaked out of my arms and walked down toward the bedroom. I followed, trying to catch every word as she spoke.

"Allie, I take care of my sister and nephew. I have a demanding job with an asshole boss, but it pays well and I can use my benefits for them. I am stuck there." She turned to me, tears streaming down her cheeks. "Don't you get it? I'm stuck."

I watched her chest heave as she cried, feeling helpless and not sure what to do next.

"I review restaurants for a living and you are a chef, the one kind of person I cannot get involved with. It would ruin everything I've worked to build. No matter what I might feel for you."

I hated seeing her like this. I tried to go to her, but she put up a hand.

"Don't. Please. I don't have the strength to tell you no right now."

I froze. "Wait. Might feel for me? What do you feel?"

She turned and started getting dressed. "It doesn't matter. I can't have this, and you shouldn't want this anyway. Trust me, if you knew me, all of me, you wouldn't want this. Let's just take the nice memory from the last couple days and leave it at that."

"I can't leave it at that. I feel like I finally just got to know you. I can't lose you now."

She turned to me, her hair over one shoulder, eyes still glistening with tears. "Lose me? Kael, this isn't real. No matter how it feels right now. You and I cannot be," she waved her hand in the air, "whatever this is."

I went to her as she turned away. I put my arms around her, pulling her close. "I don't understand why. What would it matter?"

She was stiff in my embrace. "I'm not the person you think I am. And I am dangerously close to telling you everything, but I can't. I have to go. You have to let me go."

She picked up her bag and put it over her shoulder, waiting for me to drive her back to the motel.

12

~

Helene

"I need to go."

Kael looked at me, with eyes full of longing and need. I didn't know how much resolve I had left, but it wasn't enough to combat those eyes long enough to get out unscathed. I should've never slept with him.

This was a disaster.

"Just stay for the rest of the day. You can't fly out right now anyway."

The urge to stay was too strong. This was uncharted and dangerous territory. "And do what? Play house a little longer?" He pulled back as if I'd slapped him. My words hit me deep as well. "I'm sorry. That's not what I meant."

"Just stay." His voice was soft as he spoke, sounding vulnerable in a way that almost undid me.

I shook my head. "I really can't."

He hung his head, hands on his hips. "Okay, Lena. I'll take you back."

"Hey, at least now we're friends, right?" I gave him a half smile.

He walked past me to grab his coat. "You and I both know that will never be enough," he said under his breath.

My chest hiccupped with more tears. He was right. It would never be enough. Nothing ever would again. No kiss, no romance, no anything ever again would compare to being here with Kael. It was the only place I'd ever felt I'd belonged. What was I thinking, coming back here to have the last word. *How did that work out, Carnahan?*

We rode to the motel in silence. I went back into the lobby to get another room. She gave me the same one and I was surprised to see Kael leaning against his truck when I headed to my room.

"Lena, I know you're leaving. I know you have to. And I've heard what you've said, but I honestly don't know why this can't work."

I stuck the key in the lock and tossed my head toward the room as I opened the door to let Kael know to follow me.

He quickly moved in behind me and closed the door against the cold.

"First, you live here and I live in New York. That is number one."

He pushed a lock of hair back over my shoulder, sending a ripple through me as his fingers brushed over my arm. "Travel can be worked out."

I steadied my voice or tried to. "Second, I can't date a chef. Don't you see the conflict? I have built something and I have a reputation. One word of this got out, I could lose it all. You know how this game is played."

His eyes said something much different than his words. "It might have been a problem before, but I'm not a chef you review anymore." He took another step closer. "So that can't affect you now."

And that brought me to the third point, is that I did still review him and I had a massive secret I couldn't tell him. I opened my mouth, but nothing came out.

"What's going to be your next excuse, Helene?"

I put my hand on his chest and looked up into his piercing blue eyes. I wanted him so badly. He put his hands on my waist, holding me close to him, but not close enough. "They aren't excuses." His fingers tightened their grip, and I stepped to him. "You've known me for a day. You probably won't even miss me."

He cupped my cheek then ran his fingers through my hair, to the base of my neck. "If you only knew how long I've wanted to know you. How often I regretted letting you leave my kitchen. How I wanted it to be more back when we were in school. You've dominated my brain from day one. I already miss you."

I sucked in a small breath before his mouth was on mine. I wrapped my arms around him, fingers lacing in his hair. We took a few clumsy steps back toward the bed until we tumbled down together, arms and legs intertwined.

God, I never wanted to be anywhere but in Allie's arms. But this was exactly what I needed to not be doing.

I sat up, breathless and put a hand on his chest. "I can't. This can't happen. There are parts of me you don't know and things you can't know. This won't work."

"Tell me what they are. Maybe I'll surprise you."

I shook my head, stood up and crossed my arms. "I can't. I'm sorry. I want to tell you, and that's part of the problem."

He stood, hands out. "I don't get it."

I nodded my head. "I know. And I'm sorry."

My phone rang, making me jump. "Hey Jack. Oh great. Thanks. I'll head that way."

Kael looked at me, pleading in his eyes.

"The plane is ready."

I reached out and Kael held my hand. "And you have to go."

I nodded, lips pressed together. I fought to hold back the tears. "Don't worry, in a couple days, you'll be so glad I'm out of your hair, you'll laugh about this moment."

He shook his head. "No, that's not how it will go. I'm too far gone. I think I'm in love with you."

The force of the words hit me in the chest. My heart squeezed hearing the word I'd felt the last couple days said out loud. I had to make a decision in that moment. So I decided on the path I'd taken a hundred times before. I'd give up the thing I wanted, because it stood in the way of what I had to do.

I had to end Kael's feelings for me.

I blew out a breath, ready to destroy the person I might've had a future with in another lifetime. "You need to get over that."

His head shot up, to look at me with so much hurt. "Why would you say that?"

I cringed away from his pleading stare and took a breath, but pushed on. "Because that restaurant I want to open? It's going to be all of Kitty's recipes. I have them all and that's what I plan on doing. It will be a better version of this place and that's that."

He stepped back, his face turning red. "That's been your

plan the whole time?" Disbelief colored his voice making his words feel like ice as they settled on me.

I bit my bottom lip to hold in my emotion. "Yes."

"This entire time, you sharing your dreams with me. Listening to me encourage you like the fool I am, your plan was to use my aunt's diner as a blueprint for your own?"

I nodded on stiff nod. "That is the plan. I came here the first time to see the place for myself, I just happened to find you. I would've left it alone if you hadn't brought me up in your response to that reviewer. But you didn't. You couldn't." The next words would hurt. "You were...just Kael"

He turned away. I didn't want him to go like this, but as soon as I reached out, I lowered my arm. No, this is what I was going for, no matter how much damage it did. I had to do this. He had to hate me and never want to reach out again. This was the only way my secret would remain safe and he might have a chance of getting over this and moving on.

"If you knew, what has the last two days been?"

I swallowed hard. "It's been nice. It wasn't my plan, but we're adults."

He turned back to me. "An opportunity then?"

I shored my shoulders and gave a tert nod.

"Got it. I'm the idiot who went and fell for you. Let down my guard for a second and see what I get? Won't make that mistake again. Good to see you again, Helene. You're right. In a couple days, I'll be glad you're gone."

The door clicked close behind him and as I heard his truck engine rev and drive away, I cried in the lonely room knowing I'd regret this moment for the rest of my life.

Kael

Damn, Helene Carnahan. I tried to focus on the still snowy road on the way back to the house. She was planning on using Cat's recipes that whole time. Unbelievable.

And man, I truly was an idiot to think she felt something more. As if someone like her would actually be into someone like me. I mean, how could she like me after all of our past. Like she said, I was just Kael. All that in the kitchen and the stories we exchanged, just a product of the moment. She was right, it wasn't real.

It had felt real, but clearly, I was wrong.

I slammed the truck in park and stormed into the house. I pulled the sheets and blankets from the bed and couch, shoving them into the washer. Nothing needed to smell like her. It would hurt too much. I clicked on the machine and went to the kitchen. I put everything in the dishwasher and ran that too. No trace of her could remain. I looked around the room.

A laptop was on the dining table, open, which was weird. Weirder still because it wasn't mine.

I touched it and to my surprise, the screen came awake. Who didn't lock their laptop?

I went back over the day and night. Helene had gotten up in the night and she was used to living alone.

But did she live alone? I wasn't sure if her sister and nephew lived with her or not, but either way, this was definitely hers and I shouldn't care about her living situation. *Nemesis, remember?*

She would need it for work though. I would do one last thing for her and take to the motel, then I would be done with Helene forever.

I went to close it, but a tab caught my eye. It said Small Town Eats. Where did I know that name from?

A sick feeling settled in my stomach.

I pulled up the Anon review on my phone. It was Small Town Eats. I sat back.

The feeling grew heavier.

"No, no, no."

Why would this be on her laptop? There had to be a good reason. *If you knew who I really was.*

Okay, but she is now collaborating with them at least as far as publishing, so that makes sense it would be here. Right? Right.

There's no way she could be Anon. She couldn't be. I sat at the table, staring at the screen. The little blue folder daring me to click on it.

And what would I find? Probably correspondence between her and the secret reviewer. It was published with her column now. That was all.

I got up and paced, not able to shake the feeling it was more.

I closed the computer and grabbed my coat. I tucked it under my arm and was almost to the door before I lifted the laptop and looked at it, willing it to tell me what I wanted to know.

I couldn't let it go. Why was there a special tab for that, and not her own column. That made zero sense.

I sat back down and opened it. Now it was locked. Damn. If I tried a password and it wasn't correct, it would lock up and she'd know I'd tried. But did it matter? I wasn't going to be anything to her and she couldn't be anything to me. And I had to know.

What would the password be? I thought maybe her sister's name, but I didn't know how to spell it and I wasn't sure she'd told me her nephew's name. She hadn't said a name for her restaurant so that wouldn't be it.

I growled as I thought about her using all of Cat's recipes. My brain sparked with an idea. She said Cat had saved her, and her plan was to model her place after Cat and the Fiddle.

I typed in K-I-T-T-Y-'-S and to my surprise, the page opened.

I took a deep breath and doubled click the Small Town Eats folder. All of the reviews Anon had posted were there. That made sense, she'd need them for work.

Except they only started collaborating with the last one. I scrolled down to the last entry.

My finger hovered over the file. "Now or never." I opened the last one, labeled simply – Oklahoma.

It was a new review, not finished. Some notes were there including one about changing the name of the column to Food to Write Home About. If I hadn't been so shocked, I could've appreciated the cleverness of that column name.

I closed that one and clicked on Cat and the Fiddle. Sure enough, there was the review, my response and the back and forth. There was also one labeled draft. I opened it.

"While the food was good, who can enjoy anything with Kael Fucking Ruggeman leaning over your table."
**do not mention the chef by name.*
***do not damage the restaurant in this review.*

I seethed. Helene Carnahan was Anon and not only the person who gave me four stars, but also four blue plates. And then she didn't bother to tell me it was her when she took me straight to bed for two days.

I closed my eyes. *Kael, I don't have enough Blue Plates for you.* I snapped to attention. *I need to tell you something.* And I'd stopped her. She did try to tell me. But what did it matter now? I closed the machine, watching it like a viper that might strike.

Helene wrote the review. And she was the reason I responded. And then she wrote back and had the nerve to come here and tell me off? Anger filled my insides and shoved out any warm feelings I'd harbored from the last couple days.

My phone buzzed.

> Hey. It's Helene. Did I leave my computer there?

I grimaced.

> Yes.

I tucked it under my arm, and went out to my truck, not checking the other messages coming in.

I pulled into the motel parking lot, her car still in the same spot. I knocked on her door.

She opened it with a smile on her face.

"My hero."

I held it out to her. "You'll definitely need it. Oklahoma will need to know what you think of their diner."

The color drained out of her face. "What?"

"You know, the place in Oklahoma you might want to write home about?"

She stammered. Telling her the name from her notes was probably a step too far, but in for a penny as they say.

"Kael, I..."

I stepped into the room shoving the computer at her as she backed up, holding it in her arms like a shield. "What?

Wanna defend yourself? Tell me again how you weren't sabotaging me with four blue plates. It doesn't matter. How can anyone enjoy eating with me standing right there, anyway?"

She clutched the computer to her chest, tears streaming down her face. "I wasn't. I would never want to hurt the diner."

I headed to the door. "It's just me you don't give a shit about. Got it."

"No, that's not it. I care. I care too much. I wanted to change it, but I couldn't because..."

I whirled on her. "Of your precious professionalism? But then you went and fucked the chef. Remember?" Bile filled my throat as I hurled the hateful words at her.

Her breath hitched and I watched her face crumple at my words. "I'm sorry. But please, you can't tell anyone it's me."

I took a step to her, but it was only anger between us now, nothing else. "I can't believe I thought for a second you cared about me, or that I might have feelings for you."

I turned to go.

"Allie..."

I stopped. "It's Kael. Only family calls me Allie." I looked back at her over my shoulder.

She sucked in her tears, but her face was lifeless and still. "Got it. Won't make that mistake again."

"Those recipes should've never been given to you. They are not yours to use. Goodbye, Helene."

13

Helene

I shook as the cold air blew in the open door. I should get up to close it, but I was frozen in place. I forced myself to the door to block out the cold.

The laptop in my arms weighted a thousand pounds.

Kael knew. He knew I was Anon. And he was pissed. He could ruin me, but that wasn't what hurt. The things he'd said and the anger in his voice. The way he looked at me like a stranger. That's what got me.

I'd struck the first blow, but this. There was no coming back from this. And this is how it had to be anyway, but now Kael had the power to take me down if he wanted.

He was right to be mad. I'd lied to him and let him believe I was someone I wasn't. I slid my laptop into my bag and pulled out the old recipe book Kitty had given me. It was held together with a new rubber band, the old one long gone. The note from her was tucked into it still. I pulled it out and read it for the millionth time. Her loopy hand-writing covered the creased page.

> *Lena, bake well and remember, when life gets tough, you always have the kitchen. Bake a pie. Kitty*

A tear fell as I folded it gently and tucked it back inside the band.

My phone buzzed.

"Hello?"

"Helene, you coming? We need to get off the ground."

It was Jack.

"Yeah. I'm on my way. Sorry, had to go back and get something."

"No problem, darling. But we gotta get moving."

I couldn't get up off the bed though. I made another call.

"Didi?" My breath hitched as I said her name.

"Lena? What's wrong?"

Tears ran down my face and I couldn't make words come out coherently for a second. For once, Deidre was patient and waited for me to get a hold of myself.

"I left my computer at Kael's. And I'm not sure how, but he saw my notes. He knows. He knows I'm Anon."

Silence met me from the other end.

"Didi?"

"Well...shit. Do you think he'll do anything with the information?"

When I really thought about it, no. I didn't think he would. But it was a possibility. And if he did...

"I don't think he would, but I'm not sure. He was so

angry." I cried more. My world was imploding and I wasn't sure what to do.

"Okay. For now, we're going to work under the impression he is satisfied letting it be. Is there anything you can do to make sure he doesn't say something?"

I looked at the book in my hand.

"Maybe."

"Do that. I'll come to the city in a couple days. Lena, it's going to be okay."

I nodded even though she couldn't see me. "Okay. Love you."

"Mean it."

I took a breath, shoved the motel key in my pocket and walked across to the diner.

Now I had been across this road several times in the last few days but today the walk felt long, like it might never end. Today I was walking to my doom. Kael was on the other side and I knew he didn't want to see me. *Only family calls me that.*

I pushed back the tears. He had every right to hate me. I should've never come back here. It was all my fault.

My ego and pride couldn't let it lie. If I could take back the last couple days, I would. I stopped. No. I wouldn't. Being with Kael, it was wonderful. And even though everything was shit now, I think it might have been worth it.

That's what made the pain unbearable. Now I would just go back to the city and hope I never saw Kael Ruggeman again.

The only problem with that plan? I was pretty sure I was in love with him. But what did that matter? Anything he might have felt for me was long gone. It was destroyed the minute he found out about Anon and my business plan. No. It didn't matter what I felt, he felt nothing.

I pushed open the door to hear the familiar ding. Sheila turned around to smile at me. "Hey hon. You need coffee for the road? Kael said you're leaving us today."

I swiped at a tear, turning my head to hide it as best I could.

"That's so kind, but no. Kael left something I needed to return."

"Oh, I'll go get him."

I held up my hand. "No, please. No need to bother him. I know he has opening prep. And he doesn't want...we said our goodbyes. Can you give this to him, though?"

She took the book from me and looked at it. "This is Kitty's."

I nodded, shocked she knew that. "It was, yeah. I, uh, borrowed it for a while, but it should be with family." My voice broke on the last word.

"I'll get it to him, honey." Sheila had a sad, all knowing smile on her face.

I turned and practically ran out of the restaurant just as I saw Kael coming around the corner into the dining room. I sped across the street, grabbed my stuff from the room, and headed to the airport. The faster I could get away from here, the better. I had to put this all in the past. All of it.

The diner, this town, my restaurant, and most of all, Kael.

Kael

"We're not open yet."

I caught a whisp of blonde hair heading out the door. Sheila turned around, something in her hand.

"I don't know what you did to that girl, but she left in tears."

I walked back to the kitchen. "I didn't do anything."

Sheila followed me. "She was crying for no reason then?"

I shrugged. "I don't know what's in her head. I don't know her at all."

"Kael, don't bullshit me. What did you do?"

I turned to face her, shocked by the question. "Why do you think I did something? I didn't do anything. She got a little taste of her own medicine, that's all."

Sheila stared me down with her all-knowing look. I hollered to the staff, without looking away. "Lots to do, let's get a move on. Full menu today."

Sheila was right beside me. "Yesterday you left here starry eyed. Today she's crying, telling me you already said your goodbyes, and your neck is redder than the clay. What's going on?"

"Nothing." I wiped at the stove top, making it shine as best I could.

"Kael, don't try to hide something from me. I've known you since before you were a bigshot. Talk to me."

I sighed. "Not here."

We walked back to the office much to Danny's chagrin. He was not the sneaky eavesdropper he thought he was. "Danny, get to work."

"Fuck you, Chef."

The walk to my office usually felt long, the one place I didn't want to go. But now with Sheila hot on my heels determined to know why Helene left here in tears, I was there before I knew it.

I tried to block out the thought of Helene, my Lena, crying. This time it wasn't entirely my fault but I still hated it. I wanted to apologize already for the words I'd said to her. Hold her close and make it up to her. We could've talked through it, worked it out. I was mad because she didn't tell me, but not because she kept it from me. I was mad because she didn't think she could trust me with it. I'd never done anything to break her trust, and yet, she didn't tell me.

Sheila blocked the door behind me.

I sat in the chair, head in my hands. "She's the anonymous reviewer."

"And?"

I lifted my head. "And? She lied to me about it."

"Did she?"

I didn't answer. She did deny it at first, but she'd never full on lied.

"Did she lie, or did she try to tell you and you didn't listen?"

I looked at her. "She had chances."

"When? Between you being stuck in here with no power and you whisking her off to your place?"

I hung my head. "She had time," I gruffed. "Plus, listen to this. She was going to open a restaurant with all of Cat's recipes."

"Yeah?"

"Yeah? That's it. She was taking Cat's recipes. Doesn't that piss you off?" The anger was right back there with me, burning bright.

"Cat told her to."

I looked up at Sheila. "What?"

Sheila didn't answer, just crossed her arms and leaned against the door.

"When?"

"Cat loved that girl. When you were gone doing your thing, she mentored her."

I stood up. "You knew?"

"Kitty was my best friend. Of course I knew."

I stood up, making the space tight but Sheila didn't budge. "But Cat left it to me, this place. She left it to me."

"Because she wanted Helene to open her own place, why would she leave her this? She wanted her to make something new. This place is for you to have."

I grit my teeth together, squeezing my jaw until it ached. "Great. Cat thinks she's capable and I get this place to run."

Sheila took a step forward, squaring her shoulders. "Now you listen to me. Cat left you this because it was important to her and to a lot of other people and she knew you'd do it justice. Don't disrespect her and her wishes again. Do you understand?"

I shook my head. "Yes, ma'am. But Helene's not family. She doesn't have the right to those recipes."

Sheila's jaw tensed and I flinched. I felt like a little boy in trouble. "Did you say that to her? Is that why she was crying?"

I didn't move, just a deer in the headlights.

"Family is who you choose. You don't know what she's been through." Sheila shoved a book into my hands. "She brought this to you. She said it should be with family." The last word she said with a sugary sweetness that turned my stomach.

I looked down to see a very loved recipe book.

She paused. "You really messed up with this one. She was something special."

I sat down in my chair and pulled a note from the front. It was for Lena from Kitty. I undid the rubber band and opened the book hearing a crack as the pages protested.

Cat's writing was on each page and in the margins, notes were made in another's hand though. Small drawings littered the pages. Ideas on how to make each one special. Silly names for the dishes were written, scratched out, and better ones took their place. This was Lena's concept book. And it was a gift from Kitty.

And I took it from her.

Oh god. Sheila was right. I really messed up.

14

Helene

I sat in the seat, buckled up, as Jack checked all the dials and talked to air traffic.

We were taking off, heading home, all I had wanted to do since I arrived, but I felt I was going as far from home as I'd ever been.

Kael was back there and heading away from him was the wrong direction. Words had been said and couldn't be taken back. But it didn't matter anyway. I couldn't be with Kael. These last few days were a blip in time. One moment and a sweet memory I could hold onto.

As long as I forgot the end.

I felt empty without my book of ideas. It had been as if I could keep Kitty with me as I tried to realize my dream. Could I start over from scratch again? I didn't know. This felt like a bigger loss than the other one. It was closer to real and more to lose.

Plus I'd lost Kael in the process.

But now he would have the recipes Kitty had given me and could have no more beef with me. I'd go my way and he could go his. And hopefully he wouldn't tell anyone my secret.

My lip trembled as I tried to hold back tears. All my ideas, my little homages to Kitty were in that book. The designs for a dream I'd had covered those pages. But again, it didn't matter.

Now that dream was dead.

I pushed it away and locked it far back in my mind with all the other forgotten dreams. It was time to move on and do what I always did which was what needed to be done.

But the almost restaurant circled my brain. Not that I would've ever made it a reality, but while I had her cookbook it felt like I could.

Instead, I was here going back headfirst into my own reality, and that's just how it was. How it had to be. I reviewed other people's food, half in public, half in secret. At least I got paid for both. As long I kept the ruse going, I should be able to care for my family.

You're not family.

I squeezed my eyes against his words. Trying to push them from my brain. The worst part was he was right, I wasn't family. I'd been able to pretend for a time, but the cold hard truth was, I was outside of it. He'd never even known I'd been around his aunt. What did that say about me?

I wasn't that important.

I brushed away at tears so Jack wouldn't see. The air was

so cold up here and I shivered as we headed back to a life I wasn't sure I wanted.

But like it or not, it was all I had. Kael thought I was brave for it, but I knew that wasn't it. There wasn't a way to do anything better. And I was stuck.

He didn't think that anymore, I'm sure. He probably thought I was a coward for reviewing places in secret. A laugh snuck up and out at the ridiculousness of going out to that diner to confront him. What had I been thinking?

For five seconds I'd thought maybe my life could be different, but that look on his face when he came to the hotel told me all I needed to know. The life I had was all I got, and Kael wouldn't be a part of it.

And no matter what he thought, I wasn't brave enough to try something different. This job paid the bills and got shit done. If I did something else, I could fail.

More than likely I would.

I tucked my arms around myself and held everything as close as I could to stay warm, wishing for the warmth I'd felt in Kael's arms just a day ago.

I should've stayed in bed with him that morning. And taken him on the offer to stay there all day. We could've spent more time just being happy together. I would've remembered my laptop if we hadn't been fighting and then he wouldn't have known. He wouldn't hate me.

But what kind of relationship, love or friendship, is that? One built on lies is doomed to fail. But for one moment in time, it was perfect. It was everything. And I'll miss it for the rest of my life.

That might as well have been a different lifetime, and maybe it did only exist in my mind. Maybe I'd made it out to be more than it was.

Then I thought of his anger.

No. Anger that strong only comes out of betrayal. And you have to care to be betrayed. Which is why I usually steered clear of caring.

Lesson learned.

I wouldn't make that mistake again.

~

Kael

I LAID IN BED, staring at the ceiling. All I could think about was Helene and what I'd said to her. And what an asshole I was. There was no reason for me to be that way to her, except my ego was hurt. When I found out Cat, or Kitty as Helene knew my aunt, had mentored her and given her those recipes and the permission to use them, something had flipped. A switch of some kind had been triggered and I lashed out. I always thought I was special in Cat's eyes, but I guess I wasn't as special as I thought.

But I remembered what Sheila had said. Cat thought I could do this place justice. It wasn't enough for me to be special. Why did I always need to be the only one who was special?

I wish I could talk to Cat, ask her why she never mentioned Helene to me.

I paused that thought before it left the station. I knew why. She'd probably tried to but I was very busy being important in the city and didn't listen. Hell, she'd might have even asked me to watch out for her if I had listened.

I chuckled. Helene would've hated that so much. She

didn't want anyone to watch out for her. But I would've had her back. Or would I?

I closed my eyes, rubbing the lids hard enough to make purple and green starbursts appear in the dark. I hadn't looked out for her though. I tried to take her apart because she was so damn good. And for what? To make sure she could hack it?

Why did she need to be destroyed to survive in my kitchen?

Simple answer, she didn't. No one did. I was a literal expression of "I made it through and turned out fine".

Clearly, I didn't and I wasn't fine. I swung my feet to the floor, sitting up so quickly my head spun.

I needed to talk to Helene. I was still mad at her for so many things, but I knew in the depth of my soul, Helene only did all that to protect her family. She told me over and over she had responsibilities. She did what she had to do take care of them and when I thought about it, her anonymous reviews were probably something she did for herself.

And now she didn't have that. Or her ideas for her own place.

I texted the number she called from earlier.

I'm sorry.

Who is this?

Kael

This is Betty at the motel. What are you sorry for?

I frowned.

I guess I have the wrong number.

Great. I didn't have her number and didn't know how to get it. The only thing I had was the email to anonymous. Which was Helene. I felt a little anger spike as I remembered that. She might not even read those and probably had an assistant.

It was that or nothing.

I pulled up the email.

This email is for Helene Carnahan. I understand these columns are published together, so I was hoping to get a way to contact her. I need to speak with her in a professional capacity.

OKAY, that wasn't really true, except most of our interactions had taken place in a kitchen. And my living room...and bed. I shivered as I felt Helene in my arms again. I should be kissing her right now. Getting up and making breakfast, watching her as she maneuvered around the cooktop, serving up a masterpiece.

She was beautiful and I loved her laugh. The small giggle when she felt like she'd pulled a little trick on me. I smiled thinking about it.

"Focus." I frowned, shook my head and went back to the email.

This is Kael Ruggeman. Any assistance would be appreciated. Thank you.

· · ·

IT WAS short and sweet and to the point. I took one last look and hit send. I stumbled through my morning routine, trying to not check my email every five seconds. There wouldn't be a response or if there was it would be a simple, sorry we can't help you. I drove to the diner, forcing myself to put on a smile.

I didn't need to be the way I was in the kitchen. If anything, I could learn from the situation with Helene, and then at least it wouldn't be a total loss. Happy employees would probably give better output.

Someone come hit me with a hammer, already. How hard was this to get through my skull.

Danny rolled in ten minutes early.

"Thanks for showing up early. I appreciate all you do around here."

Danny raised an eyebrow, a cigarette in hand as he headed to the back door and looked around. "Where's Kael and what have you done with him?"

"Fuck off, man. I mean it."

He chuckled as he went back out the door.

"Okay, that went well."

I greeted everyone else as they came in. When Sheila walked through the door, I motioned her back to the office. She followed.

"Did you apologize yet?"

"Hi. Good to see you too. And no. I don't have her number."

Her mouth set in a hard line. "You don't have her number."

I shook my head.

"And social media?"

"It's all private. Already checked."

She put a hand on her chin leaning against the wall. "Hmmm. Then how do we get to her?"

A glimmer of hope lit in my soul. Sheila was on my side.

"I don't know. I emailed the magazine she works at."

"Good, good. As soon as you apologize, you leave that girl alone. She's had a hard enough deal in life. She doesn't need to put up with someone who tells her she's not family."

I sat down like she'd punched me. So, not on my side then.

I should probably email the magazine too. Double my chances. I sent the same email to the main address, and the contact for Helene as well. That was three times and probably the limit before it got creepy. If after a week I hadn't heard anything, I would call the magazine. But for now, I had a restaurant to run.

THAT WAS the longest day in existence. It was possibly the busiest we'd been since I took over. Correction, since I owned this place. Wasn't sure what was in the air, but I swear every tourist in the state came in today. I wiped at my grill top, sweat soaking through my clothes.

"Wild day, huh?" Danny slapped me on the back.

"Crazy."

"See ya tomorrow, Chef."

I stopped. No explicative hurled my way. Maybe this morning was a start.

"See ya."

Once I was home, I poured a bourbon and opened my phone.

The email icon in the corner called my name so I clicked on that first.

Mr. Ruggeman,

An honor to have you email us. Here is the information requested. Please let me know if I can help in any way. Rob Clemons.

Helene's number and personal email was included. That didn't seem like information that should just be given out, but I was too happy to have a way to contact her, I let it go.

Holy shit. I had her number. *Now what?*

15

Helene

Another day, another time to not think about Kael. I had eaten at three different restaurants this week, which a was two too many and each time I consumed a scallop covered in pureed cauliflower sauce with an herb on top I wanted to scream. Kael's stupid pot pie crept into my head. Followed by the inevitable thoughts of his kiss and how he held me. How we'd laid in the comfort of his bed passing the time, cooking together in his kitchen in a routine reserved for a lifetime spent together. Some kind of dance that felt like we'd done it a thousand times.

But we hadn't. It was only a moment in time and really only a moment ago, but it was farther from me now than any distance my mind could conjure. A text went off on my phone.

I've got a new place for you. Stillwater,
Oklahoma.

I smiled at Didi's text.

Thanks. What's it called? Do you think it's
okay to do two Oklahoma places in a row?

Shortstack. They specialize in different
pancakes. Plus their omelet was fantastic.
And yes. Who is keeping track?

I grinned. There was no better food than breakfast food. I closed my eyes and again tried to push making scrambles with Kael out of my mind.

And he was keeping track, I could almost guarantee it.

I'll head there this weekend. Love you.

Mean it.

That's what I needed. A trip somewhere else to get my mind off this whole debacle. The more distance, the more time, the more I could move on and act like it never happened.

"What are thinking about?"

I jumped as Jen came in.

"You scared me. I was thinking about breakfast food." It was half true.

"The best. Where are you getting it?"

"This place in Oklahoma." The words were out before I thought to stop them. I looked at Jen. Her face didn't even flinch. She just smiled at me.

"Meeting Deidre?"

I smiled back. "She recommended it."

She sipped her coffee then said, "Can't wait to hear how it is."

I nodded. "I'll let you know. And Jen, thank you."

"I told you. I'm with you." She sat at her desk, completely unfazed by my weird behavior.

My phone buzzed again, this time a call. I answered without looking at it.

"I told you, I would go this weekend."

"Go where?"

A deep voice answered me instead of Didi. My heart beat hard. I knew the voice but it could not be him.

"Who is this?"

"It's...it's Kael."

I sat back and Jen turned to look at me. "You okay?" she said quietly.

I nodded, but I was as far from okay as you could get.

"How did you get this number?"

"I emailed you at work. And someone sent it to me."

Heat crept up my neck. "Hang on." I put him on mute.

"Did you give my number to anyone?"

Jen shook her head. "I would never do that."

I blew out a breath. "I know you wouldn't, but I know who would."

I unmuted the call. "I don't think we should speak. Goodbye."

"Wait. I just wanted to say sorry. I'm really sorry."

Kael's voice was earnest. I knew he meant it. But what did it matter now? I knew how he felt about me and he had Kitty's recipes, and all my ideas, so it was done. Sorry was only a word.

"Okay. Thank you. Goodbye."

I hung up.

"What was that about?" Jen asked, concern creasing her forehead.

"Come on. Let's go get a coffee. I need to tell you something."

WE MOVED to the table farthest back in the little coffee house. I told Jen about Anon, the storm, the whole deal with Kael, and how he'd gotten my number.

"It had to be Rob, right?"

I nodded. "It couldn't be anybody else. But I never saw those emails which means he's vetting which ones come to me and you. I know playing with fire will get you burned, but I wasn't sure how to dissuade him from running both columns without giving myself away."

She thought for a minute, leaning back in her chair. "Two questions. First, why do the diners at all? And second, why does it matter if you do?"

I blew out a breath. "Opening a small diner like that was my dream. Deidre and I were going to open one and a hotel together. But after all the family bullshit, she'd already started reviewing roadside stops and she loves it. The travel, the freedom." I chuckled. "The money. She makes a good living."

"And your part?"

"Well, I don't have the money and I take care of my Celia and Jonny. Because they are basically dependents, they can use my insurance. Rob, being the asshole he is, wants to make sure he's the only one making money, so he signed me to an exclusive contract. Honestly, when I started going to the places Didi told me about- "

"Who's Didi?"

I grinned. "Oh, Deidre, that's her nickname."

Jen smiled. "Go on."

"When I started going, I just wrote about them to bring business to them. I didn't think anyone would actually read them or care except for a couple tourists. I sent them to the local paper where the diners were and The Times. I couldn't have known it would blow up."

"Makes sense." She finished her coffee and we stood up, taking our cups to the counter.

"But now, worlds have collided and if Rob finds out its me, I'll lose my job."

Jen was quiet for half a block. "Go somewhere else. I'm sure anyone would want Helene Carnahan."

"Not after all that. I'd look underhanded and if it got out I slept with a chef..."

"That is a problem." She growled causing me to look at her.

"What was that for?"

"If you were a man, no one would give a shit who you slept with, but since you're a woman, they think some chef must've had a magic penis and it clouded your judgement."

I laughed and pulled her into a hug. "Didi said the same thing. You guys would love each other. And honestly, it was his kiss that did it. The rest was just a bonus."

She laughed, putting her arm around me. "Come on. Let's get back to the office and figure out how to get through all this."

Jen headed to our desks and I went to let Rob have it when we reached our floor.

"Did you give my number out to someone?"

"And good morning to you too."

I crossed my arms, planting my feet. "We are not good morning people. Did you?"

"You look like shit."

"Thanks, Rob. You are a shit. Where does that leave us? Oh yeah. Did you give out my number?"

He stared at me from across the desk. "So what?"

"So what?" I walked over and leaned my arms on the desk. "How dare you give out my personal number? I don't need chefs calling me. It's unprofessional."

He stood and came around to where I was. "Listen Helene, I'm your boss and while you are number one at your job, this place is mine. And it is my job to make sure we have the best and most successful publication out there. So if that means I give out a number, help make connections, then so be it."

I shook my head, which matched the rest of me vibrating with anger. "How did he ask for it?"

That took him aback. He stepped back finally. "Um, I'm not sure."

I tilted my head. "But I thought this was your job, your place? Right? You know all the outs and ins."

"I think maybe he called."

"Weird. Because he said he emailed me and someone else responded." I looked at my boss with disgust.

"Oh. Yeah, maybe." He busied himself at his desk.

"Am I getting all my emails, Rob? Because I didn't receive that one for some reason and neither did Jen."

Color drained from his face. He knew I had him. "I'll check on that and make sure you're getting everything."

I blew out a breath. "I hope you do."

"Oh, what did he want?"

I looked at Rob with disbelief. "Are you kidding right now? My personal number, personal. When I'm on the clock my time is yours, otherwise, it's none of your damn business."

I turned on my heel and stormed out, hot with anger. How dare he play with my life and livelihood like this. He couldn't know what it meant, but I certainly did. And he knew HR would have a field day with this if I pursued it.

As soon as I sat down, my phone buzzed.

> Please can we talk?

Kael. I wanted to talk to him. A part of me believed him when he said sorry. Another part wanted to hear him out, but there was too much on the line. I had to make this decision for Celia and Jonny. I didn't get what I wanted this time, just like all the other times, I did what was best for them.

> No. I can't. There are too many reasons to list here. I accept your apology. I wish you all the success. Truly.

And then I blocked his number.

Kael

I TRIED to text again only for the response to say the user didn't exist. Then I called to get the same message.

She blocked me.

I stared at the phone as if maybe she would reconsider and it would start ringing. But I knew that wouldn't happen. She'd made up her mind and now I'd have to deal with it.

I slammed things around as I prepped in the kitchen.

"What the hell is wrong with you?" Danny piped up.

"Nothing. Just get your prep done."

He made some kind of noise I was sure had a curse word

in it under his breath. My hand froze in midair as I was about to smash a pan down on the stovetop. No wonder she blocked me. This is how I acted when things didn't go my way. Like a child.

Sheila came around the corner. "Mornin', all."

"Morning. Can I talk to you?"

She raised an eyebrow but a small smile crept onto her face. We went back to my office, a place we'd been more in the last week than in the last year. I turned as soon as we got in there.

"I found her number, reached out, and then she blocked me."

Sheila shook her head quickly, as if to shake of all the information I just threw at her.

"Okay. How did you get her number?"

"I emailed her work and someone gave it to me."

"So her work number?"

I looked at the ground. "No. It was her cell I think."

Her mouth fell open. "Someone, at her job, gave you her personal number?"

When I thought about it like that... "Kinda problematic, huh?"

She nodded with her lips pressed together. "Kinda."

But she stood up straighter. "And then you called her?"

"Yes."

"Just once?"

I nodded.

"How did that go?"

My shoulders slumped. "She said we shouldn't talk."

"Did you hear her?" She cocked an eyebrow.

I bounced my head back and forth as I debated telling her the truth. "Then I texted. I just wanted to say sorry."

"Oh, Kael honey." She sat down next to me and took my

hand, just like Cat used to do when she was about to deliver a lesson. "You can't go through life like a battering ram. You need to read the nuance sometimes. Or listen when someone tells you something."

"I know. You're right. But I've never felt this way about someone and it's making me a bit..."

She chuckled.

"What?"

"That's what love is. It makes you ignore your good judgment because being with that person—"

"Is the only thing that matters."

She smiled and squeezed my hand before she let go. "Yep. That's how I felt about Cat. And she felt that way about me."

I looked at Sheila for the first time with a realization of things I hadn't even considered before.

"Oh shit. How did I never put this together before?"

She laughed, deep and hearty. "Why would you? But why do you think I'm here. This was our favorite place and she wanted you to have it. I'm here to help you succeed, but can I be honest?"

"Please."

"You gotta pull your head out of ass, honey."

My body shook with laughter. "That's fair. I am trying. Honestly."

She patted my back.

"But what am I going to do about Helene?"

"Did you say you were sorry?"

"I did. She said she accepted the apology and then she blocked me." That wasn't all she said, but it was close.

"Then that's that." She stood up. "C'mon. We gotta open up."

I sat in the quiet of the office. I couldn't let it go. I needed to tell her how sorry I was, I didn't mean what I said. That of course she was family, I was just an ass. Give her back her idea and recipe book then...then what? Sheila was right. That was that.

I'd done everything I could and unless she decided to give me another chance, our time together was over.

I turned it around and around in my mind all day. How could I get through to her? Let her know I was truly sorry. A small idea started to percolate through my mind as I cooked. Every time I flipped a sandwich, it solidified more. Piece by piece, it fell into place.

It wasn't until after dinner rush, it came together fully and I figured out what to do. I'd go to New York and apologize in person.

16

❦

Helene

It had been five days since I blocked Kael. Almost a week of checking my emails and rereading the ones he had sent. 120 hours of wishing there could be a different outcome to this. But instead of calling him, I held the door handle of the next restaurant I needed to review in my hand. I didn't want to go in. It was the latest fusion – comfort food in an upscale atmosphere.

The idea sounded dangerously close to my idea but those two things were the antithesis of each other. How could that even work? One small piece of pork chop in a too rich sauce with a designer dollop of mashed potatoes? If they didn't have mac and cheese on the menu, this place was not getting five stars.

I gave the door a tug and walked into a dark room

straight out of the 1960's. If I hadn't just walked in, I'd be convinced I was in someone's living room. Coffee tables and couches were strewn about, divided from the others with plant stands and small bookcases. This was upscale?

I look over to see a bar straight out of Mad Men. Some spots around it had two recliners and a smaller table between them. Clearly, this area was for cocktails and apps, not a meal.

I had to admit, there was a charm to it. A petite woman walked up and smiled at me. She couldn't have been more than five foot tall, but she had a commanding presence.

"Welcome to Comfort. Do you have a reservation?"

"Yes. Helene Carnahan."

She smiled again. I felt at ease with her in a way I didn't normally in these restaurants. She wasn't freaked out by my name and honestly, it *was* comforting in here. "Follow me."

I was seated at one of the couches. "Is this okay?"

I nodded as I hung my bag and coat on the wooden coat rack directly beside my chair.

"Can I get you a drink?"

"I'll take a water and your signature cocktail. Thank you."

She nodded. "When will your guests be arriving?"

"My guests?"

"Yes. Your reservation is for three."

My stomach turned as I shook my head. Restaurants made mistakes, but not like that. Why would there be a reservation for three? "No. That isn't correct. It should just be me."

"Of course. I'll make that adjustment." She returned to the host stand. I noticed it wasn't just the couch in my little alcove. There was also a recliner.

What was happening? Why would my reservation have

three on it? I texted Jen to verify she made it for only me. She sent me the screenshot of the confirmation – one.

I tucked my phone away and pulled out my notebook.

The host returned. "I'm Henny. Sorry about the mix up. Your drink will be out soon, but here's your menu. Is this table still acceptable?"

I took the two sided menu from her. "Thanks, Henny. And yes, this is fine if I'm not taking up too much table space."

That disarming smile again. "Not at all. We're excited you're here. Don will be your server."

The menu was unfortunately what I expected. Small plates and underwhelming sides. The branding of this place was fine, but comfort was supposed to fill you up and stick to your ribs, not leave you wanting when you go.

But I was surprised once again when my cocktail came out. It was in a Tiki glass, one of the molded ceramic ones. A small umbrella stabbed some fruit and graced the top. I assumed it was Don that sat it down.

"Mai Tai, our specialty."

"A Mai Tai is your comfort drink?"

He nodded. "It's the vacation drink of choice."

I took a sip. It was delicious. Wow. I took a second drink. It was really good.

"I'm Don. Can I tell you how our menu works?"

I looked at him. "How your menu works?"

He nodded and pointed to the page with all the small bites. "You choose a main dish, three sides, and then we have a dessert option on the other side for your final selection. If you so choose, we have a sidecar drink menu to enhance your choices."

Okay, that was interesting, but harder to really critique the normal way. I looked over the menu. "I'll take the pot roast, sides of green bean casserole, mac and cheese, and mashed potatoes."

"Your dessert?"

"I'll take the most popular please."

"That will be our cherry cobbler."

I handed him the menu.

"Do you want the drink sidecar and is brown gravy okay?"

"Yes please."

Don turned to go as three people came into view. Henny, the lovely host, led the others over with a confused but determined look on her face.

"Ms. Carnahan, these men say they are on your reservation? Is that acceptable to you?"

Henny was a girls' girl. She might be tiny, but clearly this woman kept the ship afloat.

I took a breath. Rob stood there with a smug look on his face and Kael Ruggeman was just behind him.

I looked at Henny directly. "Thank you for checking. It will be fine. I apologize for this."

"You have no need to apologize." She handed menus to the men and gave me one last look that said, let me know if they need to go. Henny was getting a shout out in this review.

"What are you doing here?"

Even though I said it to Kael, Rob answered.

"I've been wanting to see my star critic in action and Kael came into town this afternoon, so I'm treating him to dinner."

I pursed my lips together and a deep, dark heaviness landed right in my stomach. This was a disaster in the making. But I put a smile on my face and held out my hand to Kael. He shook it and electric sparks shot through my body. I looked up to meet his eyes. They were full of yearning. So strong it almost matched mine.

I directed my gaze to Rob. "Can I talk to you?"

Rob nodded and looked at Kael. "Get what you want to drink."

He put his hand on my back at we went over to the bar. I felt Kael's eyes burning through us as we walked away.

"Could you be more unprofessional?" I whipped around to face him, to find a self-satisfied look on his face.

"He's been asking for you. And he's not here in the city anymore, so what does it matter?"

"It matters. I am working and rating this restaurant. And now a chef I gave four stars is sitting right there for a front row seat. It's beyond uncomfortable."

He motioned to the bartender. Rob was under the delusion he was a big roller-type, making things happen. But did I have news for him. He was more like an obnoxious lackey no one could stand. The bartender glared at him.

"Bourbon, neat."

The bartender looked at me with an eyebrow raise. "Nothing for me, thank you." He smiled and turned to his work. Rob's eyes came back to me. I felt like a mouse in view of a hawk.

"Is it uncomfortable or unprofessional?" He didn't wait for an answer. "Having him here could be great publicity."

I crossed my arms. "Do we have a circulation problem? Are our numbers bad?"

He sipped his drink. "Not really. But every view helps."

I leaned my back on the bar and crossed my arms as Rob threw down a couple bucks.

"You need to respect my work and what I do." I looked over to Kael sitting alone. "We should get back to your guest."

"Our guest."

I breathed deep. "Your guest."

As we headed back that way, I looked at Rob. "Keep your hand off my back."

He held up his free hand, his glass in the other.

"Sorry about that." I said as we sat down. Kael smiled and I melted into the booth.

"No worries. I told the waiter two more of what you ordered. I knew you'd order the best thing on the menu."

I wanted to bury myself in my cocktail but remembered I was here to work and sat it down after a small sip.

"How are you?" Kael's voice was low and touched a place in me that had been lonely. He was the thing missing and the only cure.

"Fine, thanks. And yourself?"

"Good. Good."

Time to be a professional, Carnahan. "What are you doing in town?"

Rob looked from one of us to the other. "You two know each other, more than professionally?"

Kael kept quiet, but his look said it all.

Yes. We knew each other.

I broke the silent tension. "We were in culinary school together."

Rob's face was hilarious. If the situation wasn't such a shitshow, I would've laughed. "Oh." was all he could get out.

"I also had the pleasure of having Helene in my kitchen."

My mouth fell open. The statement was loaded and I fought a shiver thinking about being in his arms.

"Before she started reviewing," he added quickly, the implication of his words landing in front of us.

Rob grinned. "Wow. I've learned more about you in five minutes than the whole time we've worked together."

"Work is for working, not for making friends." I looked away.

"It can't be both?"

I shot a look at Rob but before I could say anything Don appeared with our food.

"Here's your appetizer."

I held up a hand. "I didn't order an appetizer. That wasn't on the menu."

He smiled. "Everyone gets one. It's different each day. Today is a cocktail party sampler. Swedish meatballs and a wedge salad with a multi dish of dressings."

He sat down a two-tiered dish. I turned it one direction, then the other. It was very cute and on theme.

"And it's included in the meal?"

He nodded and walked away.

I made a note in my small notebook.

On the bottom tier, the wedge salads were plated side by side. A three-divided dish that turned held different dressings.

"But what are the flavors?" Rob asked pointing to the silver and wood dish. I picked it up and took a sniff.

"French. Blue cheese. And a vinaigrette – raspberry maybe?"

Kael took it from me. "Cherry."

Rob's head swiveled as if he was watching tennis.

"Mm. Yes. I bet you're right, because dessert is cherry cobbler. That would make sense." I made a few notes as Kael dipped a fork into the dressing and took a taste.

"Definitely cherry." He made a face.

I couldn't help but grin. "Not for you?"

He shook his head as if he could dislodge the taste. "No. Not that. Acid is off. Way off."

I froze. His thoughts could influence my review if I wasn't careful. Okay, no more talking to him at all.

"Please don't tell me your thoughts on the food. I have to make an impartial judgment on it."

He nodded and held up his hands.

The meatballs were on the top tier with a fancy spoon and small boats for them. We each got our own. It reminded me of Salisbury steak, but in the best way possible. The salad was a wedge of lettuce with bacon crumbles. Nothing exciting.

"This place isn't what I expected," Rob said.

I looked around. "It's cute though. Quirky."

"What do you think?" Rob turned to Kael.

I held up a hand. "Please don't answer that. I respect your opinions, but we haven't even had the main course, and you are not the critic. Anything you say could influence my thoughts or if we have the same thoughts, I wouldn't want anyone to think I'm using your words."

Kael nodded with a smile on his face. "Absolutely. You're really good at your job, Helene."

Rob drank his bourbon, trying not to smile. Then turned to me.

"What do you think then?"

I took a breath and thought for a second. "It's trying to be something casual in a fancy world. I'm not sure it works. It might be better as just a theme restaurant."

Kael nodded in agreement. "Yeah. You can't have a family style restaurant in uptown."

I shook my head. "You just can't help yourself, can you? Have to have your two cents?"

"What? I agreed with you."

Under my breath, I said. "Well, you know all about family."

His head snapped to me. "What was that?"

I shook my head again right as Don and two other waiters placed our food and drinks on the table.

I did a double take. It looked like a TV dinner. Each item I'd ordered was in its little square or rectangle of the dish. It looked like foil, but when I tapped on it, I found it was ceramic. A smile filled my face. I was...charmed.

Don smiled at my reaction. "The pot roast is marinated and slow roasted for hours with onions and herbs. The green bean casserole uses locally sourced vegetables and is served crusted in onions and pan seared. The macaroni and cheese is made with a four cheese blend including an aged cheddar and baked with a breadcrumb crust. The mashed potatoes are blended fully with cream and butter.

Your side car of drinks includes an Old Fashion, a Gimlet, a Manhattan, and a Mint Julep. The Julep will pair excellently with the Cherry cobbler."

"Thank you, Don."

He refilled our water glasses and left the table.

I took a sip of water to clear my palette and took my first bite. The pot roast was divine. "Oh god. So good."

I tried each of the sides, all rich, all delicious. I took notes and savored each bite.

Rob looked at me like he'd never seen anyone eat. Redness rose up Kael's neck. I swallowed and wiped my mouth.

"What? You can't appreciate good food unless you make it?"

He righted himself. "No. I appreciate it. That wasn't it..." He faded out.

I realized too late the heat had risen all the way to his

face. He wasn't angry, he was turning red for another reason. I watched him lick his bottom lip, just a dart of the tongue, but I got it. He wanted me.

And I wanted him. This was torture. I was surprised to learn I wanted to hear his thoughts on the food, too. To do this together was something I hadn't considered, but it would be so fun. I thought about his frozen meals and pretend cooking show. A small giggle bubbled up in my throat. I swallowed it and tried to keep my face neutral.

"Do you always eat like this?"

I looked at Rob, remembering he was there. "Like what?"

He cleared his throat. "So...into it?"

Kael answered as I opened my mouth. "Helene gets food in a way most people don't. That's why her stars mean so much. She tastes and enjoys it in a way few do. It's remarkable. It's no exaggeration when people say she's the best."

I smiled at Kael, beaming from his compliment. Rob grinned. "And she works for me."

I slumped against the chair. That was depressing.

Kael frowned. "You're lucky then. I bet every place in this town would like her to work for them."

He was defending me against Rob. My heart melted. "Sorry I snapped at you. I'm not used to people watching me work."

Kael had a playful look on his face. "Yes, we know you don't like a hoverer."

I tried to hide my smile. I should be irritated, but he was so gorgeous and genuine, plus the food was good. I was giddy.

"Now what?" Rob asked.

"Well, I've had a bite of everything. So now I need to try each one with the drink sampling. Then dessert."

We worked our way through the meal and by the end I was stuffed.

Kael piped up. "How's the cobbler?"

I bit my bottom lip. "It's good. I've had better pastry."

He smiled as he took another bite. The chef came out from the back and asked how we liked everything. After some small talk, we finished up and paid, leaving a hefty tip for the impeccable service.

"Ah, that's how it's done. You let them eat first." Kael joked. I smiled at him. Why couldn't it work for us again?

"Where did you have better pastry than this?" Rob asked, breaking into my thoughts.

Kael grinned. "A little diner she happened upon."

Alarm bells went off. I tried to tell him with my eyes to stop, because I knew what was coming.

"Oh?" This perked Rob's ears. "Where? We'll have to get you over there."

"Kansas."

Rob turned to me. "When were you in Kansas?"

"I went to visit my friend. I travel a lot to see her." I needed Kael to stop, but the drinks had gotten the better of him I suspected.

Rob's wheels had started to turn. "Where in Kansas?"

"You know, I don't even remember."

Kael clicked his tongue. "So rude. You were stuck there for three days."

Rob crossed his arms. "You were stuck with him for three days."

"Who said that?" I headed toward the door. "I got snowed in. You knew that."

We stood out on the sidewalk. "Where's your restaurant, Kael?" He leered at me, even though he directed his questions to Kael.

"What are you doing, Rob?"

"In Salina, Kansas as a matter of fact."

"You know he's not in the city anymore." I tried to smooth it over before it got worse.

"It wouldn't be the Cat and the Fiddle by any chance?" Rob's voice was low and menacing.

It was as if I wasn't there. "Yes! It is the Cat and the Fiddle. My aunt owned it and passed on. I took it over."

Rob turned directly to me, a smug look on his face and in that moment, I realized he'd played me for a fool. He'd known the whole time. He set this up to out me as Anonymous. It all made sense.

"Four Blue Plates." Rob stared at me as my lips trembled.

Lightbulbs went off for Kael in that exact moment as to what had happened. "What are you talking about?"

"Oh, you know. You wrote in to an anonymous reviewer complaining about your four blue plates asking for another chance and then this one just happens to wind up at your restaurant? What a coincidence."

Kael came over to stand by me. "It wasn't like that."

"Then how was it like?"

Kael opened his mouth but he clearly couldn't think of anything to say.

"Helene, you might be good at what you do, but I promise I can find another reviewer that will be a fraction of your price and won't be in breach of contract."

My mind went blank with panic and rage.

Rob clicked his tongue. "The next reviewer probably won't sleep with the chefs either. That's a big no-no. What a conflict of interest. I really hope people don't find out."

Kael looked at Rob, his arms flexing as he clenched and unclenched his fists. "This isn't on her. You set this up. You're an—" I stepped in front of him before he did something dumb.

"Please, I need this job. I will quit the other thing. And no one said I slept with anyone."

"So you admit it's you, then."

"You already knew it was when you showed up tonight." I felt the tears brewing.

Kael looked at me, apology all over his face. Rage, anger, and hopelessness filled me.

"Ms. Carnahan. I say this with great pleasure, you are no longer needed at Food, Drink, Air. I'll expect your keys, card and anything else in the morning. You have until noon to turn in this review and clean out your office."

With that he turned and walked down the street, whistling as he went. I looked at Kael, tears streaming down my face.

"I'm so sorry." He tried to put his hands on my arms, but I shook them off.

"I told you no one could know I knew you. I told you this couldn't happen," I waved my hands between us, "but you always have to have your way. You think you know best. Just because you've been untouchable your whole life doesn't mean the rest of us are. Are you happy now? Please leave me alone, Kael Ruggeman."

I heard Kael calling my name as I headed to the subway, but I ran on and jumped on the train as soon as I hit the platform.

All the warm fuzzy feelings I'd felt a little bit ago were gone, a stark reminder of why we couldn't be together.

Damn him. And damn Rob for playing us both. What was I going to do? The bottom had fallen out of my world again, and this time I didn't know if I could get back up.

17

Kael

I stood on the sidewalk, reeling from the booze and what just happened. I'd really screwed up. I had to find Helene. I called her name as she ran to the subway station. I was hot on her heels but as soon as she reached the platform, she was on the train and gone. I had to no idea where to find her. I walked slowly back to my hotel, going over the whole evening. Rob was an absolute asshole.

Helene was right, he had set this up from the beginning. But why did he want to get rid of her so badly? Surely, he knew she could go get a job anywhere else and be welcomed with open arms.

But not if people knew she was, shall we say, familiar with the chefs.

Damn it. I was an idiot. Everything she'd ever said about

me was true. I was selfish and self-absorbed and jumped before looking.

Okay, she hadn't said any of those things directly out loud, but it was inferred, and I might be an idiot, but I wasn't stupid.

It still bugged me, why did he want her gone so badly?

At the hotel, I pulled out my phone and decided to dig. It didn't take but five minutes to see that Rob used to review restaurants - and was a spectacular failure. I called my old boss.

"Hey Stef."

"Ruggeman? How the hell are you?"

"Good, I'm I the city." If anyone had the goods on Rob Clemons it would be Stef Goldman. "I've got a question for you."

"You're in town? Come over to the restaurant."

I took a breath. Did I want to step back into a kitchen I'd never be a part of again?

"I mean if you're free. If not, what's your question?"

My pride wasn't going to stop me from seeing a friend. "I'm on my way."

I hung up and ran a hand through my hair. Stepping out on the sidewalk I hailed a cab and headed to London House.

I went back over the evening once more time, getting angrier by the minute.

Entering the restaurant took me straight back, and to my surprise, it filled me with an anxiety and tension I hadn't anticipated or remembered feeling when I was there before.

But that wasn't why I was here. I was here to fix things for...no, with Helene. I was sure she could take care of herself. But I had to remedy my part of this.

Allison was still the hostess and smiled when she saw

me. "Kael Ruggeman in the flesh. I didn't believe it when Goldman said you were coming by."

"And yet here I am."

"He said you could go on back."

I nodded and pushed through the steel door. The roar of kitchen noise soothed my edges even as it took me back to a place I no longer belonged. It was surreal. I had my own kitchen now, and this felt foreign.

"Hands."

"Yes chef."

The usual chorus followed by a flurry of moment. Stef came around the corner and stopped when he saw me.

"Kael," he called, waving me over, and I joined him in the back.

"Hey Stef." We hugged. "How are you? Looks great in here."

He nodded looking out over his flawless staff. "Yeah. It's been good. It was tough after you left, but we finally found someone to fill your shoes."

A woman with brown hair and a furrowed brow nodded one curt head bob at me and got back to work. It was a Chef named Destiny and she had a reputation as a hardass in this business, and that is saying something.

"Really?" I looked at Stef.

He winked. "Don't believe everything you hear. Let's go get a drink."

We moved out to the lounge area at the bar and settled at a table off to the side. This was clearly Stef's table.

"Where's Lou?"

"Heading up What's at Steak."

"Is that seriously the name?"

He nodded. "Tell me everything," he said with his usual flair, after ordering our bourbons.

"I can't drink anymore tonight."

Stef laughed and pushed a glass in my direction anyway.

I looked around, sipping the rich beverage. "I thought I'd be sad coming back here."

"But?"

"It's not mine anymore. I have something else."

"And it is yours. That's what no one gets. You don't know what yours is until you hold it in your hand. But why are you in town?"

I leaned forward, setting down my glass and putting my head in my hands.

"Wait." Stef sounded serious. "Is it the restaurant?"

I shook my head. "No. That I would know how to fix."

He leaned back in his chair. "Now I'm intrigued. Go on."

I looked at my old friend. "I can't believe you used to scare the shit out of me."

He chuckled. "Times change and so do relationships. We both run our own kitchens now. It's different."

I shrugged. "I guess. So there's a woman…"

"Yes. I got that part from the sick-puppy-in-love look on your face."

"Now I can't believe I call you friend."

He laughed again. "Come on, Kael. I know you. Out with it."

I told him the whole story.

He leaned in. "Wait. Helene Carnahan is Anonymous?" He smacked his knee. "Of course she is. She's such a badass."

I looked at him. "I know. But here's the thing. Her boss was gleeful in firing her. I think he set up this whole night just to let her go."

He frowned. "Why the hell would Food, Drink, Air get

rid of her? She has to be the only thing keeping them afloat."

I shook my head and took a drink. "That's what I don't get. I looked him up and he used to review, but he basically got laughed out."

"Who is it?"

"Rob Clemons."

It was a rare thing to see Stef get serious, but when he did it was something to behold. His lips pursed together, jaw set. Red crept into his glare. "Rob Clemons is a fucking joke. I cannot believe he's running that place. I wonder what he did to get there."

"Tell me what you know."

"He doesn't know food. He was let go from a couple kitchens. Terrible work ethic and has no instinct for food. He started reviewing, but they were laughable. And what's more is he tried to take down the kitchens that let him go. All nonsense, of course, but that isn't how you make friends in this town. And everyone knew it. I didn't know he was still here, to be honest."

I swirled the ice in my glass as I thought. "So why would he want to take down Helene?"

He laughed again. "Oh, that's easy. She was the one who called out his bad review. He was writing under another name then, so I doubt she knows it's the same guy, but she ate at the restaurant after him. It was one of her first big reviews. She contradicted everything thing he said, and of course she knows food—"

"Like no other." I closed my eyes, recalling eating a meal together. Watching her savor the food, talking through the experience.

Stef snapped his fingers a couple times. "Still with us?"

I opened my eyes. "Yep. Then what happened?"

"He disappeared. Except I guess he didn't."

I sat back. "And he's been waiting to take her down and he used me to do it."

It still didn't make sense. Why would he care? It wasn't like he'd get the critic spot if she were gone.

"Okay, so what does he have to gain here?"

Stef rubbed his chin, deep in thought, and for a minute I was positive he was a TV character I'd conjured to help me with all this. Then he gasped.

"I bet he gets her column."

I nodded. "I got there five minutes ago. Is that enough to do this to someone? And how do I fit in?"

Stef laughed. "You let him go from here."

My mouth dropped open. "I've never seen him before tonight."

He stood and I followed him back to the kitchen. "Yes, you have. Don't you remember the guy who couldn't do the carrots right?"

I rolled my eyes. "That's half of them."

"Okay, but this one in particular. He couldn't do the julienne properly and quickly."

I raised my hands. "Still, nothing."

"Next day, onions. No good. So you put him on stock and—"

"He dumped it and I knew he did it on purpose. It was too convenient the way it happened."

"He had to go home to change and you told him not to come back. That's the same guy."

"Bobby...something."

He nodded. "I think he was out to get Helene and her job and you were just a happy coincidence. How did he find out you two knew each other again?"

I hung my head, hands on hips and sighed.

"You were Kael. Got it."

He gave some orders to the staff while I stood there offended. "What the fuck does that mean?"

"That means you got your ego hurt and decided you would prove how you were right and not a jackass while actually proving you are one. The mind blowing thing is, you're the real deal. You don't have to prove yourself to anyone." He leaned on an incredibly clean counter.

I wanted to be mad, but he was right. "I need to prove myself to Helene."

"Why?"

I turned to go. "Forget it. How do I take down this Rob guy?"

Stef touched my arm, so I turned.

"No, why do you need to? What else happened you haven't told me about?"

Moment of truth. "I wrote in after Food, Drink, Air posted the anonymous review and then Helene popped up at Cat and The Fiddle. I didn't think about it at first. And all those old feelings, and some new ones, were still there."

He was rapt. "We should have stayed out there with the bourbon. Did she feel the same?"

I shook my head. I wanted to pace, but there was nowhere to go to stay out of the food path. "She came there to yell at me for owning my aunt's place. And then she got snowed in."

He waved his hand in the air. "I get the rest and that also explains the look on your face. But why did she care about you owning Cat's place?"

I weighed my words carefully, not wanting to tell Helene's story for her. "She knew my aunt, I guess. And it felt personal to her."

He moved back to his office. "Interesting. Let me look into this Rob person. How long do I have?"

"Until nine tomorrow morning."

He looked at the clock. "Shit. Okay. I'll call. And Kael, it's really good to see you."

We hugged again and I stepped out through the back like I had done a hundred times.

As I made my way to the hotel, I formed a new plan. Get Rob out of his job and Helene back into hers, say I was sorry, and then I guess I'd see where the chips would fall.

~

Helene

TEARS RAN down my face as I rode along in the almost empty subway car. It felt unusually sparse for this time of night, but maybe it reflected how I felt inside. Just an empty train moving through a dark tunnel lacking anything of substance.

Damn Rob and damn Kael and damn everything straight to hell. How did this happen?

Oh yeah. I couldn't be satisfied with my real job and had to do something else. And I couldn't leave well enough alone when Kael responded to my review.

And then I slept with the chef.

So really, it was my fault. I brought this on myself. And Jen most likely too.

Jen! Oh no. I pulled out my phone and dialed her.

"Are you okay?"

"Did you hear already?"

There was a pause. "Hear what? It was just that you don't usually call."

"Oh. Rob fired me."

"That piece of shit. What happened?"

I took a big breath and spilled everything. "I went to Comfort and he showed up with Kael Ruggeman in tow."

She interjected. "I have a question about that, but we'll circle back."

"He ordered food for them and the whole nine yards, but it was all a ruse to out me as—"

"Anonymous. That bastard. How did he find out?"

"Jen, you're the best. Thanks for being on my side."

"Why wouldn't I be? I am irate Rob fired you. What the hell?"

My shoulders hung. "I don't know. He's had it out for me. It was probably just a matter of time. Breach of contract for the other column."

"But why would he really care? He had both columns in his magazine and it could have been an absolute coup to eventually reveal Anonymous. Zero sense."

"I don't know. Anyway, I have to have my office cleared before noon tomorrow. Can I bother you for one more thing and ask for your help with that?"

"*Our* office cleared out. I believe I told you I was with you."

Now the tears that rolled down my cheeks were grateful ones. "Thank you. You're such a good friend. I'll see you there when the office opens."

My phone rang immediately after I hung up.

"Hello?"

"Why was Kael there?"

I chuckled through my tears. "Rob figured out I was Anonymous through the letters Kael sent and my little snow delay. He may be a dick, but he's pretty clever."

Jen clicked her tongue. "Bastard. He planned this."

I nodded to no one. "Yeah. I think so."

"Send me a copy of your contract if you don't mind. There has to be a loophole."

"Thanks, Jen. You're truly the best."

I emailed her a copy and stood to get off the train. What the hell was I going to do? I had to take care of my sister and nephew.

My shoulders dropped. The money from Kitty would have to get us by. Kael's words about being brave and strong and doing what had to be done bounced around in my brain, but they were no consolation. I might be doing what needed to be done, but it was just one more time my dream was in reach and now it was gone. And as much as I wanted to blame someone else, this time it was all me.

I trudged up the stairs to my apartment, hating my walk up more than usual. The TV spoke to me through the door and I braced for the conversation I was about to have with my sister. It surprised me she was still up, but I took a breath and opened the door.

Relief poured over me as the reality of what I saw before me sunk in. Deidre sat on the couch, arms outstretched. I dropped my bag on the floor and ran to her arms. Every emotion I'd been holding in came flooding out. She gently rubbed my back and didn't say anything. She kept me together by letting me fall apart.

Finally, I pulled back and she wiped the tears off my face. "I'm so happy to see you."

She smiled and handed me a glass of vino. "I told you I'd get here as soon as I could."

"Didi." I lowered my voice just in case Jonny or Celia were awake down the hall. "Rob fired me. What am I going to do?"

She tilted her head and closed her eyes. Her "let's

fucking go" face. I couldn't help but grin. "He did what now?"

I told her about the entire night, Kael showing up, how it was a trap, and that Jen was leaving with me.

She chewed on her bottom lip, thinking it through. "First, great that Jen is getting out of there too. Second, what the hell is that guy's problem?"

I frowned. "Which one?"

She raised her eyebrows and hit me with a "are you kidding me" look. "Your ex-boss. I know what Kael's problem is."

"You do?"

She laughed and grabbed my hand. "Yes. The same as you. You're in love with each other."

I pulled my hand away. "Yes, that is a problem, except it's not true."

She took a drink of wine but didn't say anything.

"And even if it was true, there's nothing to be done about it."

She smirked at me. "You're proving my point."

I stood and paced. "How? I just said it wouldn't work."

"You've mentioned that repeatedly. But perhaps the lady doth protest too much."

I shook my head and sat back down. "I don't. I'm not. Didi, how could we be together? I've done all the math and it doesn't add up. Or to put it in cooking terms, not enough eggs for this cake."

"There has to be-"

I held up a hand. "I can't worry about that now anyway. How am I going to take care of them?" I tossed my thumb in the direction of the hall.

"Do you have anything saved up?"

My shoulders slumped. "I have a little and what Kitty gave me."

"So your restaurant money."

I nodded, a tear slipping down my cheek.

Deidre grabbed my hand again. "We'll figure this out. Maybe this is the moment we've been waiting for. We can finally start our business together."

I looked at my oldest and dearest friend. "I thought you loved the travel and freedom."

She dipped her chin. "I do. For sure, but after a while, it's hard living out of a suitcase."

The lightbulb went off. "You met someone."

She smiled, wide and vibrant. "I might have."

I thought back over the last six months. "He's in Oklahoma."

Her mouth dropped open. "How the hell did you know that?"

I grinned. "The last three diners you sent me were there."

She smacked my leg playfully. "I don't know that it's anything, but I know it's big enough to explore."

"That's all that matters. But I don't think Celia will want to leave the city."

She looked down and then back up. "I don't mean this in a bad way, but don't you get a say?"

I shut my eyes against the world and the crushing weight of my responsibilities. "I don't know."

"Have you asked Celia?"

I shook my head. "If I did she'd say we could go anywhere because she'd want to do what I wanted even if it wasn't the best thing for her and Jonny. I know she feels guilty for how much she needs. But I truly don't mind taking care of her."

"I know you don't, but you get a life too, Lena. You get a life too."

18

Kael

I paced the coffee shop waiting for my latte. The barista behind the counter eyed me, my nervous energy leaking over and making her uncomfortable. I sat down at a table instead, taking deep breaths to soothe my nervous system. I'd decided to go to Helene's office and apologize one more time. If I could take Rob down at the same time, then great. Two birds, one stone.

The girl behind the counter called my name and I flashed her a smile as I took the cup to let her know I wasn't a jerk.

Or at least was actively trying not to be one.

I walked the five blocks to the building that housed Food, Drink, Air and crossed the street, just in time to get to the door at the exact moment Helene did.

"Lena."

Her head shot up and she pulled out her earbud. "What are you doing here?"

"I wanted to apologize. That's why I came here to begin with. To the city I mean. And I made it worse."

She crossed her arms. "Yes. You did."

I knew she was right, but it stung none the less.

"I know. And I'm so sorry."

"You couldn't have known Rob would do that though."

I half smiled at her, so much regret knocking through me. "I didn't. But still, I'm so damn sorry."

The second of her soft nature I'd just felt dried up and ice came from her. I recognized this as Helene's armor. She did that to detach.

"Okay. You're sorry. You said it. Now go."

I reached out to touch her arm, but she drew away. "Please forgive me."

She shrugged and half-laughed. "Forgive you? Why would I do that?"

I shoved my hands in my pockets so I wouldn't pull her into a hug but I wanted to hold her close and tell her it was going to be okay. To get on my knees and beg for forgiveness. To go up and give Rob all the pieces of my mind I had left. Instead, I stood mute, not knowing what to say.

She nodded twice, her lips pushed together in what I now recognized as her fighting back tears. I was learning her. I wanted to know all of her.

But this wasn't the moment for that revelation.

When I still didn't say anything she said, "That's what I thought. Look, I have to go in there now and clean out my office. I get to put all my stuff in a cardboard box and carry it out in front of everyone I work with while Rob stares and smirks. The ultimate walk of shame. And then I have to figure out how to take care of my sister and nephew with no job. Oh, I know. Maybe the money I'd put back for my restaurant. I'll use that. Again."

She leveled me with her eyes as a single tear ran down her cheek. I was frozen in her gaze.

"I know I keep saying it, but I am so sorry. What can I do?"

She tilted her head back to the sky and I wasn't sure if she was looking for the words, or the strength to not murder me. I wouldn't blame her if she did.

I tried to reassure her. "You'll get another job. Why not go out on your own? Everyone loves your work."

She looked at me with vitriol. "Not anymore. Rob started the whisper network last night. The texts have already started. People know I am 'friendly' with a chef and they suspect I slept with them. They don't trust me because I broke a contract, and..." she looked away.

"And what?"

"It been suggested I only got where I am because I slept my way here."

Anger burned in my veins. "But none of that is true. You've earned everything you have."

"Kael, I don't have anything! Everything I thought I'd built was swept away in a second. As if it never existed." Her chest rose and fell as she yelled at me. "I have nothing." Her voice fell off into tears and she put her head in her hands.

"And I told you. I told you if this happened between us and people found out I would be left with nothing."

I pulled her into a hug, closing my arms around her. She sobbed against my chest as I held her close. She looked up and raised her face to mine. I wiped her tears away. Our lips were so close, about to find one another when I felt her stiffen and pull away. "What am I doing?"

She swiped at her cheeks with the backs of her hands. "I need you to go."

"What? Why? Let me help you."

She shook her head. "Get out of my life. You did nothing but tear me down in your kitchen. During the hardest time of my life, and you did nothing but tear me down. And for what? To make yourself feel better? Look better? Feel like a big man?" She advanced on me as she spoke until I stepped back.

"Then you openly criticized my review and told people I still shouldn't be in the kitchen. You asked for a gift I held so dear, which I gave to you, and with it, you took all my ideas and work. Now you've helped the man out to get me do exactly that. I lost my job, Kael. I lost everything."

"I know, I didn't—"

She held up a hand. "I don't want to hear your apology anymore. You got your way. You destroyed me. You promised you would, even though you didn't know you were writing to me that day. It took a long time, but you did it. You can go now, knowing you took down Helene Carnahan, just like you promised you would."

She turned to head into the building but turned back at the door. "I can't believe I ever felt anything for you."

And with that, she was gone.

As I stood there dumbfounded, my heart in pieces. My phone buzzed scaring the shit out of me.

"Hello?"

Stef answered. "I have the info you wanted. And it's good. Or bad, depending on which side you're on."

Stef went on and on about all the shady shit Rob had done and used to get his position and keep it. No wonder he wanted Helene out. She'd never be a part of his schemes.

"Holy shit."

"Yeah. Stop back by before you leave town."

"Thank you, Stef. I appreciate this."

"Anytime."

I had the info I could use, but now I needed a plan. I dialed the diner and only to get no answer. I called Sheila.

"Why isn't anyone at the diner?"

She paused before answering. "Kael, honey."

"Oh god. You never say honey to me unless it's bad news."

"There was a fire and it didn't level the place but it was bad."

My stomach dropped to the floor. "Is everyone okay?"

"Everyone is fine. But the kitchen is all but gone and the dining room..."

I ran a hand through my hair. "I'm on my way then. Why didn't you call me?"

"It happened yesterday and I was about to. It's really early here."

I forgot about the time difference. "Oh yeah. Why was there so much damage? Was it that bad?"

"It wasn't initially but we couldn't find the fire blankets and then once it found the grease..."

The fire blankets. Shit. I had sent them to be cleaned after the night Helene and I had spent in the freezing cold.

"That's on me. I sent them out and forgot to pick them up."

"The repression system came on, but it didn't make a difference I don't think."

I took a breath. "There's still a building standing, it made a little difference. I'll be home soon."

Home. First time I'd called it that without my mind revolting. Interesting what time will do. But I would go

home, take care of this, then come back and deal with Rob
Clemons.

Helene

As I rode in the elevator for the last time, I fought every
urge to go back down to Kael. His arms were so strong and
secure as I cried in them before I remembered why I was
crying. Because he was here in the first place.

Damn him.

Damn his lips, and his pretty eyes, and that piece of hair
and how it fell across his forehead when he focused on
something. The way he looked at me as if he'd never seen
anything better. His voice saying my name. Damn all of it.

The ding on my floor brought me back to the moment. I
straightened my shoulders and stepped out into the office.
Whispers among colleagues and a few looks of pity met me.
Good, then everyone already knew.

I blew past them straight to my office. Jen was already
there with most everything in boxes.

"You're the best."

She smiled at me. "Rob's been waiting for you, but don't
worry, I found a loophole."

She passed me a very official looking document and I
glanced over it right as Rob rounded the corner.

"I have been looking forward to this moment for so long.
Ready to hand over those keys?"

I leaned back against the desk that was recently mine. "I
have until noon to turn in my last review, but first, I'd like to
discuss my severance."

"Ha!" He tossed his head back like a super villain. I was

half-surprised he didn't laugh like Lex Luthor. "You were fired. Fired people don't get severance."

"Actually, according to my contract, I do since I'm being fired without just cause."

His face clouded before he regained his composure. "No. You're in breach of contract. I have just cause."

"The cause can't be because you don't like me or you want my column, and I'm not in breach."

"Yes. You are. You can't work somewhere else and here at the same time. It's a conflict of interest."

I nodded and sat in my chair. "True. That's why I posted the other reviews anonymously. But the thing is, I didn't work for anyone. I never got paid for them."

"But we paid you here." When the words left his mouth, he realized what I'd said.

"Right, I've only worked for you with both things. You hired me and offered the money for it. This is the only place I'm employed. And there's no conflict because I only reviewed out of state and a different kind of eating establishment than what I do here." I looked at him with a smirk on my face as I watched the color drain out of his. Jen crossed her arms and leaned on the desk next to my chair.

"Is that right, Jen?" I asked without taking my eyes off Rob.

"Yes, I think that's correct."

"So again, let's discuss a package for me to go away."

He shrugged. "Fine. Not that it will make a difference. You don't have a reputation to go away with, so money doesn't matter."

A little of my bravado left me. "What does that mean?"

Now it was his turn to look self-satisfied.

Jen stood up. "What the hell did you do?"

"Not much. Just a few well-placed blind items and it won't matter where you go, you won't find a job."

And that's when I broke, the wall I'd put in place came crumbling down. "What did I do to you to make you hate me so much? I don't even know you. I have come in and done my job and consistently brought in numbers for this place. What the fuck is your problem?"

A voice in my head told me to control myself but I was past listening. I seethed as I looked at him.

"I don't have a problem. Maybe your temper is why I fired you."

"No one would believe that."

He got close to my face, his voice low. I fought to hold my ground and not back down. "Helene, I can't wait to get rid of you. You are the thorn in my side, and now that I have respect in this town, whatever I say people will believe. Your time is over. Run along to your boyfriend and maybe if you ask real nice, he'll let you in his kitchen this time."

I could feel the anger boiling over into tears, my least favorite thing about me. I cried when I was mad. But I would not cry in front of Rob. He would see it as weakness. Instead, I dug in and stayed right there with him, staring him down. "What are you going to give me?"

"I'll give you 25 grand if I never have to see you again. I never want to hear from you. And no lawsuits."

The last part tripped me up. Why would there be a lawsuit? I looked at Jen and she gave a small head nod.

"Deal. You can't talk any more shit about me. No comment if people call or ask or anything. You let it die. Otherwise, I will sue your ass."

He pushed his tongue in his cheek, debating whether he would agree or not. "Fine. I'll get the paperwork drawn up."

"Today. I want it today."

He stepped aside and made a call and with one more look he left.

"Should he be able to just make a call and get that done that fast?"

Jen shook her head. "No. But let's make sure you get your money and then we'll figure out how to take the bastard down."

"I can't do anything. My agreement ties my hands unless there's mutual destruction."

She smiled at me. "Why do you think I kept my mouth shut? I didn't agree to anything."

I impulsively pulled her into a hug.

"I don't know what we're going to do now, but want to go start a business? Deidre is on board too."

Jen smiled and it stretched across her face. "You bet your ass, I do."

19

Kael

The smell of charred remains and smoke met my nose. It twitched with the acrid scent. I walked gingerly through the blackened wood and darkened, warped counters. The walls were scorched, the paint bubbling up in places, completely gone in others. I felt someone at my shoulder.

"It's not a total loss. That's the good news."

Sheila stood with her arms crossed, staring at the remains.

"Then what's the bad news?"

She waved her hand across the mess. "This isn't enough?"

I nodded. "It's plenty, but I thought you were going to drop something else on me."

She patted my back gently. "Just let me know what you

need. We're all here for you and want to get this place back up and running if that's what you want."

I turned to look at her. "Of course that's what I want." I stepped outside, pulling my coat close around me and hopping up to sit on my tailgate. Sheila joined me. "It's the only thing I have."

"It's not all you have. You have a house and a staff that believes in you. And what about Lena? You have her."

I shook my head, lowering my chin. "No, I don't have Helene. I should've left her alone. Maybe I could have done something if I'd been here. Maybe I could have stopped it. Maybe..."

"Stop that. You don't need to go down the what if path. I thought you went to New York to make up with her."

I looked over at Sheila. It was so close to having Aunt Cat with me. Man, I missed her so much. Tears welled in my eyes. "I miss..."

She put her arm around my shoulder. "I know, honey. Me too. Every minute."

"I'd give anything to ask her about all this. What would she do?"

Sheila laughed, and it was just this side of bitter. "She'd probably already be in there with a paint brush."

Now it was my turn to laugh. "You're definitely right."

We sat in silence for I'm not sure how long before Sheila spoke up. "Tell me what happened and what's going on in that head of yours."

"Short story: I fucked up."

"I'd like the long version." She slid down from the tailgate and lit a cigarette, her bright red nails tapping off the ash every couple drags.

"I lost Helene. Forever. I went there after she'd asked me

not to and her boss had it out for her, which I didn't know by the way, but he used me to out her as Anonymous and then he fired her on the spot, right in front of me."

"What an asshole."

"Right? Anyway, I was trying to save her job so I found out the dirt on him. It's enough to get him fired, and then some, but went there to tell her, she was having none of it. She told me to go away and she never wanted to see me again."

Sheila opened her mouth, but the flood gates had opened.

"And then you called and I came home to a shell of Cat's diner. The one thing she left me in charge of, I destroyed. And I did it from many states away." I heard my voice growing, like a dam had broken. I hopped down from the gate, walking trails in chat under my feet, hands waving in the air. "Jesus, I can't do anything. Helene was right. My ego gets in the way, I don't listen, I just barge in like a bull in a China closet." My chest heaved.

"How is this your ego?"

"This whole thing started because she was so good I basically bullied her out of my kitchen. Then she wrote that review and that also pissed me off, even though I only wanted to impress her. Then when she came here and gave me four blue plates, even though I didn't know it was her, I had to go and respond, which is a no-no."

"And you know that." She lit another cigarette.

"I know I do." I paused for a minute.

Sheila held up a hand before I could get going again. "You don't need to be telling me this, you need to tell her. Lena should hear this from you."

"She won't talk to me."

"Give her a minute. I bet she comes around."

I shook my head again. "I don't know how to make it up to her."

"What did you do with the info on her boss?"

I leaned against the tailgate and blew into my hands to warm them. "Nothing yet."

She smiled. "Start there."

I hesitated, then I pulled her into a hug. "Thanks, Sheila. I'm so glad you're here."

"Me too, honey. Now let's get this diner up and running and you need to get your girl."

I looked at her. "She's not my girl, and it's not about that. But I, for sure, want to make it right."

I roamed through the debris now that the fire department had deemed it safe. Climbing over all the things that used to be a kitchen, I forced my way into the little office. It was a place I'd hated, but now I'd give anything to sit in there doing mundane tasks knowing it was mine.

I up righted my chair and took in the scene. Papers were singed on the edges, the middles still untouched. Great news to the people I owed money. A filing cabinet looked covered in black spray paint but it was the remnants of the fire. Stuff had fallen behind it, so I scooted it away from the wall only to find a small metal box by the baseboard. I pushed away the scatter of papers. It was a fireproof container you use for special documents and things. It was light and a small metal plate had been attached to the top with my name on it.

Heading back out to my truck I placed the box gently in my front seat. My heart pounded in my chest, but I didn't start the engine. The drive home would take too long and I had to find out what was inside.

Flipping open the small latch, I lifted the lid. A couple pictures of me and my sister as kids. One of her and Sheila in a park, arms around each other. Another of Cat in front of the diner, a big smile on her face. It wasn't recent. I turned it over to find 1967 written on the back.

A ring with three diamonds in it just lay in the bottom of the box and a letter. I lifted the envelope and held it in my hand.

For my Allie Bear.

Tears pricked at my eyes. I gently opened the sealed edge. I pulled out the contents. Three recipe cards fell in my lap. One each for the favorite dishes Helene and I had talked about and one for something called a pancake cake.

A few papers were folded together. I caught her scent as I unfolded them and read the words they held.

Allie Bear,

I know by the time you find this, if you ever do, the diner has been running well and I'm long gone. I'm sure you'd disagree because you've never once in your life thought anything you ever did was good enough, but if you're there doing it, that's enough.

I wish I could see you there at the stove. I loved that little place. I hope you're happy here, but I wanted to tell you a few things.

Over the years, I hoped to instill these things in you, but you were always so busy trying to show you were good enough, that didn't leave a lot of time for listening. Here's Aunt Cat's rules for life. (And I need you to listen to the last one.)

Follow your heart. Your heart has always been big but you try to fight it. Don't.

Trust yourself. You are really good at what you do, but you've always needed validation. Here it is from me. You're great. So now, you can trust yourself.

When in doubt, bake a pie. It'll fix anything. (Just don't over work the crust.)

This is my place, Allie. And thank you for keeping it going, but if the time comes for you to make a place of your own, you can. And you will. And you should.

I love you Allie, and I'm so proud of you.

Cat

I TURNED to face the restaurant, tears running down my cheeks. The neon feline on the sign still survived. I smiled. "Thanks, Aunt Cat. I'll make it right."

I opened my phone as I got in my truck after waving bye to Sheila. "Stef? I've got a favor to ask."

"If it's take down, Rob Clemons, then my answer is yes."

"Great. On my way."

Helene

I SAT IN MY APARTMENT, dreading the moment I would have to tell Celia I'd lost my job and I wasn't sure what we'd do. I mean I was getting a huge sum from Food, Drink, Air but was that plus what I'd saved enough to take care of them and start up a new place? I wasn't sure. Or I could review, if I could get a job. That was really the key point, because how much damage had been done to my reputation by Rob I wasn't sure. Even though he'd agreed to let it die, I couldn't trust him any further than I could throw him.

I wish I had something on him. That would help at least. If I had some dirt, it would make him harder to believe. I sat up taller.

I could tell everyone I was Anonymous and go that route. Simply come clean and beat the rumor mill. But was there enough there to make a business? Maybe take up the mantel of travel Deidre was ready to put behind her. But I couldn't start a place and be gone all the time.

I slumped back on the couch. I doubted I could be away from Celia and Jonny that much. No. That wouldn't work. Unless I had help.

Kael came to mind instantly. No. I'd been burned by him for the last time. He only thought about himself and every time he stepped in, I lost something more. My job, my recipes, my heart.

I'd have to go it alone. My phone buzzing gave me a start, snapping me out of my spiral.

I didn't recognize the number, but I answered anyway. Why not? How could this day get worse?

"Hello?"

"Is this Helene Carnahan?"

"This is she. Can I help you?"

The voice on the other noticeably brightened. "This is Chef Stefan from London House."

That caught me off guard. My mind raced. "Yes?"

"First, big fan. You are the best at what you do and I'd love to have you back in my restaurant for a meal. But I'm calling on behalf of a friend of mine."

"Thank you, sir. But if that friend is Kael Ruggeman, I'm afraid I'm not interested."

He chuckled. "I like you already. But please hear me out. One, he'd like to meet with you wherever and whenever you'd agree to it. He just needs five minutes. Two, we have some information you might be interested in."

What good could come out of giving Kael five minutes?

But what harm would it do?

I put that aside. "What kind of info?"

"Something that will take down Mr. Clemons."

"Nonna's. 6 pm."

"We'll see you there."

I texted Jen and asked her to come along too, but she already had plans. Right as I sat down my phone, Celia and Jonny came through the door. He ran over and climbed in my lap. "Auntie Leen."

"Hey, JonJon. How was school?"

Celia didn't speak when she came in which told me she was having a rough day. She smiled and went straight to her room.

Jonny told me all the details of his day, and then all the details of the week, and I made him a peanut butter sandwich.

"I can make you something else. Want anything?"

"Auntie Leen, I know you make fancy food, but this is my favorite."

I cleaned up the small mess. "I write about fancy food, there's a difference."

"Mama says you make food too and that she's scared you aren't making food because of us."

I turned to look at my nephew. "She said what?"

He laughed. "I told her she was silly because you make me food all the time." He held up his sandwich with a goofy smile on his face.

I sat by him. "Did she tell you this or was she talking to someone else?"

"Leen, can I watch cartoons?"

I nodded and he ran off to turn on the tv. In a fog, I walked down the hall. I thought I'd kept everything inside, close to the vest. Never letting on that I was unhappy around them. Unhappy is a rough word. It wasn't that. I simply wasn't fulfilled. I gently knocked on Celia's door.

"Come in," she said softly.

She was lying on the bed in the almost dark, only a small illumination from her bedside lamp lit the space. Weird shadows danced on the wall and ceiling.

"How you doing, sis?"

"Same old. Just a rough day."

"Can we talk for a minute?"

She moved her arm from her eyes and looked at me. She sat up and patted the bed next to her.

I sat down and took her hand. "Jonny just told me you think you're holding me back."

She hung her head. "I didn't mean that. I was talking to a friend and said you'd have a restaurant of your own if I could be on my own."

"Sis, I don't mind taking care of you. You know that right?"

She nodded but I saw the first tears fall. "I know. But I want to be on my own too. I feel like a burden. You shouldn't have to be a caregiver. It's not your job."

I wiped her tears. "It's no burden. I love you and Jonny. Plus, you're my only job now."

"What?" She sat up straight.

"Rob fired me."

"Oh god. Are you okay? What happened?"

I held up my other hand. "I'm fine. We're fine." I gave her all the details of the last couple days.

"Hmmm." She rubbed her chin with her hand. "What can I do?"

"Hold down the fort for a bit. Is that doable? I'm meeting with someone tonight that might be able to help, but I'm not sure what the next few days will look like."

She nodded.

"You have someone you can call if you need something?"

"Yes. Do what you need to do."

I kissed her cheek and went to the door.

"Lena?"

I turned at the doorframe. "Yeah?"

"I'm so proud to be your sister."

That hit me square in the feels. "Right back atcha."

Time to let Deidre know what was going on.

I think I'm getting some info on Rob.

Good. Nail him to the wall.

That's the plan.

> Need me there?

I think I'm good, I'll call you after.

> Let me know what I can do. Love you.

Mean it.

I cleaned the apartment, unloaded my boxes from the office, and made lunch. Now all I had to do was wait for six o'clock.

20

Kael

"**S**it down. You are stressing me out."

I looked at Stef. "What else am I supposed to do?"

He sighed and walked to the host stand. "Can we go ahead and be seated? Our other member is walking down the block and we'll order drinks right away." He smiled his smile that always got him his way.

The hostess smiled back and said, "Follow me."

I shook my head with a grin. He knew all the things to say to get around the "whole party must be here" and it worked. We were seated toward the back and as promised he ordered a bottle of wine as soon as we sat down.

I checked the time and as if on cue, the front door

opened. Helene was there, lovelier than ever. She scanned the restaurant as my heart beat hard in my chest.

"You were right."

Stef looked at me. "I know. About what am I right?"

"I'm in love with her."

"Yes. Obviously. I thought we'd established this." He rolled his eyes.

Her eyes found mine and a smile spread across her face. But clearly, she remembered who she was looking at, because as soon as it had come, it was gone, replaced by a dark cloud. She spoke to the hostess and I saw her point to us before she bee lined to our table. Stef stood and I struggled with my chair but tried to do the same. Why was I a freak show around her. I lost all my self-control.

Stef held out his hand. "Stefan London. Owner of London House. Pleasure to meet you. I meant what I said, come in for a meal on the house anytime."

She smiled and I fought to keep my legs from going to Jell-O. "Helene Carnahan. So nice to meet you. And now I get the name."

Stef raised an eyebrow.

She nodded toward me and we all sat down. "I could not figure out why a New York restaurant that served no English dishes was called that. Your name isn't on the proprietor listing."

Stef laughed loud and hearty. "That's hilarious. Yes. It is listed under my partner's name." He turned to me. "Do other people think this about the name?"

I nodded sheepishly. "It's been mentioned."

"Well, damn." He laughed again. "Helene, we will be fast friends. But we have business right now. Let's order. No sense in talking on an empty stomach."

The wine arrived. Stef ordered a second bottle and we

selected our food. Helene crossed her arms and stared at me.

"I'm here. What do you want, Kael?"

I cleared my throat. "I know I've said I'm sorry. But I truly am. It's so good to see you. I've missed you."

She turned her head partially away, closing her eyes and then looked back at me. "And?"

Her eyes bore into me as sweat dripped down my back with nerves. She was terrifying when she was angry. She waved her hand.

"And?" She said a second time with exasperation.

"Right. Um, Stef found out some things about Rob. I think it can take him down and get your job back."

She lifted her wine glass and swirled it. "I don't want my job back." She shifted her gaze. "But I do want to take him down."

Stef opened his mouth but I cut him off. "You don't want your job back?"

She shrugged and it was the first crack in her demeanor. "What's the point? He's killed my reputation. I look like a fool. For some reason, people are under the impression—"

"Nothing he's said or done is going to mean dick." Stef interjected. We both snapped our heads to him.

"What?" Helene sat down her wine.

"He's shady and a liar. His word doesn't mean anything."

Helene sat up straight, color filling her cheeks. "Tell me."

"He has a hefty financial stake in several restaurants around town. He's promised them good reviews, five stars to be exact, if they will buy advertisement in the magazine and I suspect he's getting a kickback from his monetary input."

"That's disgusting." Helene tapped her chin. "Let me guess. Steaks on Fifth, Noodle Bar, and Fire are on that list."

Stef pulled out his phone. "Yes. How did you know?"

"Because they were all...not great and he was adamant I go back. Then those reviews magically didn't get printed for some reason. He had a list of reasons. That's why he wanted me out. I interfered with his money and power."

Stef nodded. "He wants someone to control, not someone good at their job."

"Then why not let me go outright? He could've made up a million reasons."

I put my hand on her forearm. She looked at my fingers on her skin, then met my eyes. "You're too good. He couldn't risk you going somewhere else to work. He had to destroy you."

She pulled her arm gently away. "That's kind of you. But it doesn't seem like enough. There has to be something more."

Stef laughed. "There's the whole Kael kicking him out the kitchen and you taking his job, too."

"What?" Her voice was low and whispery. She looked from Stef to me.

"Apparently, he couldn't cut it. I don't even remember him. And then you... left the restaurant and went to work at the magazine. I think that was supposed to be his gig, too."

Her face flushed red with anger. "Kael Ruggeman." Her voice was low and even. "I rue the day I laid eyes on you. You have caused me nothing but heartache since day one."

I took her hand and pulled her to standing. "Stef, we'll be right back."

She followed me out to the sidewalk. I took a deep breath of cool air. Trying to steady myself.

"Helene, I could not have known what would happen, this chain of events. No one did, not even you. I came to your office the other morning to tell you about Rob and try to make it right. But there was...I was needed back at the diner and I had to go. But I'm here now to tell you all this."

"I don't need you to fix it. I need you to leave me alone." She turned to head back in, but I grabbed her hand and she looked at me, really looked at me, not through me. I pulled her close, holding her as I spoke.

"I didn't say I came to fix it. I said I came to tell you what I need you to hear."

Our breathing was heated, bodies close. My eyes flicked down to her lips and back up to her eyes. They burned with desire.

"I'm so, so sorry. I couldn't have known the repercussions of you leaving the kitchen because of me. I was worried about me and my life. I was young and scared I wasn't going to be taken seriously if I wasn't a hardass. You were too good, and I knew it wouldn't be long before someone noticed. I knew someone would snap you up and put in you in charge somewhere else. How could I know you'd have to leave cooking altogether? If I had it to do over..."

Tears ran down her cheeks, but she didn't speak.

"Then there you were, eating my food for a review, and that review." I clenched my jaw but continued. "Everything you said was right and that made me more insane. I only acted that way because I wanted to impress you, get a chance to say sorry. But seeing you again, I didn't know how to deal with what I felt."

She stepped back, still holding my hands. "What you felt?"

I nodded. It was all on the table now. I couldn't back down. "Yes. I felt it then, and now, and in between. You have to know that's why I'm here."

She bit her bottom lip. "Go on."

"And when I thought I had put this place out of my

mind, and you were out of my mind, another review pops up and it said all the things I was insecure, *am* insecure about. Your words came rushing back and I responded. God, I'm an idiot. I know better and you know I do and it's all shit. I'm so sorry. But then you walked back into my diner. I couldn't believe it. I'd dreamt of that moment, but when you were standing there I didn't know what to do."

She stepped closer. But I squeezed her hands, let go, and paced as I spoke.

"Now, I've lost you, the diner is in question, and all because I couldn't stand the idea of someone else making Cat's recipes, even though I don't want to make them, mind you. That's the real stupidity here. I want to make something of my own. I don't have your vision to take her stuff and make it yours. You're better than me." I looked at Helene who stood there dumbfounded. "But Cat wanted you to, and she knew you could, and I want you to now, too. Ahgghh-hh." I yelled into the air, my breath visible in the night.

Tears glittered on her eyelashes as she watched my breakdown, but the look on her face gave me the strength to go on.

"But I fucked that didn't I? You're the one person who appreciated her in the same way I do. We could've done all that together, but I always get in my own way. As Stef says, I was Kael." I ran a hand through my hair, feeling more manic by the second.

"I can be myself with you but I lost you before I even got a chance to love you. And I do love you, Lena."

Her breath hitched. "You do, don't you?"

I nodded, hands on my hips in defeat. "I do."

She stepped close to me. "What do you mean the diner is in question?"

"It doesn't matter right now." I thought about the

charred remains I'd walked through a day before. "I know I don't deserve it, but can you at least forgive me and let me try to help you now?"

"Come on. Stef's right. We can't do this on an empty stomach." She wiped the tears from her cheeks then mine.

"Shit. Am I crying?"

She laughed, soft and caring. "It happens when you care."

"Huh. Who knew?"

Our food was ready for us when we walked back in.

"I didn't wait." Stef said as we sat.

"Why should you?" Helene answered. "What can we do with what we know about Rob?"

Stef drank down his wine and poured another glass. "It's already done. I did it this afternoon. He's also getting nailed for tax evasion and falsified documents. He did all that to, ironically, not have a conflict of interest with his job."

Helene and I stared at him. "Then what was all this for?" I waved my hand between us.

"So you could say what you needed to say and she would listen. How else was that going to happen?" He twirled his noodles on his fork and consumed a mouthful.

Helene chuckled. "Fast friends, indeed." She raised her glass and they cheersed each other.

After a quite pleasant meal, Stef left us, and I walked with Helene as we made our way to the subway.

"Any word on the forgiveness?"

Her hands were in her pockets, guarding against the cold. "I want to, Kael."

"But?"

She turned to me. "I know you didn't know any of this would happen. But it did. And part of it happened because you didn't listen to me. You put yourself first and there's a part of me who is scared that's what you're doing now. How do I know this is for real?"

"I understand that. You don't really have a reason to trust me. I have been selfish."

"Can I think about it?"

I nodded. "I have something for you that might help."

I pulled Cat's recipe book, now Helene's, out of my messenger bag.

Her mouth dropped open. "But you said—"

"I know what I said. I'll never be able to forget hurting you like that, but this is yours. Cat wanted you to have it and you are family." I handed it to her.

She ran her hand over the top as if it was a precious artifact, the greatest treasure, instead of a beat up, old book.

"Thank you."

I nodded. "Good night, Helene. Thanks for hearing me out. If you're ever in Kansas…"

"You'll be my first stop." She smiled and it took all my energy just to smile back and not pull her into a kiss. I turned to go to my hotel, heart heavy.

"Kael?"

Helene surprised me by being right there when I turned around, a look of longing on her face. This time, I pulled her to me, our lips crushing together. I curled my arms around her, the taste of her kiss filling my senses. The softness of her lips on mine, her curves flush against me. My fingers wound in her hair, holding her as close as I could. The kiss went on, heating me from the inside out. A part of me thought of the possibility within the kiss, but that was covered by the goodbye I felt. Helene pulled away, our foreheads leaned together.

"Thank you. I mean it."

"You're welcome."

She snaked her arms down mine and squeezed my hand before she turned to go, the recipe book tucked in her other arm.

And with that, it was done. I'd told her all the things I needed to. I'd done what I could to discredit and take down Rob, and now I could go back to see if I could salvage some semblance of my own life. The fact I would be doing that without Helene would take longer to accept.

Helene

I HEARD Celia pad softly down the hall. She sat on the couch beside me.

"How's it going?"

Tears sprung from my eyes instantly. "I don't know. I don't know what to do next. I feel lost."

I often felt like the older sister in our relationship. I was the caregiver, the one in charge of things. I paid the bills and made the appointments. If school called, I showed up. When we needed milk, I put it on the list.

Now I was floating, adrift, and I felt like anything but the responsible adult. I was a child. The little sister not knowing what was next.

Celia put her arm around me, allowing me to sink into her embrace. "We will figure it out. I know you always do, but this time we can do it together."

I'm not sure how long we sat there before she spoke up.

"Can I ask you something?"

I nodded into her shoulder. "You know you can."

"Are you intent on staying here, in the city, now that you don't have your column?"

I sat up. I'd never considered moving because I thought this is where she wanted to be. I'd always pushed on to figure out how to make it here. "Um, I don't know. Do you want to stay here?"

"Truthfully, no. I don't. I'd really like to get away from all the memories and our past. But this has always been where you wanted to be, and I want you to be happy."

I turned to her. "I stayed here for you and for Jonny because of school and doctors. I thought this is what you wanted."

She laughed and it ran over into me until laughter bubbled up and out of me, too. "Oh, sis. We are a mess."

"Aren't we?"

I sat with it for a minute. "Where should we go?"

She looked at me and shrugged. "I didn't get that far."

"Fair enough."

"Oh hey, one more thing."

I moved to the kitchen to make coffee. I pointed to a cup to ask if she wanted one. She nodded. "Shoot."

"How would you feel if I was dating?"

I turned to see a goofy grin on her face. "Oh, Celia! That's amazing. Tell me everything."

"Well, that's what I need to tell you. It's someone you know. A friend of yours."

"Deidre? My only friend here is Jen."

She looked at me and I looked at her, until finally the lightbulb went off.

"It's Jen? That's the best news I've heard in a while." I hugged my sister, then pulled away.

"But that means you probably don't want to move. She would likely stay here."

She took the fresh coffee and headed back to her room. "You should ask her that."

"What does that mean?" I called after her but got no response.

I sat at the kitchen counter stirring my coffee aimlessly. Bringing up Deidre, I realized I hadn't called her in too long.

"Hello? You do still exist. I've called and texted."

I smiled at her greeting. "Yes, hi, hello. I do exist and sorry. This had been a nutty few days."

"Nutty how?"

I gave her all the details.

"Holy shit. I'm coming to see you."

"What? Why? You were just here."

"Lena, that's best friends do. Booking now."

"Love you."

"Mean it."

After I hung up, I cleaned the kitchen, looked through my idea and recipe book, and drank another cup of coffee. I was restless.

"Going down to get the mail," I called down the hall and made my way to the mailboxes on the first floor.

My mind turned over the conversation with Celia. We could go anywhere. And it would be way more affordable than here. I'd already received my check from Food, Drink, Air. Basically, I now knew it was a pay off, but whatever it took to move on. I had that plus a little saved up. And the money from Kitty. I pulled a huge wad of mail from the box. I hadn't been down in a few days and clearly Celia hadn't either.

Once back upstairs, I dropped it all on the counter and sipped more coffee. I pushed the cup away, pretty sure I could now see sound due to all the caffeine I'd consumed. I filed through bills and ads and random political flyers.

At the bottom of the stack Food, Drink, Air sprawled open in its shiny glory. The latest edition I wasn't sure I even wanted to look through.

Would I be mentioned? Probably not. I was a blip on the radar.

But I flipped it open. A few pages in, a picture of Rob caught my eye. At the bottom of his photo the article was titled *HAND IN THE COOKIE JAR.*

I leaned closer. A detailed account of his underhanded dealings followed. The article ended with his dismissal. No mention of me at all. Interesting.

I flipped back to the review section. The last review I'd turned in that morning of Comfort was there.

Under that a small note was added. *We wish Helene Carnahan the best as she fulfills the next step of her journey. It's been a pleasure experiencing food with her and we look forward to doing so in her next endeavors.*

Who even put this issue together? I flipped another page. Ice ran in my veins.

Tragedy: Loss of an American Icon.

A photo of Cat and the Fiddle was there, but it wasn't the bright vibrant place I'd spent a night inside of with Kael's arms wrapped around me. It was ash and rubble. The cat still played its neon instrument, but only the walls stood. Kael was in the foreground, a desolate look on his face as he surveyed the scene. I scanned the article. He said he planned to rebuild his aunt's place, determined not to let it go.

The look on his face broke my heart. I checked the date of the fire.

I froze.

It was while he was in New York. But he still came back.

He came here to help me, even though his life was in shambles.

And he did it to ask for forgiveness that was already given. But I didn't say it to him. I was stubborn and hurt and I made him keep paying.

And he never even said...

Yes, he did. *The diner is in question.*

I was a royal jackass sometimes. I should've pressed and found out what was wrong. And he still gave me the recipe book back.

I pulled out my phone but I'd deleted and blocked his number. Damn. I could call Stef and get it most likely. Instead, I put my phone down as a plan formed.

Jen, Celia, Jonny, Deidre, and I sat around the table. Fried chicken, mashed potatoes, cornbread, and veggies were passed around.

"Aunt Leen, this is so good. I want you to make this every day."

I smiled. "I thought peanut butter sandwiches were your favorite."

"Not now. This is. This every day."

I looked at Celia and she shot me a sympathetic look. "Sorry, sis. Now you have to make a big meal every day."

I smiled and took a breath to steady myself as Celia grabbed my hand.

"You're probably wondering why I gathered you here." One beat of silence filled the room followed by laughter. "Sorry. I've always wanted to say that. Anyway. Celia and I have been talking and we've decided to move from New York."

Jonny looked at me, worried.

"Don't work, JonJon, we'll still be all together." He smiled and shoved more potatoes in his mouth.

"Jen, I'm going to start a business. Not sure what yet, but will you go with us? I know you have an extra stake in this now, but I'd love you to be there."

Her mouth dropped open and she looked at Celia. "You told her?"

"I tell her everything." She shrugged.

I laughed. "And I'm so happy for you both. But Deidre and I need a business partner. How about it?"

"I told you before, Helene, I'm with you."

Deidre raised her glass. "To adventures and endeavors and whatever lies ahead."

We all raised our own glasses in turn, even Jonny with his iced tea.

"Didi, still want to do something together? I didn't really ask you." I raised an eyebrow at her as I asked my question.

"You know I do. And I have some ideas, too."

I beamed at my little family. Emotions threatened to boil over as I looked at them. I had a family. After all this time.

"Where are we going?" Jonny asked excitedly.

I looked at everyone. "I was thinking Kansas."

Jen smiled. "You saw the latest issue then?"

I nodded. "It's so awful. The diner burned. And he didn't say anything while he was here. He only tried to help me."

She agreed. "And I knew when you read that letter, you'd see the light."

"What letter?"

Jen got up, handed me the magazine, and opened it to a page in the back. The opinion column.

An open letter to the food community.

This is Kael Ruggeman. I was most recently the head chef at London House. After my aunt passed, I moved to the middle of America to run her diner Cat and the Fiddle. Before leaving the city, I had the pleasure of having Helene Carnahan in my kitchen. She was dedicated, driven, and most of all a fiercely talented chef. I was intimidated by her innate look at and knowledge of food, tastes, and skills that seemed to come naturally to her. I knew she would be the best thing to happen to the city's food scene and my ego couldn't take it. I was hard on her, telling myself it was to her benefit so she would know what's coming.

Instead, she left the kitchen totally.

Lucky for all of us, she decided to review food. We still got a look at her brilliance every few weeks as we experienced the meals she ate and the stars she gave. And one day, she walked into my restaurant. I admit, I was nervous. But she gave a fair and accurate statement of my food and, to my chagrin, my demeanor. You all know how that played out. I got four stars and many people thought that's why I left the city.

But it was to run my aunt's diner. Then one afternoon, Helene happened into that small town diner. I didn't know it at the time, but she was there to review me once more. Again, I did not achieve the rating I wanted and once again it was because of me, not the plate I offered.

This time, I did the cardinal sin. I responded to the review. Everyone reading this magazine saw the play by play. But what you didn't see was how much Helene puts into this and everything she does. She was even doing it without her name attached, just because she loves it so much. She came to defend herself and I was, well, me. I did see how great she is, how she knows food inside and out, and how well she can handle herself in

*the kitchen. Being me, my ego overstepped and caused her a
headache, or a heartache, or maybe both.*
*Because of my recklessness she lost her job and I lost a friend in
her. Now, she'll probably kill me for writing this, but what Helene
really wants to do is cook for you, not just write about other
people's food. And believe me, you want her to.*
*I've never seen someone put so much love into a dish, except my
aunt, and even that is a tie.*
*Helene is selfless, choosing others over herself time and again. She
hasn't spoken out against any of the people who led to her losing
her column and her job, because that isn't who she is.*
But trust me when I say, none of it was her fault.
*She takes care of her family and maintains her professionalism on
a level I can only dream one day to achieve.*
*So, fellow food community, let's rally around Helene and help me
help her. I've told her fifty times how sorry I am, but now I'm
telling all of you, too. Details of how to help are below.*
*Helene – you deserve the world, and I can't wait to see what you
do in it.*
Kael

I LOOKED up in stunned silence. Celia and Jen waited for me
to say something, but I couldn't. There were no words. He'd
put himself out there, ego aside, laid himself bare. For me.

"The link is a fund. Helene, it's for you. And your restaurant." Jen watched me closely.

"He didn't need to do that, he's the one who needs the
help right now."

She smiled. "Then let's go help."

Deidre held up her hands. "Hello? When do we leave?"

21

Kael

I t had been four days since the publication came out and I hadn't heard anything from Helene. But the fund I set up seemed to be gaining steam. To be honest, I could use a fund myself. I looked around at the progress being made on the diner. It was small and going slowly, but there was progress.

I kept thinking about that letter from Cat, about me doing my own thing. Maybe rebuilding this place wasn't the best plan.

Danny came out to what was once the lobby, covered in paint. "Hey, Bossman, want to come check my work?"

I followed him into the kitchen. "What are you painting? Are we to that yet?"

Half the kitchen was back in shape, ready for new appliances and a fresh coat of paint on two of the walls glistened in the bright room.

"They said we were." He pointed to the construction crew.

I clapped him on the back. "Great work, my friend."

He smiled at me. "Thanks, man. I'm going to get lunch. Want anything?"

I shook my head. "I'm set, but thanks."

I spent the next few hours doing small tasks around the restaurant as it slowly came together. I ordered new pans, confirmed the stove and oven installation, and most importantly, planned the new fire suppression system inspection.

Sheila came in and jumped on board too.

This was the first time I felt like it was mine. I was building something here and a pride I didn't know I could have vibrated through me.

Was this mine now? Or was I simply rebuilding something that already existed? I didn't know the answer and I was so tired from all of it, I had no energy to puzzle it out.

It was a full and rewarding day and once I was home, I collapsed on the couch.

It was only a couple minutes before the loneliness and ache took over.

Helene. God, I missed her. I'd kept my part of the bargain and except for the letter to the magazine, I'd stayed away. I hadn't called or emailed or anything.

But I thought about her every day. How was she? Did she have a new job yet? I thought about all the things I've never had a chance to ask about, like her sister and her nephew. Why did she take care of them like she did and more importantly, why did she have to. What had happened in their lives to create that situation?

I hoped the fund I'd set up was helping her. But what

was she going to do with it? If she opened a place, would I be invited to see it?

The desperation to have these answers and so many more ate at me.

"I should probably eat," I said out loud to no one.

In the kitchen, I opened the freezer to find some frozen TV dinners. Now even that reminded me of Helene and the things we'd confessed in the freezing restaurant that night.

I tossed one in the microwave and poured a glass of bourbon. I looked around. The house was clean. I was the only one here and even that was a stretch because I'd almost exclusively been at the diner lately.

I could do laundry, maybe.

Instead, I turned on the tv. Some cooking show was on. I turned it back off. Nothing I did distracted me from Helene.

I wanted to talk to her, hold her, hear her voice. Just know she was alright.

I ate quickly and after another fifteen minutes, I got back in my truck and returned to the diner.

No one was there which I was grateful for. I needed some time alone with the place. I walked the kitchen pattern we'd decided on. The sink was now in that plan and I smiled. Helene would like that.

I closed my eyes. *If you're ever in Kansas... You'll be my first stop.*

Our last kiss held me in thrall. I should've held on longer. Or asked for just a little more time. I should have done anything but let her go.

No. That's what she asked me to do. I respected her and her wishes. No sense dwelling on this.

And being here wasn't helping either. She was everywhere and all over me.

I heard the door ding. I jumped because I didn't know

that had been repaired. Danny must've forgotten something. I rounded the corner to the front of house and stopped cold.

A bunch of things sat on the counter I knew weren't there when I left the first time. I saw the door closing but didn't see anyone. I ran over but by the time I got there, no one was in sight. What the hell?

I turned my attention to the counter. Whoever left this here must've been in here when I came in the back. I made a mental note to check the whole place next time.

On the counter, or at least the plywood that would become a counter as soon as the Formica came in, sat an artfully arranged bag of kitchen utensils. Some were new, some well-loved. Next to that was a small wooden crate with a smock, paintbrushes, a putty knife, and a hammer. A couple other things were in the crate at the bottom but I couldn't see them without unloading it.

A blue blanket folded with a ribbon around it was next to that. I picked it up and I swore I could smell Helene on the fabric. My head spun as my heart squeezed. An envelope was propped up against the crate. I ripped it open and pulled out the letter.

DEAR KAEL,

I got your letter (as everyone did in this month's edition) and decided to take a page out of your book. I'd write you back.

First – What you said, how you said it, what you did for me, it touched me. And I want to say thank you. I heard what happened to the diner and I wish you would've told me. When you were in New York, I mean. You didn't have to go through this alone.

See, I realized some things when Rob fired me and one was, what's the point of doing this life if you hate the life you're making. The thing is, I didn't know I hated it. I felt stuck, no doubt. But then I met you.

It was the first time I knew what I truly wanted.

And more importantly, felt like I could achieve it. You told me you thought I was brave. Then I proceeded to turn you away, shut you down, and not give you the one thing you asked for — my forgiveness.

And Kael – My Allie – you had that before you asked. I was simply being stubborn because I was hurt. And for that, I'm sorry.

But to my point, I brought some things for you. And a proposal of sorts.

First, kitchen tools. I'm sure you've ordered new, but here's a few you can use now. A crate of stuff to make it new again. They are my tools, I figured you've have your own, but with these I can help. In there, you'll find a new Chef's cover (I wasn't sure if yours was lost in the fire) and some concept drawings for things to come.

This letter has gone on too long. I'm in room five at the motel. If you're interested in learning the rest, come find me. If not, I'll understand. But if you do...

With hope, Lena

P.S. THERE'S one more thing in that crate I thought you might want.

I STARED AT THE LETTER. It didn't tell me what the blanket was nor why there were concept drawings. Did she think I should change this place? I was trying to build it exactly as it was.

I tucked the letter back in the envelope and took things

out of the crate. All the tools I could see, then as promised a folder of drawings, menu layouts with funny names for dishes. I felt the biggest wave of Cat being with me when I read those names. She's had a whimsical edge to her and she'd love this.

In the bottom of the crate was something wrapped in paper, the way you'd wrap a dish when you moved.

I lifted it out and carefully took off the protective coverings.

It was a blue plate. Speckled and vintage, exactly what you think of when blue plate comes to mind.

I held it in my hands, the weight of what it meant hitting me dead on. Helene had given me a blue plate.

A small note was taped to its center.

Here's your fifth blue plate. You deserve it.

My heart cracked open. I sat it down gently and practically ran across the street.

Helene

A knock on the door made me jump even though I'd been hoping to hear nothing else.

"Hello?"

"Helene?"

Kael's voice filled me with warmth and I threw open the door. He smiled so wide when he saw me. It touched his eyes and all the way into my soul.

"Hi." His eyes glistened with unfallen tears.

"Did you get my gifts?"

He nodded and took a step in. "What are you doing here?"

I put my hands in my back pockets, feeling shy and unsure out of nowhere. "I went looking for the owner of the diner. I heard he suffered a huge loss and thought I could help him out." I grinned.

He shut the door behind him, a look of desire on his face. "I'd be open to some help. But New York is a long way to travel back and forth to help."

He put his hands on my waist and I put mine on his shoulders. "I recently moved."

Shock made his features go slack, then excitement as the news sunk in. "You what?"

I shrugged as he pulled me closer. "I wanted to open a diner, but there's already a great one in town. I thought maybe we could collaborate."

"We did just get our fifth blue plate." He smiled the cutest smile I'd ever seen on his beautiful face.

I pushed a wayward curl out his eyes and bit my lip. "Good. I only want to work with the best."

"You moved here." He repeated it as if saying it again might make it real.

"Well, I'm here for now. With my whole crew in tow. I didn't know if you were rebuilding or going somewhere else, but I thought we could talk about it. Maybe. I don't know, it's sounds nuts when I say it out loud." My stomach flipped with nerves.

"And you want to rebuild this place and run it together?"

Worried knitted my brow making my head ache. "That was just an idea. If you don't want—"

He pulled me to him, kissing me deeply. My arms wrapped around him tightly, holding him close. I would never let him go this time.

He broke the kiss and hugged me. "I can't believe you're here. Am I dreaming?"

I leaned into him. "If you are, so am I."

He moved back just a step. "Wait, what was the blanket for?"

I pulled him close again. "Winters can be brutal here. We might need it. What if we ever got snowed in."

Tears leaked out his eyes. "Lena." He held me close, my arms locked around his neck. He pressed his face in to my hair, taking big breaths.

"What are you doing?"

"Taking you in. I have missed you so much. I thought I might have imagined how great you are. But my mind didn't do you justice."

I held him tighter. "Allie, want to do this thing?"

He leaned back and met my eyes with fire in his. "Define thing."

"You asked me once why we couldn't be together. And I gave you a million reasons."

He waited, not rushing me as I gathered my thoughts.

"But all of them are gone. Distance is gone. The job I was glued to is gone. I have a chance, thanks to you and Kitty, to do something new, and I forgave you before you asked. I'm sorry I didn't tell you. I was being stubborn and you'd hurt my feelings so badly. But still, I shouldn't have kept that from you."

"Thank you." He pressed his forehead to mine, a wave of relief washing over me.

"So, how about it? Want to give us a go? I think we'd make a pretty great team."

"Helene Carnahan, nothing would make me happier."

Our lips met once more, but this kiss was full of promise and a new beginning. In that moment, the world seemed full of possibilities I wasn't sure existed just an hour ago.

"Mmmm." Satisfaction covered my face, I could feel it. It was the way I felt after I'd eaten the most delicious meal.

"What's that for?"

"You, Allie. Five stars." He spun me around and I squealed. "Let's get to work then."

His look changed, charged. "I think I know where to begin."

"Oh yeah?" I raised an eyebrow.

He nodded and stepped closer. He cupped my cheek, taking his time. His lips met mine with a softness, a gentleness, a longing. I pulled him against me as I melted into him, his kiss growing stronger. We took a step toward the bed before he rested his forehead on mine.

"I have spent every minute thinking of you, missing you. I can't believe you're really here in my arms."

I moved his hand to my heart, and mine to his. "I'm here."

He pulled me tight against him and crushed his lips to me.

"You feel so good in my arms," he managed to get out between kisses.

I wound my arms up and around him until there was no space between our bodies. I licked at his soft lips, coaxing his mouth open once more. I pushed my tongue in, tasting him. The heat, the sensation, it was perfection. He tasted like bourbon and peaches.

"Did you have pie today?"

He laughed. "I have pie every day. Why?"

"You're sweet like peaches...with cinnamon and clove."

He buried his face in my neck, his mouth hot on my skin. "God, I'm in love with you."

I pulled away to look in his eyes.

"You love me?"

"You know I do. How could I not? You're everything." He looked at me soft and dreamlike, in a haze of sorts. Then, his eyes darkened. Desire poured from them lighting me on fire.

He advanced as I took a step back, and he nipped at my lower lip. The kiss was enticing and I wanted another taste of him already.

But he moved his lips across my cheek, capturing my earlobe in his teeth and giving a gentle graze to the skin. He kissed just below it, his breath warming the tender skin there.

I moaned softly.

A sound rumbled from his chest in response. "Lena, you make me crazy with every little thing you do."

I sat back on the bed as Kael knelt in front of me. He closed his hands on my hips and looked deep in my eyes.

My legs parted as he slid close, his hands in my hair. This kiss was rough and needful and I didn't want it to end. I grabbed big handfuls of his shirt to drag him closer to me. One of his hands brushed my shoulder and down my arm. He reached down and squeezed my calf then ran his hand up my leg, grabbing my thigh tight.

I tipped my head back in his hand as his mouth moved across my neck, down to the hollow of my throat. His thumb grazed my jaw, his fingers on the back of my neck as he held me there, weak in his arms.

"Lena, you're perfection."

I felt my cheeks rise, but he didn't stop to notice. He

kissed along my jawline and followed with his fingertips as he laid me back gently on the bed. He rose over me, looking in to my eyes.

"What are you thinking about?" I played with his hair as he hovered over me.

He shook his head. "It's cliché, but I've never wanted anything more than you. And this is wonderful but it's not just this. It's all of you. I wasn't sure I'd see you again, and now you're here, and we can be together."

A tear rolled from the corner of my eye. "That's beautiful, Allie." I wrapped my arms around him and held him close to me, our hearts beating as one.

Kael rose up on his side and trailed his fingers over my cheek, until he found my breast. He cupped it with his strong hands, kneading it until he kissed my chest. Pushing my shirt off my shoulder, he covered all the skin he could find, his tongue running along the top of my bra. I drew in a breath and felt his cheek rise against me.

He nipped at me through the fabric, driving me wild. "Kael, don't tease me."

He looked up at me, a devilish grin on his face. "What's your rush? We have all the time in the world."

I smiled at him and reached for the bottom of his shirt. "Fine, but this has to go."

He helped me pull it over his head and toss it to the side. My eyes swept over him. I would never tire of this view.

Kael returned the favor and soon we were skin to skin, electricity snapping between us. He cradled my face to kiss me once more, our skin burning hot against each other.

He lowered his head, working his way down. He reached behind me and unhooked my bra and moved it out of the way.

He took my breast in his mouth. The warmth and pressure of his tongue took over me. I arched my back as he wrapped his arm under me, holding me closer as he had his way with me. I felt the heat of his mouth moving down my stomach as he ran a thumb over my sensitive nipple. I drew in a breath, needing him more than I thought possible.

His kissed from my ribcage to the top of my jeans.

He pulled me to sitting, back on his knees in front of me.

He held my face. "Lena."

22

∾

Kael

Helene was here with me. I kept getting lost in the passion because I couldn't believe it. She came here to be with me. Not just be with me, but to start a life together. I pulled on her lips as she bent over me, her hair falling on each side of my face.

I pulled at the button and zipper on her jeans and tugged at the bottoms, until she fell back and lifted her hips so I could pull them off. She laughed, carefree and full of joy.

I gripped her hips, pulling her to the edge of the bed. With a thigh on each side of my head, I kissed up one thigh and ran my tongue along the other. She writhed in my arms as I held my grip firm on her.

"Need something?"

She leaned up to look down at me. "It's going to be that way now?"

I leaned my face against her leg. "It's going to be a lot of ways if everything goes to plan."

With that I pushed the thin fabric of her panties aside and closed my mouth over her most delicate spot. She sucked in a breath and her fingers closed in my hair, holding on tight. My scalp tingled as she pulled at my hair, directing me to the best spot. I pushed two fingers deep inside her heat and no matter what grand plans I had, I knew I wouldn't last too long. My want was too much and too deep. I forced myself to stop and stand. I took my own pants off with no ceremony, closed an arm around her waist and moved us both back upon on the bed. Her hands closed on my shoulders as she held on. My fingers laced in her hair, turning her face in to my kiss, taking everything I could get from her. I didn't want to stop until I got enough.

And let's face it, I'd never get enough. Our bodies were so close together, burning. Then I froze.

Helene looked at me, worry wrinkling her brow. "What's wrong?"

"I...uh, I don't have a condom."

She grinned and pushed me off her as she rolled out of bed. I watched her hips swish as she moved easily across the room. "Just when I was thinking you were perfect."

She held one up between two fingers she'd pulled from her bag. I tried to reach for it but she dodged my hand. "I don't know, couldn't have been thinking about me that much if you weren't even prepared." She dropped it back in the bag.

"Are you kidding me right now? I'm not a boy scout."

She shook her head. "Disappointing." She reached for her shirt.

I lunged her direction, lifting her in my arms. "Not a chance." She squealed then laughed as she dropped her shirt. It was drowned out as we kissed again. She reached back into her bag as she broke off the kiss and held it up. I took it from her hand and sat her on the bed. I rolled it on as she laid back, pure sexual desire meeting me.

I moved in between her welcoming legs, getting back to where we were. I paused for a second, before sliding inside her. She let out a soft moan and opened fully to me. Our eyes never left each other as we moved together.

Slow and gentle at first, suspended in a moment of longing for the love of my life. But after a few minutes, desire and need took over and our bodies moved more forcefully, but together.

Heat grew, the want exploded but on and on it went. Limbs tangled, bodies crushed together, mouths connected. She moaned and grew louder as my thrusts got harder. I moved against her, feeling her legs close around me, pushing me in deeper. I was close.

"Helene."

Her fingers dug into my back. "Yes."

The passion erupted in both of us, rippling out as our bodies rocked together until we slowed and settled, still in each other's arms.

"Allie..."

I kissed her nose. "What's next on the menu, Chef?"

She laughed, her body softly shaking the bed. "That's the beauty of it. Anything we want."

EPILOGUE

~

Helene

I stood in the parking lot, Kael's arm around my waist holding me close. The crew led by Sheila and Danny stood by my family– Celia, Jonny, Deidre, and Jen.

"I can't believe it took so long for this sign to come in."

"Didi, it was custom work. It takes time," I said over my shoulder.

She waved her hand. "Yeah, yeah. But still."

Celia held hands with Jen on one side and Jonny on the other. "Isn't this exciting?" She asked Jonny.

He shrugged. "I guess. When do we get to eat pie?"

We all chuckled. Jonny had grown quite fond of being Uncle Kael's official taste tester. We watched as the workmen hung the new neon sign on the building. It was still a cat in an apron, but now it held a plate with a piece of pie on it.

"The Blue Plate." I read the words, my chest swelling with pride and love as they installed it.

Deidre surveyed the scene. "This property was really a find. A place for our office right next to the new diner and a motel in need of renovation."

I smiled at her. "Made just for us."

"Hopefully the other signs will come in soon, too."

"They will, Didi." That was the sign I couldn't wait for, the one that would top the office building. It was just a logo of the plate but it had a hotel key chain next to it. It would be the home of my new column, *Food to Write Home About* and Deidre's reviews of *Places to Rest Your Head.* Jen managed all of it and kept us on track.

She looked on as the sign went up. "I hope we can find as good of a deal in Oklahoma for the next one."

Kael squeezed my hand and whispered in my ear. "I can't believe we'll have a second one."

I wrapped my arms around his neck. "We really did it."

I took in all the people I had in my life and the love I was surrounded by. "Thanks everyone for making this dream happen. How should we celebrate?"

Kael smiled at me and I saw Deidre give him a small nod. "I have the perfect plan."

"Oh, do you?" I laughed thinking about all his crazy ideas he'd come up with over this project. But I turned to see him down on his knee, all the people I loved right behind him. He held a small box with a ring set with three diamonds up to me.

"Yeah. I think it's pretty perfect. What do you think?"

I leaned down, my hand on his cheek. "Perfect. Chef's kiss."

ACKNOWLEDGMENTS

So many people to thank! Derek - thank you for being a true partner, never getting frustrated when I say I need to write, and also asking - hey, do you need to write? I can't ever thank you enough.

Nashville Girls Night (the ultimate group chat) - You have talked over every detail of this book, cheered me on, and wiped my tears - thank you endlessly.

Jaime - for being there for literally everything. Jean - for the daily chats. My kiddos and mama - for believing in me.

Last to my Grandma - I'd give anything for one more day making cinnamon rolls with you while sitting on your countertop. This book is for you.

ABOUT THE AUTHOR

Angi N. Black(she/her) is a romance author. She has been writing her whole life. She studied creative writing at LSU and owns an editing business, Editor Around The Corner. She is a dance and theatre instructor at Missouri State University. A proud member of the LGBTQIA+ community, she loves to bake and cook, make art, and listen to good music. She has grown kiddos she adores and a husband who makes her laugh. Prone to breaking out in show tunes and proficient in the art of the mix tape, she makes an excellent road trip buddy. Oh! She did win a write-your-own-book contest in 4th grade, so like Bill Murray in Caddyshack, she has that going for her. Which is nice.